DEATH'S BRIGHT ANGEL

DEATH'S BRIGHT ANGEL

ANGEL

J. D. Davies

The Sixth Journal of Matthew Quinton

First published in 2016 by Old Street Publishing Ltd,
Yowlestone House, Tiverton, Devon EX16 8LN

www.oldstreetpublishing.co.uk

ISBN 978 1 910400 46 3

Printed and bound in Great Britain

Typeset by Martin Worthington

For Jon, Debs, Thom and Maddie

We all have sinn'd, and thou hast laid us low,
As humble Earth from whence at first we came:
Like flying Shades before the Clouds we shew,
And shrink like Parchment in consuming Flame.

From John Dryden, *Annus Mirabilis* (1667)

Mars and Venus were in conjunction at his birth, and Love and War's his business.

Description of Willmore, 'the rover', a naval captain
From Aphra Behn's *The Rover, Part 2* (1681)

It may be that death's bright angel
Will speak in that chord again,
It may be that only in Heav'n
I shall hear that grand Amen.

Adelaide Anne Procter, *The Lost Chord*, 1858
(Later set to music by Sir Arthur Sullivan)

AUTHOR'S NOTE

The Great Fire of London began at about one in the morning on Sunday, 2 September 1666. By the time it was extinguished, some eighty hours later, about 13,700 houses had been destroyed, along with the Royal Exchange, the Custom House, fifty-two livery halls, eighty-seven churches, and St Paul's Cathedral. Sixty to seventy thousand people were displaced, becoming refugees in their own city. Moorfields and the other open spaces in and around the City became vast camps for the homeless. Miraculously, the official death toll was fewer than a dozen, although it is possible that the number of unrecorded deaths was higher.

For centuries, it has been accepted that the Fire was an accident, caused by the carelessness of a baker in Pudding Lane. Many contemporaries, though, were convinced that the Fire was started deliberately. The year 1666 had seen several plots, real or imagined, and countless intimations of imminent disaster. There were many predictions that London would be consumed by fire, as punishment for England's sins (specifically, for those of her king, the notoriously immoral Charles II); indeed, Mother Shipton and Nostradamus were supposed to have predicted the fiery destruction of the city in this, the year that contained the Number of the Beast in its date. Above all, though, at a time when the British Isles were engaged in a colossal naval war against both the Dutch and the French, many blamed enemy action – especially deliberate arson by foreign and/or native Roman Catholics. This opinion was reflected in a rabidly anti-

Catholic inscription placed in 1681 on Sir Christopher Wren's monument to the catastrophe; and although the inscription was removed in the nineteenth century, the monument itself still survives, giving its name to one of the busiest stations on the London Underground. Meanwhile, a French watchmaker, Robert Hubert, actually confessed to starting the fire, and was hanged as a result. But all modern books about the subject agree that he did not arrive in London until after the fire began, and the full reason for his pointless martyrdom remains a mystery.

The Great Fire of London is one of the most famous events in British history, one of the very few that still fulfils the age-old criterion of 'what every schoolchild knows', and its consequences still shape the cityscape of the United Kingdom's capital to this day.

Rather less well known is the fire that destroyed the Dutch town of Westerschelling, known to contemporary Englishmen as Brandaris, just over three weeks before the Great Fire took place. Whereas the conflagration in London is generally regarded as the result of an accident, that on the Frisian island of Terschelling was a deliberate act of war, carried out by units of King Charles II's Royal Navy. About one hundred and fifty Dutch merchant ships were torched in the adjacent Vlie anchorage, and the town was burned to the ground. The only known fatal casualties on the Dutch side were a watchman and two old women. The event is still remembered in the Netherlands as 'the English Fury', and its 350th anniversary is being commemorated on the Frisian Islands during 2016.

There is no known connection between 'the English Fury' and the Great Fire of London, although many at the time speculated that the latter was revenge for the former.

Prologue

Fire is a temptress.

To be sure, in childhood you learn very swiftly indeed that going too near her will burn you. Keep your flesh in her flames, and it will roast like that of a hog on a spit. When you are older, and witness such an event, you learn that if a living body is burned, as in a Spanish *auto-da-fé*, then the flesh will peel from the bones, and the sickly-sweet stench will attract the attention of dogs two miles downwind.

But there is that moment when you are close to the fire, but not too close. She warms you. She embraces you. She dances her seductive dance for you. She waves her red-gold locks at you, as brazen as a Dublin harlot. She lures you in. And you remember the scriptures' talk of the refiner's fire, the fire that cleanses, the fire that takes away your sins. In that moment, before your flesh blackens and the pain becomes unbearable, you want nothing more than to leap into the flames, to be consumed, to be at one with the temptress.

So it was with me, that September of 1666, when London burned and I felt the flames singe my face and hands as houses collapsed all around me. When I saw great Saint Paul's, which had stood for half a millennium, crumble to ashes. When I thought, more than once, that this was justice: divine retribution for the flames that we, the English, had inflicted upon others. The flames of countless ships, burning upon the sea. The flames that I, Matthew Quinton, had inflicted upon peaceful innocents. The flames that, perhaps, provoked the most terrible of retributions. And vengeance, too, for the very personal sin that I had committed, the sin that could be purged from my body and soul only by cleansing, redeeming fire. In those moments I wanted to turn, to fling myself into the fire, to feel the embrace of the temptress.

Sometimes, when I have business in the City – in other words, when I have to berate my brokers on the Exchange for swindling what they perceive to be an ancient, bent, senile creature out of a proper return on his investments – my coach takes me past Wren's preposterous Monument to the Great Fire that consumed London, more than sixty years ago. (In England, we erect memorials to disasters. *O tempora, o mores.*) When I was younger, I would climb out from time to time, and read the inscription on the west side:

This pillar was set up in perpetual remembrance of the most dreadful burning of this Protestant city, begun and carried on by the treachery and malice of the Popish faction, in the beginning of September, in the year of our Lord MDCLXVI, in order to the effecting their horrid plot for the extirpating the Protestant religion and English liberties, and to introduce Popery and slavery.

Of course, those who consider themselves wise scoff at this. The Fire was not begun deliberately by the Papists, they say, but was a mere accident, all the fault of a baker in Pudding Lane. The inscription has become an embarrassment, and there is talk of altering it, or removing it altogether. But the mob, the many-headed monster that still sees the sinister arts of France and Popery behind every accidental kitchen fire in Shoreditch, will not hear of it. And, of course, our so-called politicians become craven when confronted by the mob, and the wrath of the so-called 'news-papers' that pander to it.

What a country we have become!

So, whenever my coach takes me past the Monument, I think back to those strange days in the summer of 1666, the year that incorporated the Number of the Beast, and I think upon the truth of the Great Fire of London. The fire that I saw consume old Saint Paul's, and dozens of churches, and street after street, and which threatened so much more, so much that was dear to me.

A great Popish conspiracy? The stupidity of a careless baker? Or something else altogether? Now there's a question.

Perhaps it is time that I, one of the last who remembers the days of flame that consumed a great city, provided an answer.

Chapter One

'Never thought I'd see the day when those colours flew proud in these seas,' said Urquhart, the taciturn Scot who served as sailing master of my command, the King's ship *Royal Sceptre*.

She was a fine sight indeed, the great sixty-gun man-of-war coming down at us upon the wind, exactly one month to the day before London began to burn. She heeled slightly to starboard, her sails filling with the breeze, the bow wave breaking around her cutwater as she surged through the swell. Her cannon were run out, ready for action. Her men were working the clewlines, leechlines and buntlines, gathering in the fore and main courses, a sure sign that she was intent upon a fight.

From the glorious ship's ensign staff streamed a vast banner of pure white, interrupted only by fleurs-de-lis.

The royal ensign of France. Flying in the middle of the North Sea, at the very heart of what we captains of King Charles the Second regarded as our British seas. The France of King Louis the Fourteenth, now allied to our mortal foe, the Dutch Republic, against whom we had just fought two colossal sea-battles, one of four days and one of two. So the great ship coming towards us was an enemy, and we were closing to engage it.

'We' being not just the crew and guns of the *Royal Sceptre*, irreverently by-named 'the King's prick' by her crew, but our consort too, the nimble Fourth Rate frigate *Association*. We two ships had been detached from the main fleet to cruise southward, toward the Straits of Dover, expecting to arrest a few Dutch merchantmen disguised as neutrals, and maybe to fight a Zeeland privateer or two. Certainly not expecting to come face to face with one of the leviathans of King Louis' brand new navy. Five years before, France's entire navy could have been defeated by a single Thames barge. Now this titan was coming straight for us, and we knew that somewhere behind her – hours? days? weeks? – was an entire fleet of her vast sisters, commanded by the Sun King's bastard uncle, the Duke of Beaufort.

Our ship's chaplain emerged from the steerage, strode up to the quarterdeck, looked over at the Frenchman, and nodded at me.

'Now, Sir Matthew?'

'Now, Francis, if you please.'

The Reverend Francis Gale, a stocky fellow fast gaining on his fiftieth birthday, with yet a slight trace of his native Shropshire in his voice, went up to the rail and looked out over the ship's waist. Warrant and petty officer's whistles brought forward a makeshift congregation of those who could be spared from their stations. My officers and I removed our hats in due reverence.

'Thou, oh Lord, art just and powerful,' Francis began, embarking once again on the great prayer before battle enjoined in the Book of Common Prayer. 'O defend our cause against the face of the enemy. O God, thou art a strong tower of defence to all that flee unto thee; O save us from the violence of the enemy. O Lord of Hosts, fight for us, that we may glorify thee. O suffer us not to sink under the weight of our sins, or the violence of the enemy. O Lord, arise, help us, and deliver us for they name's sake. Amen.'

The men in the waist echoed the amen.

When I'd first encountered him, four years before, Francis Gale had been a hopeless drunk, broken by the memory of his true love's death during Cromwell's assault on Drogheda. Now he was the vicar of Ravensden, the family living in the gift of the tenth Earl of that name, my brother. He was also the deeply respected chaplain of my commands whenever he could obtain leave to accompany me to sea.

'Oh Lord, we beseech thee,' he said, moving on to the extemporised portion of his prayers, 'to grant us victory over the Frenchman, yonder. The true and natural enemy of all Englishmen, against whom our ancestors strived and triumphed at Crécy, Poitiers and Agincourt. The embodiment of the Popish tyranny that burned honest Protestant folk at the stake in the reign of Bloody Mary. That wooden hull, oh Lord our God, is the very embodiment of Popery and France! Popery, that consumes all before it by fire and treachery! Popery, that pretends to serve thee, yet is naught but the Whore of Babylon! France, that seeks universal monarchy over the world! France, that persecutes her own Protestant children, the godly Huguenots, more and more every day! Lord God of Abraham, Isaac, and Israel, grant us the battle this day! God, grant victory to England, King Charles, the *Royal Sceptre*, and our noble captain, Sir Matthew Quinton! In the name of the Father, the Son, and the Holy Ghost, amen.'

A growl, composed in equal measure of devotion and national fervour, came from the men in the waist. We officers made our own amens dutifully, if less fulsomely. As Francis turned toward me, I said, 'A little strong today, Reverend Gale?'

He shrugged. 'My mother never liked the French, Sir Matthew. Lost a lover in the Breton war in the old Queen's day, or so she said. Besides, the men have got so used to fighting the Dutch, they might have forgotten they're dealing with a different coin here. A very different coin.'

'She's changing course, Sir Matthew!' cried Lieutenant Julian Delacourt. An eager but woefully inexperienced young man, only son and sole heir of an impoverished Irish nobleman, he had taken up his post in this ship just over a week before.

Indeed she was. With the wind south-westerly, the Frenchman was starting to turn north-east, giving us the advantage of the wind.

'Running for the coast,' I said to my officers. 'Brave, to make for a lee shore. But he'll have a shallower draught than we do, maybe even than the *Association* does, given how lightly the French build and arm their ships. A bold captain, this, my friends – running for the shoals, hoping he can outrun us as the flood sets to the northward, and thus get into the mouth of the Scheldt. But we'll disabuse him of the notion, by God!'

Not many years before, Matthew Quinton would not have been able to make a speech like that. In those days, I could barely tell where north-east and south-west were. Yet even then I was already captain of one of the King's men-of-war: a King's man-of-war and a crew, by far the greatest part of which did not survive to tell of my failings.

'Gentlemen,' said my not much older but infinitely wiser self, 'we will clear for action, if you please. Mister Delacourt, we will signal to the *Association* –'

Just then, and only for a moment, I caught a glimpse of the splendid white-and-gold carving upon the French ship's sternpiece: a maid in armour, being wafted to heaven by angels. So this was our foe, as recorded in the latest list of King Louis's men-of-war. The *Jeanne d'Arc*, new-built at Toulon. In our tongue, the *Joan of Ark*. Well, we English had roasted the namesake, and now we would burn the ship named after her, too.

That said, I prayed that the *Jeanne d'Arc* was not commanded by either of the French naval captains whom I knew well. Roger, comte d'Andelys, was a good friend, who had served me in the disguise of a sailmaker's mate when he was in disgrace at the court of King Louis. Whereas Gaspard, Seigneur de Montnoir, a knight of Malta, was a mortal enemy, a fanatic who had once attempted to convert me to Rome when I was in his power.

I dismissed the thought. Roger was at his château in the valley of the Seine, trying to find a wife and fulminating against those rivals at court who had ensured he held no command at sea during this expedition. Montnoir, meanwhile, was supposed to have died aboard a great Danish man-of-war that I had fought some six months before, the Danes, like the French, having joined the war on the side of our Dutch enemies. But although there had been no word of Montnoir since, there was no confirmation of his death, either. And while a part of me would gladly have fought the Seigneur de Montnoir once again, another part prayed fervently that such a truly malevolent and implacable enemy was indeed already dead.

'Fighting sails, Mister Urquhart!' I shouted. 'Master gunner, car-tridge and shot to the guns! Half pikes between decks, if you please! Case shot to the swivel guns! Loose the tackles, open the ports, thrust out the main battery!'

Our drummers beat to quarters, our trumpeters sounded our ship's challenge to its enemy, and the *Royal Sceptre* sailed into battle.

* * *

The *Association* engaged first. I had ordered her captain, Walton, to take a more direct easterly course, intercepting the Frenchman's route to the Flemish shoals. This brought the frigate directly across the *Jeanne d'Arc*'s bows, and she fired a raking broadside at the enemy. My orders were for Walton to stay ahead of the French ship, blocking her course and forcing her to turn back towards the *Royal Sceptre*.

'What in the name of Christ is he doing?' said Delacourt.

The youth had been at sea no more than a few months, a lieutenant for just a few days, but even a babe-in-arms could see that Walton was not bearing away to the north-east, as he should have done if he was following my orders.

My telescope was pressed hard against my eye. I could see the men adjusting sail in the *Association*'s tops and yards. I could see Walton on his quarterdeck: a rough old Yorkshireman, a veteran of the

Commonwealth's Navy and Blake's campaign in the Mediterranean. I could see his arm pointing toward the *Jeanne d'Arc*.

I knew what he was doing, and I knew why he was doing it. I lowered my telescope.

'He's tacking,' I said. 'Disobeying my orders. He wants her for himself.'

The bows of the *Association* were coming round into the wind.

'He's giving the Frenchman the wind,' said Delacourt. 'He's conceding the weather gage!'

'Intends to thwart her hawse,' I said. 'Grapple onto her bows, and board. Take her prize before we can even get close. But it's a dangerous manoeuvre, Mister Delacourt – desperately dangerous, even for a man as experienced as Captain Walton.'

A rotund, bald figure came onto the quarterdeck, carrying my breastplate and my grandfather's sword – the weapon with which Matthew Quinton, eighth Earl of Ravensden, had fought against the Spanish Armada. He looked out toward the other two ships, shook his head, and said, decisively, 'Rebel fuckwit.'

'Thank you, Musk,' I said. 'You know the opinion of the King and the Duke of York about the raising of past differences.'

'Beg pardon, Sir Matthew. Plain, unvarnished fuckwit, then.'

He began to buckle the breastplate onto me. Phineas Musk: long-time retainer to the Quinton family, steward of our London house, nominally my captain's clerk. Very nominally.

'Mister Delacourt,' I said, 'let us make one last attempt to bring Walton to his senses and his duty. Signal in accordance with the thirteenth instruction, if you please!'

'Aye, aye, Sir Matthew!'

A white flag was hoisted to our mizzen topmast head. If we had been in the fleet, and I an admiral, the signal would have been unambiguous: the thirteenth fighting instruction specified that the frigates in attendance on the great ships should come under the admiral's stern for new orders. With no specific fighting instruction that fitted our particular circumstance, it was the only signal I could think of that would order Walton to break off his proposed course of action immediately. I could only hope that the captain of the *Association* would recognise my intent.

Instead, we looked on with horror at the spectacle unfolding before us. I do not know whether Valentine Walton saw the signal, or recognised its purpose; but I suspect that he did, and deliberately ignored it. Walton was not only displaying utter contempt for me, the jumped-up young sprig of a Cavalier who had been a sea-captain for twenty years fewer than himself, yet who commanded the larger ship and was thus his senior; he was also deliberately ignoring the fighting instructions laid down by the Lord High Admiral of England, the Duke of York. If he survived, nothing was more certain than that I would accuse him at a court-martial. He would know that, but, doubtless believed that a famous victory would see him acquitted. Above all, though, Captain Valentine Walton was displaying scant regard for the fighting qualities of his French opponent. By tacking back toward the *Jeanne d'Arc*, he was not only giving the Frenchman the advantage of the wind: he was exposing his own bows to a raking broadside. Perhaps he assumed the French captain was too incompetent, or too cowardly, to react.

The main and fore courses of the *Jeanne d'Arc* fell, and were sheeted home with immaculate speed and precision. As the ship gained momentum from the great new spread of canvas, she turned more northerly, taking her bows away from Walton's intended attack.

'Now we'll see your measure, *monsieur le capitaine*,' I murmured to myself.

I knew exactly what I would do in the circumstances – or at least, what I would attempt to do. I watched the sand running through the nearest glass, judged the wind, estimated the effect of the flood tide, watched the relative positions of the *Association* and the *Jeanne d'Arc*, checked the glass again –

Now.

Just as though I had given the order myself, in that exact moment the mainmast sails of the French ship swung around, into the wind. With the sails backed, all the momentum abruptly came off the ship; came off it so that it was in the ideal position to rake the *Association*.

The *Jeanne d'Arc* opened fire.

We could not see the flames from the starboard broadside, but we could see the smoke rolling toward the *Association*. A moment later, we heard the thunder of the blast.

I raised my telescope again. Slowly, the smoke cleared.

'Dear God,' I murmured. 'Walton's foreyard has gone. Looks like his bowsprit's shattered, too.'

Both the standing and running rigging in the forward part of the *Association* was largely torn to shreds. Braces, bowlines, foreclue garnets and all the rest flew free, dancing upon the breeze.

'Put on sail, Sir Matthew?' asked Urquhart.

'Of course,' I said, angrily. 'We must save Valentine Walton from himself – if the old fool still lives.'

* * *

The *Jeanne d'Arc* fired again. We were closing her larboard quarter now, and I could not see what the consequences were for the *Association*. But the long delay before her guns responded, and their raggedness when they did, told an eloquent story.

'Mister Lovell!' I cried. 'Marines to the tops, if you please!'

An eager, yellow-coated young man doffed his hat in salute.

'Aye, aye, Sir Matthew!'

He was impossibly young, this Ensign of the newly formed Lord Admiral's Regiment, yet older than I had been when I, too, was an Ensign facing my first few tastes of battle. Lovell had been thrust into the command of the Marine detachment aboard the *Royal Sceptre* a few days earlier, during the St James' Day fight, when his superior officer had been killed, and there had been no opportunity to appoint a new captain with more experience. But he and his Marines had proved their worth in that action, and I had faith in them now. On Lovell's command, musketeers began to climb the shrouds to the tops. Others manned the starboard rail, taking their positions between the seamen on the swivel guns.

We had the advantage of the wind, and edged toward the Frenchman's larboard side. If the *Association* could still engage, we would be able to trap the *Jeanne d'Arc* between two broadsides. But I was not going to repeat the mistake of depending upon Valentine Walton.

'Mister Burdett!' The Master Gunner of the *Royal Sceptre* looked up at me from his place alongside one of the starboard demi-culverins. 'Chain and bar from the bow chasers, if you please! Round for his quarter-gallery!'

He knuckled his forehead. Burdett was a steady, quiet man, a veteran of the New Model Army's mighty artillery train, and knew his business. In truth my order was superfluous, since Burdett had anticipated what needed to be done, and already had the necessary guns loaded with the relevant shot.

Our first shots roared out. Glass shattered in the stern windows of the *Jeanne d'Arc*, and splinters of timber flew from her quarter-gallery. Mizzen shrouds tore and sprang free as our chain and bar shot severed them, and holes peppered the mizzen sail itself.

My officers moved among the men, bawling encouragement as guns were hauled back, reloaded, and hauled into position to fire again. Delacourt was on the forecastle, waving his sword and showing no fear. Burdett took a final look around the guns in the waist, then went below to ready our main armament of thirty-two pound demi-cannon and eighteen pound culverins. Martin Lanherne, acting boatswain, blew his whistle and yelled fortifying words at the men on the yards. He had been with me nearly since the beginning of my time at sea, this veteran of both the King's Army and Navy in the Civil Wars.

Lanherne led the large, unruly Cornish following that I had inherited from my murdered predecessor as captain of the frigate *Jupiter*, four years before. For some reason I had never quite been able to fathom, the Cornishmen had attached themselves to me, following me from ship to ship ever since.

The sternmost larboard guns of the *Jeanne d'Arc* opened fire. The hull of the *Royal Sceptre* shuddered as four, perhaps five heavy iron balls struck oak.

'Not what I'd expect from the French,' I said to Urquhart. 'A mistake, or bad aiming?'

'Neither,' said the ship's master in his Scots brogue. 'Look, Sir Matthew, they're adjusting some of their barrels even lower. They're going to fire for the hull. They're going to fight it out English-fashion.'

I shook my head. It was an article of faith among we English captains that our enemies in this war, the Dutch and French, fired high, on the uproll, trying to cripple the rigging and dismast our ships. If they succeeded, they could board, if they felt so inclined; if not, they could simply sail away. Whereas English ships, with heavier scantlings and heavier guns, mounted much closer to the waterline, fired low, aiming to shatter the enemy's hull and, if possible, sink it.

Our own forward guns fired again. I saw the flames, felt the deck shake beneath me, inhaled acrid gunsmoke. I saw our shot strike the hull of the French ship.

A young midshipman, Stockting, ran onto the quarterdeck, knuckled his forehead, and reported the situation below.

'One upper-deck demi-culverin dismounted, Sir Matthew,' he said. 'One man wounded. The Scot, Macferran.'

'Badly?'

'Splinter gash in his side. Taken below to the surgeon in the orlop.'

Rage surged through my blood. An unreasonable amount of rage for the wounding of one man; a wound that he might well survive, if the surgeon did his business properly. But Macferran was part of my following-within-a-following, the curious gaggle of ill-sorted creatures that seemed to consider it their principal duty in life to protect mine. When I had first encountered him, having been ordered to the west coast of Scotland by the King on what proved to be a desperate and bloody business, Macferran had been nothing but a poacher-cum-fisherman. Now, he was an able seaman and a credit to the Navy. More than that, he was part of my strange, surrogate, seaborne family.

I drew my sword, went to the quarterdeck rail, and bellowed as loudly as I could.

'Sceptres! Time to show the Frogs the quality of English hearts and English blood! For God, Saint George, and King Charles!'

I brought my blade sharply downwards, and the *Royal Sceptre*'s full broadside opened fire.

* * *

'Give fire!'

On my command, the *Sceptre* fired again. The quarterdeck demi-culverins spat flame, a near-deafening blast thundered across the waters, and smoke billowed across the deck. And once again, almost as though they were responding to my own order, the guncrews of the *Jeanne d'Arc* responded. The two ships were so close that neither of us could miss. I felt iron balls strike our hull, low down, and felt the hull shake beneath my feet. Men screamed.

A youth of no more than eighteen ran up and knuckled his fore-head in salute. I recognised him as one of the carpenter's crew.

'Word from Mister Richardson, Sir Matthew. A second hole below the waterline. Bad one, just forward of the mainmast step.'

I glanced at Urquhart and Francis Gale. We all knew what that meant. Even the arch-lubber Phineas Musk, standing nearby and firing off pistols at the Frenchman's quarterdeck, frowned, for he knew, too.

'Mister Lanherne!' I cried. The boatswain, down in the ship's waist ordering men to repairs of shattered rigging, looked up. 'Look to the pumps! Every fourth quarter to man them!'

'Aye, aye, Sir Matthew!'

Such bad damage below the waterline was sure to force us out of the engagement, and sooner rather than later, especially as the *Association*, out of sight on the starboard, leeward side of the Frenchman, had been entirely silent for an hour or more. If we were going to win, rather than withdrawing in dishonour, we would have to do so in short order. Very short order.

All along the starboard side, gun crews were cleaning, loading, ramming, ready to run out the guns for our next broadside. And all the while, the relentless popping and puffs of smoke from the firing of pistols and muskets. Until now, our quarterdeck had received relatively little attention; the Frenchmen in their tops seemed intent principally on exchanging fire with Lovell's Marines in ours. Suddenly, though, a volley of lead balls struck all around us. Baines, a master's mate, fell to the deck, clutching his thigh. Francis Gale went to him, offered him words of Godly consolation, then set about the more worldly task of bandaging the wound.

I put down my sword, drew out my two pistols from my belt, and fired them in the general direction of the enemy. From a deck that was pitching and rolling in the swell, and with the target doing exactly the same, I found it impossible to be more accurate than that. But Musk, alongside me, steadied himself, took lengthy aim, and fired. We saw the head of a Frenchman shatter, a good two hundred yards away.

'Bravo, Musk!' I cried.

He shrugged.

'Bit of weight, Sir Matthew. What the uncharitable call "fat". Makes a man steadier for the aim.'

But that was not all, and we both knew it; Musk's youth, a dark age over which he drew an impenetrable veil, had seemingly embraced activities that bestowed all kinds of unlikely, but generally violent, skills upon him.

I went to the quarterdeck rail, and waiting for the signals from the gun captains and the Master Gunner. Wait for the downroll…

'*Give fire!*'

This time, our shot seemed to have more of an effect. There was a noticeably longer interval before the Frenchman replied, and when he did, his broadside was more ragged. A part of me wanted nothing more than to close and board. It was what my grandfather would have done, but the science of naval warfare had moved on since the time of the great Elizabeth's sea-dogs. Boarding was a deeply unpredictable business, especially against large and determined crews, as that of the *Jeanne d'Arc* clearly was. There were great holes in the enemy's larboard side, and his rigging was in tatters. No doubt ours appeared in a similar state, when viewed from the Frenchman's quarterdeck; but we were more heavily built, and could take more punishment. Above all, we had a greatly superior weight of broadside to the Frenchman, together with a more practised crew possessing substantial recent experience of battle, which was certainly not true of our opponent. In the end those considerations were bound to tell: bound to, that is, as long as we stayed afloat long enough for them to do so.

There was a sudden, colossal roar –

'The *Association*!' I cried. 'Dear God, she's rallied!'

Why had our companion been silent for so long? I had wondered more than once whether Walton, or whichever officer had succeeded him if he was dead, had surrendered. What had enabled her to rejoin the battle now? But this was not the moment for speculation. It was time to strike.

'Faster, Mister Burdett!' I called to the Master Gunner. 'One more effort! One more broadside! Come on, men! A double ration of wine, at my expense! One more broadside for England, the King's prick, and your doxies!'

All over the deck, exhausted gun crews redoubled their efforts. I had no doubt that the same was happening on the lower gundecks.

There is nothing on earth more determined than an Englishman who scents victory.

The *Jeanne d'Arc* had not replied to the *Association*. And she did not reply now, as the broadside of the *Royal Sceptre* thundered for one final time. Moments later, the tattered white fleur-de-lis ensign came down. A ragged cheer broke out in the waist, and was echoed by the men below decks. Phineas Musk punched the air, while Francis Gale offered up prayers of thanksgiving and for magnanimity in victory. I fell to my knees, leaned heavily on my sword, breathed deeply, and joined in Francis' prayer.

'The Lord hath appeared for us; the Lord hath covered our heads, and made us to stand in the day of battle. The Lord hath appeared for us; the Lord hath overthrown our enemies, and dashed in pieces those that rose up against us. Therefore not unto us, O Lord, not unto us: but unto thy name be given the Glory.'

Perhaps it was the influence – or the ghost – of my French Catholic grandmother, or even of Shakespeare's King Hal, but I found myself mouthing the last part of the prayer in Latin.

Non nobis, domine.

Chapter Two

'God willing we can keep her afloat,' said Richardson, the carpenter of the *Royal Sceptre*, 'but we can hope for little better than that, Sir Matthew. The ship has to be docked, and as soon as possible.'

I stood alongside him – or rather, crouched alongside him, for I was nearly doubled over – by the starboard side of the ship's hold, well below the waterline. The stench from the bilges was overwhelming. Two members of Richardson's crew were hammering a makeshift fix of timber and canvas over one of the three holes in the lower part of the hull. There was a distant sound of hammering above, too, as the great gashes in our starboard side were repaired.

I climbed back up to the orlop deck, where Lanherne awaited me.

'The pumps are coping?' I asked.

'Barely, Sir Matthew. But it's better now than it was, as long as the carpenter's repairs hold. More a case of if the men can cope.'

'They'll cope. Tell the cook to be generous with the beer – I know stocks are low, but I doubt if we'll be needing to keep the sea to wait for the victualling ships.'

'Aye, aye, Sir Matthew.'

I went astern, to that part of the orlop reserved for the surgeon. Rowan, who held that post on the *Royal Sceptre*, was a venerable fellow who claimed to have stitched up a gash in the arm of the Duke of Buckingham during the La Rochelle expedition in the year Twenty-Seven. But he was still nimble and steady, and his patients trusted him.

Two of the patients were well known to me. Macferran tried to sit up as I approached, but I raised a hand.

'Not yet your turn to stand before Saint Peter, then, Macferran?'

'Seems not, Sir Matthew.'

'Painful?'

'As if I've been ripped open, sir.'

'You have been. Be thankful that Master Rowan, there, knows what he's doing. There's not a few sawbones in the fleet whose attentions would have seen you slipping beneath the waves in weighted canvas long before now.'

I went over to the other member of my personal following who lay among the twenty or so men in the surgeon's care. He lay on his back, unable to raise himself thanks to a bad wound in his right thigh, which was heavily bandaged. Even so, his head was still well off the ground, supported by a rough pillow, because he was so shaped that it was impossible for him to stand wholly upright.

'*Fatla genes, Jowan?*'

'*Pur dda, meur ras, Syr Mathi.*'

John Treninnick spoke no English, only the tongue of his native Cornwall, where he had spent too many years bending in the low seams of tin mines. But his strange shape, and the astonishing strength he had in his arms, made him perhaps the best topman in the fleet. And I now had enough rudimentary Cornish to ask him how he was, and to understand his obvious lie about being very well.

'He'll live?' I asked Rowan.

'God willing, as long as gangrene doesn't set in. That wound would have killed nine men out of every ten, but Treninnick isn't like other men.'

'Keep him alive, Master Surgeon. Keep them all alive, if you can.'

'That I shall, Sir Matthew. If I can.'

I went back up to the lower gundeck, where the gunports were closed. The ship was listing slightly due to the holes below the waterline, and although it was a hot, sunny day at the beginning of August, I dared not order the ports to be opened. Consequently, the deck was dark, and resembled the inside of an over-coaled bread oven. The fetid smells from the bilges and the stench of rotting flesh from the surgery below permeated the entire space. Sweating, half-naked men were scrubbing blood from the planking, and resetting two of the thirty-two pounder demi-cannon back onto new carriages. Three of Master Carpenter Richardson's men were putting the finishing touches to the repair of one of the great holes in the ship's side. I walked among the men, speaking some words of encouragement. Some of them, especially the Cornish, I knew well: good men like the tiny John Tremar and the giant George Polzeath. It was good to see that both still lived, and, God willing, would return to their homes over the winter for a few months of – well, fishing, if I believed what they told me, or smuggling, if I believed my own instincts.

To the upper gundeck, where at least the ports were open, although the culverins and demi-culverins had been hauled inboard. A few messes were at rest around their tables between the guns; we had little sail aloft, although many men had been transferred to the pumps, where the off-watch men would soon relieve them. Some were smoking clay pipes over tubs of water, up forward, as the regulations of the Navy demanded. Some played board games, one or two who could do so were reading. Ali Reis, the Moorish renegade, was playing a few soft notes on his fiddle, too rapt in the music to notice his captain's presence.

I climbed back into daylight, and breathed deeply, ridding my lungs of the between-decks stench of gunsmoke, sweat, blood, and death. I looked across to the other ships in our little squadron, inching north-west toward the safety of our fleet, and prayed that De Ruyter and the Dutch did not appear on the northern horizon, nor the Duke of Beaufort and the French on the southern. For our condition was dire. In one sense the *Association* was in a better state than we were, intact below the waterline. The French captain had clearly adopted a different strategy for each of his opponents, choosing to attack us in the hull but Walton's ship in the rigging, as his nation was wont to do. And the effect of that attack had been truly shocking. I now knew that Valentine Walton had been killed by the very first broadside, his body smashed into three pieces by barshot. Almost all his officers, over-confidently and foolishly massed together on the quarterdeck, had been slaughtered by the same cannonade. This, of course, explained the ship's inaction during our own engagement with the *Jeanne d'Arc*. One of the two master's mates who survived fled to the hold and hid himself there, shitting himself and moaning piteously the whole time. The other attempted to surrender, but was shot through the head by a fifteen-year-old midshipman, who valiantly took command and attempted to fight the ship. To fight it for all of ten minutes, it seemed, before a musketball fired from the *Jeanne d'Arc's* maintop struck him in the forehead, leaving a blind ship's cook as acting captain of the King's ship *Association*. It was he who had somehow rallied enough men to fire the decisive broadside that convinced the Frenchman to surrender. I had sent over Urquhart to assume temporary command, along with some thirty of our men and Francis Gale, who felt it his duty to offer spiritual succour to men who had witnessed such slaughter.

Behind the frigate, the great French ship wallowed in the waves, listing to larboard. Julian Delacourt was commanding the prize crew, no doubt revelling in his first independent command. Ensign Lovell and most of his Marines were aboard her too. But it was time for proprieties to be observed, and for Sir Matthew Quinton to meet the worthy captain who had proved such a formidable opponent.

'Mister Carvell, there! Ready the longboat!'

A tall black man grinned impudently, despite knuckling his forehead with appropriate deference. 'Aye, aye, Sir Matthew.'

Julian Carvell, now coxswain of the *Royal Sceptre*, sometime slave in Virginia and sometime killer of his owner (if lower-deck rumour was to be believed), went off to assemble a boat crew. I retired to my cabin, now restored to a vaguely habitable and respectable state by young Kellett, the only survivor of my little band of captain's servants. A band of four that had been halved in the Saint James' day fight, when two of them were killed; a third had developed the bloody flux a few days later, and was either recovering, or dying, or already dead, aboard the hospital ship.

As I entered, Musk seemed to be explaining the facts of life to Kellett.

'So then the man puts –'

'Yes, I know *that,* Master Musk, done it often enough – beg pardon, Sir Matthew, never heard you, sir!'

'Evidently. And God help you, Kellett, if you are learning the delicate arts of love and frigging from Phineas Musk. Best shirt, breeches, frock coat and wig, lad, and smartly, if you please!'

'Yes, Sir Matthew!'

The boy flung open my larger sea chest and began to extract the clothes.

'Off to see the Frog, then, Sir Matthew?' said Musk. 'Ready for a touch of arrogance, Popery and strong perfume?'

'I take it, then, that you won't be accompanying me, Musk?'

'Can't abide the French.'

'Is there any nation on earth, other than the English, that you *can* abide? But remember that my grandmother was French, and a Catholic. You served her devotedly, as I recall.'

'Ah, but she was a great lady, your grandmother. Besides, she was the Countess of Ravensden. That cancelled out the rest of it.'

'Let the world be truly thankful that you never became a judge, Musk. I dread to conceive of the even-handedness of your justice.'

* * *

The longboat took me across to the *Jeanne d'Arc*. As we approached, I attempted to calculate her worth in prize money. A tidy sum, that was certain, and I had already done well from prize money in the present war. Or rather, I had done well *in theory*. Quite when the permanently straitened Treasury of King Charles II would pay me the sums due to me was another matter. This was a source of some friction in my domestic life, as my wife Cornelia had designs upon a country estate for us once the war ended. Being Dutch, and thus a native of a tiny, sodden, crowded country where land was as scarce as gold dust, she dreamed of broad acres and spacious gardens, where we could take her leisure and bring up our unborn child. It was a pleasant prospect, and one I shared; but I also had a better grasp of the tortuous workings of the prize system, and of the price of land in the more tolerable shires of England.

Aboard the Frenchman, Lovell had assembled an impromptu side party of Marines, and he and Julian Delacourt saluted with their swords as I stepped aboard. Groups of French sailors looked on sullenly.

'The French captain's below, in his cabin, Sir Matthew,' said Delacourt. 'Took a wound during the fight – his surgeon's attending to him.'

'Very good,' I said. 'And his crew are co-operating?'

'As much as Frenchmen ever co-operate.'

'Ah. Carry on, then, Mister Delacourt.'

'Aye, aye, Sir Matthew.'

I went below and entered the captain's cabin of the *Jeanne d'Arc*, or rather, what was left of it. There was no glass in the stern windows, both quarter galleries were gone, and a huge hole in the deck allowed a clear view of blue sky. In the middle of the cabin, what could only be the surgeon – a fussy little man with red-black ooze on his hands and a blood-stained apron at his front – was stitching a gaping gash in the left shoulder of the man who must have been the ship's captain.

He looked up at me as I entered, and smiled.

I am a tall man; or at least, I was once a tall man. In my prime, in those faraway days of which I write, I was one of the only men at court able to look his lofty Majesty, Charles the Second, in the eye. But the French captain dwarfed me. He was a veritable colossus, a full hand's width taller than myself, and perhaps twice as broad. Worse, he was sculpted like an ancient statue of a Classical god – strong features, piercing eyes, close-cropped grey hair, a bare chest like the breastplate of Hercules himself. He must have been twice my age, yet whereas most men so ancient were wheezing their way rapidly to the grave, the gallant Frenchman sprang to his feet with the ease of a hare.

He bowed in the extravagant French fashion, the smile on his face so broad that an observer might readily have assumed he was the victor here, not the vanquished.

'Sir Matthew Quinton!' he exclaimed in English. 'A true honour to meet the acquaintance of such a brave and famous officer! Why, Sir Matthew, your praises are sung daily at court by your friend, my friend, the noble and excellent comte d'Andelys –'

'Forgive me, sir,' I said, 'but whose surrender do I have the honour of accepting?'

My slight peevishness upset him not a jot. Instead, he bowed again.

'Jean-Paul Ollivier, Sir Matthew, of Quimper in Brittany. Captain in the service of His Most Christian Majesty, Louis the Fourteenth, King of France and Navarre.'

That would explain his English, I thought: the Bretons were famous linguists, no other race on earth except the infernal Welsh (and my Cornish, come to that) being able to understand their native tongue. It would also explain the remarkable sailing and fighting qualities that Ollivier and his crew had displayed during the battle, for the Bretons were renowned seamen, forming the backbone of the manpower of King Louis' mighty new navy.

'Well, Captain Ollivier, I regret to have to inform you that you are my prisoner, sir.'

He inclined his head. 'Of course. It is, as I say, an honour. As it will be to accept your hospitality, Sir Matthew. The noble *comte*, our mutual friend, speaks very highly of it.'

'My – hospitality, Captain?'

'Indeed,' said Ollivier, grinning broadly. 'I will happily give my parole, of course, until such time as an exchange is arranged, or the war ends. But I will give it on condition that I serve that time as your guest, trusting that you will forgive my presumption. Else, of course, I shall be compelled to attempt to escape, and to kill as many Englishmen as I possibly can in the process.'

The impudence of the man! And yet there was an irresistible quality to him, the grin remaining firmly in place as he delivered his threat…

'With respect, Captain, that will be a matter for my superiors to decide.'

'Oh, I envisage no difficulties there, Sir Matthew. I served under your admiral, you see, as a kind of *chef d'escadre* – with Prince Rupert, back in the year Fifty-Two. He will vouch for me. Above all, he will vouch for my religion.'

For the first time, I realised that the captain's cabin of the *Jeanne d'Arc* contained no Romish paraphernalia, such as crucifixes and statues of saints. That, presumably, was why Jean-Paul Ollivier had been able to serve in the tiny Royalist fleet commanded by Prince Rupert, son of one of Europe's greatest Protestant heroes, in those dark days of the usurping Commonwealth.

'You are a Huguenot?'

He inclined his head. 'So you see, Sir Matthew, you need have no fear of being accused of harbouring a Papist.'

This altered the case. The French Protestants, or Huguenots, were tolerated by King Louis, but only barely. It would be instructive to learn more of their true condition. Roger d'Andelys, my French friend, was a good man, but he was also a Catholic, and thus not necessarily an impartial source. I was also eager to learn more of the French navy, namely how it had been transformed almost overnight into such a power upon the seas. Naturally, I did not dishonour myself and embarrass Captain Ollivier by demanding to know how far behind him sailed Beaufort's fleet, what the Duke's objective might be, or why the *Jeanne d'Arc* had been sent on her lone mission. But I sensed that the Breton would be good company at a dinner table, a house guest who might keep Cornelia entertained as her full term approached, and a man who might both inform and amuse me during the months ahead, after the fleet paid off. True, Captain Ollivier's presence would very probably annoy Phineas Musk, but that in itself might create some amusing entertainment.

After all, it was bound to be another long and uneventful winter in London.

Chapter Three

Our return to the fleet, with the shattered *Association* in tow and our prize, the *Jeanne d'Arc*, sailing in our wake, was marked by huzzahs and gunfire salutes, the smoke rolling across the gently swelling waters. Cheers rang out from every ship, from the mighty *Sovereign*, the largest and most famous ship in the world, down to the humblest victualling hoy and ketch. We sailed into the midst of our three squadrons, the Red, White and Blue, and slipped into the wake of the flagship, the *Royal Charles*, the Union flying from her main. The Navy Royal of England was sailing proud, just out of sight of the Dutch coast, having taken command of the sea after the Saint James' day fight, the second of that summer's great battles. Our enemy had retreated to his harbours to lick his wounds, giving us free rein.

I ordered the ship's longboat made ready to take me to the flagship. When we were roughly half way across, I noticed another boat pulling away from the side of the great vessel, her crew rowing her toward the *Loyal London*, flagship of the Blue, perhaps the most laughably misnamed vessel in the entire history of the Navy Royal – London having been anything but loyal to the Stuart monarchs, rather than the seething hotbed of sedition, dissent and rebellion it still was.

'His Grace don't seem keen to see you, Sir Matthew,' said Carvell.

'Keep your eyes on our course, Mister Carvell,' I said, although I could not resist a slight smile.

Julian Carvell knew, as did every man on the *Royal Sceptre*, that the Duke of Albemarle, joint admiral of the fleet, heartily detested me, and that the feeling was entirely reciprocated on my part. I had recently bested and embarrassed His Grace, which rather fewer knew; and Valentine Walton had been a protégé of his. So it was no surprise that the portly figure of the erstwhile General George Monck, the man who had restored monarchy to England, should be sitting in the stern of a boat pulling away swiftly from my own, not deigning to cast a backward glance in my direction.

Our boat came alongside, I acknowledged the boatswain's pipe and the salute of the flagship's side party, and went up to the quarterdeck.

'So, Matthew Quinton,' said a sharply-dressed, long-nosed fellow in his mid-forties, who possessed a pronounced dimple in his chin. He spoke with a German accent. 'You leave the fleet to cruise with two fine, intact ships. You return with three wrecks. Will my cousins think that a good return, do you think?'

I bowed to the other joint admiral of our fleet, Rupert, Prince Palatine of the Rhine. He still had about him something of the air of the impetuous young cavalry general who had nearly won the civil war for his uncle, King Charles the First, but the rings around the eyes were dark and tired.

'My apologies, Your Highness,' I said. 'The Frenchman, yonder, put up a stouter resistance than many of the Dutchmen we encountered in the late fights.'

Prince Rupert nodded.

'I would have expected nothing less. I know Captain Ollivier of old, as I expect he told you – we sailed together, for a time, back in the days when my cousin's royal cause comprised my single ship, and that alone. A good man, and a good fighter. He and I will sup together tonight, and you must join us, Matt Quinton. We shall be a merry company, I think. So you must tell me how the fight went here and now, so we do not embarrass our guest at table.'

The Prince led me to the starboard rail, and listened intently as I regaled him with the account of our battle with the *Jeanne d'Arc*. As I did so, I reflected on the fickle nature of destiny. I had spent most of my life blaming and hating Rupert of the Rhine for the death of my father, when I was only five years old. James Quinton, Earl of Ravensden for just one hundred and eighteen days, had perished in the Battle of Naseby when Rupert failed to support him during their fateful cavalry charge against the rebels' left wing. But a little over a year before, the Prince had astonished me by apologising fulsomely for his failure on that fateful day, and by revealing that he had been my secret patron in the Navy. During my recent confrontation with the Duke of Albemarle, Rupert had taken my side without hesitation. So now I spoke to him openly and enthusiastically, man to man, warrior to warrior.

'Excellent,' said the Prince as I concluded, 'most excellent, Matt. But troubling, in one sense. The fact that King Louis was willing to send this ship through the Channel demonstrates that the Duke of Beaufort and his fleet will not be too far behind. This time, I think, the French really will join with the Dutch, if we do not take steps to prevent it.'

I knew he had the same thought in his mind as I did. Earlier in the summer, our fleet had been divided due to a rumour that the French fleet was approaching the Channel, intent on joining with the Dutch. Every man in the fleet knew what that meant. The Dutch were unlikely to invade England, but the French were a very different coin, the possessors of a vast and terrible army that had trounced even the invincible Spanish, so the prospect of the *mousquetaires du roi* marching up Ludgate Hill chilled every English heart. The rumour of the approach of King Louis' fleet had proved false, but the Dutch fell on Albemarle's weakened fleet while Rupert was away in pursuit of the illusory French. During a ferocious four-day fight, our ships had been shattered and many good men killed, including one of my dearest friends, Sir William Berkeley.* So the prospect of an actual conjunction between the two enemy navies was bound to concern any Englishman – or an adopted Englishman, as Prince Rupert undoubtedly was.

'As Your Highness says. But I fear my ship is too shattered to play any further part. The French prize, too. Both of us are holed below the waterline, and much shattered in our hulls.'

We looked out toward the two badly damaged ships. A busy little royal yacht was approaching the quarter of the *Jeanne d'Arc*, no doubt to take off the estimable Captain Ollivier and bring him to the flagship.

'Losing a ship of such force as the *Sceptre* will be a grave loss,' said Rupert. 'But you are right. There is nothing for it. She and the prize must be sent into the river at once, and then up to one of the dockyards for repair.'

I bowed my head. I knew the order was inevitable, but hearing it from the lips of my admiral still felt like a hammer striking my chest. England was still in grave danger, there was still a possibility of carrying out some great and glorious service against the French, or the Dutch, or both, and yet Matthew Quinton would play no part in any of it. I would be confined ashore for the remainder of the summer, with nothing to do but to bellow at idle dockyard shipwrights and rage against the endless dockets, musters, and papers that would be demanded by the officious Navy Board clerks.

Still, I supposed that my wife would be happy to have me at home.

'Tell me, Matt,' said the Prince, as though reading my thoughts, 'your lieutenant, young Delacourt. Is he an able man?'

'He is no seaman, Your Highness.'

---

* See *The Battle of All The Ages*

'Neither were you, once. Neither was I. No, I do not mean able in that sense – I care not whether he can set his own course, or name every sail or rope. Does he have the respect of your crew, Sir Matthew?'

'He does. He proved himself a brave and resourceful fighter in the last battle, and the men took to him.'

'And you have experienced and reliable warrant officers, do you not?'

'I do, Your Highness.'

My heart lifted. I had a sense of what the Prince had in mind.

'Very well. It seems to me, then, that there is little to be gained, and much to be lost, by Sir Matthew Quinton leaving the fleet, even if his ship must. Besides, there is a little scheme afoot which would benefit greatly from your experience and resourcefulness. A little scheme which would greatly confound our Dutch friends, if it succeeds. I am due to talk with the instigators of that scheme this very hour. Might you be interested in such a scheme, Matt?'

I knew I was grinning like a schoolboy, but could not stop myself.

'I would be interested, Your Highness.'

'Excellent. And, of course, your remaining in the fleet will quite confound His Grace of Albemarle. When the scout came back with news of your action, he was beside himself with delight. Not at the capture of the Frenchman, but at the thought of you having to leave for England.'

* * *

The great cabin of the *Royal Charles* was palatial, as befitted the ship that had brought His Majesty the King back from exile six years before. As we entered, two men, who were deep in conversation by the stern windows, turned and bowed to the Prince. One of them I recognised immediately. Square of stature, with a great nose, a scarred chin, and remarkably broad and long hands, he was really too old to wear the loose satin sleeves that were then in vogue at court. But there was still more than a little of the roguish young gallant about Sir Robert Holmes, rear-admiral of the Red Squadron, an old cavalry companion of Prince Rupert and an old drinking companion of mine.

'I give you joy of your victory, Sir Matthew!' he cried with unfeigned delight, stepping across the deck to shake my hand vigorously with his iron grip while slapping me heavily on the back.

'My thanks, Sir Robert.'

'So you'll be joining our little expedition, then? Taking a great Frog man-of-war not enough to slake your thirst for action, Matt? Good man. Now, let me have the honour to name you to our friend, here. Sir Matthew Quinton – Captain Lauris van Heemskerck, late of the Admiralty of Rotterdam, now as true a subject of King Charles as you or I.'

The other man stepped forward, and bowed his head slightly. He was a small fellow with pronounced cheekbones, close-cropped grey hair, and a slightly nervous, hunted air. As well he might have. I had heard of Captain van Heemskerck during the previous weeks, but our paths had never crossed until that moment. My opinion of him had been formed long before our meeting, though. Discontented at his Admiralty's failure to promote him to the rank he thought his due, and swayed by the amount of gold that my king's agents offered him, Lauris van Heemskerck had quietly despatched his family to safety in Dover, then deserted the service of the United Provinces for that of the King of England. In short, he was a traitor; and even though we were at war with his homeland, and by rights I should have rejoiced at any defection that benefited our cause against the arrogant Dutch butterboxes, I hated traitors more than I hated nearly anything else on this earth.

'Captain,' I said, as neutrally as I could manage.

The Prince must have detected my mood, for he drew us at once to the chart on the table beneath the stern window. I recognised it straight away: the north coasts of the Dutch provinces of Holland and

Friesland, including the islands that lay offshore like a string of pearls guarding the approaches to the mainland. Flat, featureless, muddy pearls. My wife, who hailed from the more southerly and sophisticated Zeeland, once told me that the islanders were all related to each other within the canonical decrees, and had six fingers on each hand.

'The Frisian Islands,' said Rupert. 'Here, Texel, which we know all too well.'

He pointed to a large oval just off the northern tip of the peninsula that stretched up the west side of the Dutchmen's inland sea. Yes, we knew it all right. The Dutch fleet invariably anchored behind Texel, venturing out against us through the sea-gate between it and the mainland. We had spent entire weeks at a time during each of the last two summers cruising off that shore, spying out the masts visible above the low shape of the island, wondering if and when the enemy would come out.

Rupert's hand moved north and east, a little closer toward the coasts of the Holy Roman Empire and Denmark.

'The next two islands, Vlieland here, Terschelling here. These are the objects of our current interest, Sir Matthew. Captain van Heemskerck, explain if you will.'

'The islands are undefended,' said the traitor in a thin, reedy voice, although his English was excellent. 'Or at least, defended only by small companies of militia and perhaps a handful of small frigates and privateers. High Pensionary De Witt – the devil take him and all his fawning True Freedomers – he believes that if you English decide to attack the coast, it will be somewhere between Den Helder and The Hague. So most of the army is drawn up there, where it can move north or south as needs must. Besides, they believe that the English will not be able to get within the sea-gates, to the waters behind the Frisian Islands, because you do not know the safe channels. But I do.'

I looked at van Heemskerck anew: perhaps he had not sold his country for forty pieces of silver after all. If he hated Johann de Witt and the craven republican scum who ruled the Netherlands entirely in the interest of Amsterdam and its money-brokers, then he was surely an Orangist – one who sought the promotion to his family's lost honours of Prince William the Third, our King's nephew. As was my wife.

'We've had scout ships out,' said H olmes, 'and there are hundreds of masts behind the Vlie. Not warships, Sir Matthew. They're merchantmen, including plenty of fat ones. Levanters for sure. West Indiamen, certainly. East Indiamen, perhaps. Rich trades, waiting for the winds and tides to be right for them to get over the Pampus and up to Amsterdam. Destroy them, and all the warehouses their trading companies have on the Vlie, and at the very least, it'll cause a panic in the States-General, and on the Amsterdam bourse. At best, their losses will be so huge that there'll be a revolution against de Witt and his coterie. The States-General will have to send for the Prince of Orange, and the Dutch will have to make peace on His Majesty's terms.'

'And, God willing,' said Prince Rupert, 'we can accomplish this in a matter of days. Certainly long before Beaufort's French fleet comes into the North Sea and joins with the Dutch. If this scheme prospers, there might even be no Dutch fleet for the Frogs to join with. Who knows, perhaps Beaufort will be isolated, far from friendly harbours, and will fall easy prey to us. If that happens, who is to say that England will not defeat *both* of its great enemies before the summer is out?'

I looked at the chart. It all seemed so tempting, so very easy. Yet I remembered something my uncle Tristram had taught me when I was no more than ten or so, when news came that the Scottish royalist army had somehow lost from an impregnable position against Oliver Cromwell at the Battle of Dunbar.

'General Leslie should have remembered to put himself in the shoes of the Emperor Xerxes, young Matthew. Even if you're faced with only three hundred Spartans, it doesn't mean that victory is assured.'

And yet, the militias of Vlieland and Terschelling would hardly be Spartans. Perhaps some victories really could be bought so easily.

'The scheme is this,' said the Prince. 'Sir Robert, here, will command an expedition to go close inshore. There will be eight of our best frigates, a dozen or so ketches and hoys, perhaps fifty boats. Some one thousand men, divided into ten companies – each company to consist of both soldiers and sailors. A further company of gentlemen volunteers, to be commanded by Sir Philip Howard.' Holmes and I exchanged glances. Here at last might be some justification for the hordes of titled wastrels who had come to sea for the campaign, hoping for glory and honour, yet who had done little but take up precious space on the ships that bore them. 'The names of the ships and the proposed commanders of companies are here, upon this list.' He handed us three identical copies. 'That will be sufficient, Captain van Heemskerck?'

'More than sufficient, Highness.'

'Very well. Before we discuss the detail of times and dispositions, there is one matter to resolve. The expedition needs a second-in-command. A man of experience, and of sufficient seniority should the admiral fall. Now, Sir Philip Howard is a good man, but he is a soldier, and this is a position for a seaman.' The Prince did not need to add that Howard was Albemarle's man, formerly the captain of his personal guard; Rupert of the Rhine would rather have had the King's latest doxy as second in command than hand a chance of glory to any protégé of the rotund Duke. 'Sir Matthew, it seems to both Sir Robert and I that the *Royal Sceptre*'s disability is surely a sign of God's divine purpose in this matter. You are available for the task, and no man in the fleet is better suited for it. If you are willing to take it, the honour is yours.'

Holmes was grinning, Rupert serious. For my part, I doubted whether God's divine purpose had anything to do with the matter. But the prospect of playing my part in an action that might, God willing, put an end to this war, was one that no man with Quinton blood and the Quinton name could refuse.

'I accept, Your Highness,' I said. 'And if you and Sir Robert will permit it, I wish to make my choice of my headquarters ship from the frigates listed here.'

'And that would be?'

'The *Black Prince*,' I said. 'Captain Christopher Farrell.'

Chapter Four

Dawn on a fine early August morning, a marked contrast to the previous day. The sun began to rise in the east, dead ahead, revealing the two long, low islands barely a couple of miles away. The islands of Vlieland and Terschelling.

Now was the hour. We were about to invade Holland.

I stood on the quarterdeck of the *Black Prince*, a fine-lined Fourth Rate frigate mounting some forty-six cannon, the ensign of the Red Squadron spilling out over her stern. Her captain, a stocky fellow of my own age, wearing a plain russet coat, stood at my side. How matters had changed for both of us since that fateful day, five years earlier, when the young gentleman captain of His Majesty's ship the *Happy Restoration* was saved from drowning during her shipwreck on the Irish coast by an equally youthful master's mate from Wapping named Kit Farrell. A shipwreck that had been caused entirely by Captain Matthew Quinton's utter ignorance of the ways of the sea and ships. We had come to an agreement that day: Kit would teach me those ways, and in turn I would teach him to read and write. Since then, he had served under me in various ships and posts, latterly as my lieutenant, until his bravery in the Four Days' battle eight weeks earlier led the joint admirals to promote him to this, his first command.

Captain Christopher Farrell still looked about his ship with a sense of awe, as though he could not quite believe or comprehend what had happened to him. And, if truth be told, there was still a part of Captain Sir Matthew Quinton that could not quite believe or comprehend what had happened to the two of us in the space of a mere five years.

'Sir Robert's hoisting a signal!' shouted Kit's boatswain.

'I see it, Mister Kendall,' cried Kit. 'The red at the mizzen – the command to fall into the admiral's wake. We're forming line!'

Holmes had shifted his flag to the *Tyger*, a frigate of similar force to the *Black Prince*, in which he was leading the rest of us towards the channel between the two Dutch islands. This followed the previous day's debacle, when, as Holmes later told me, Lauris van Heemskerck had listened to each successive, troublingly shallow, sounding by the *Tyger*'s leadsman, shaken his head, murmured that the sandbanks must have shifted since he was last in those waters in April, and avoided Sir Robert's furious gaze for the rest of the day. Fortunately, a small Danish craft, approaching the sea-gate and blissfully unaware of the presence of our squadron, had blundered directly into the path of the *Garland*, and her skipper proved eager to win his release in return for piloting us into the anchorage.

Kit Farrell took up a voice trumpet and began shouting orders to his crew. Many more orders than I would have issued myself. I inclined to the view that if a captain had faith in his warrant officers, they could be left to issue the great majority of commands; and perhaps there was still a part of me that secretly sympathised with the views of my friend and fellow gentleman commander, Beaudesert Harris. Beau was by no means alone in his belief that captains of good birth should not sully themselves with such artisan tasks as mastering the name and purpose of every rope and timber on the ship, with writing up their own journals, or with checking the gunner's and carpenter's stores. Instead, he contended, they should adhere only to the traditional role of the warrior-knight, namely that of leading by example in battle. Or, as we both put it when we were in our cups, standing fearlessly upon an exposed deck, waving a sword, shouting very loudly, and being shot at.

'A fair wind for it, Sir Matthew,' said Kit, who knew every rope of his ship, every timber, and everything else to do with it. 'South-westerly, not strong enough to trap us behind the shoals when we want to come out again.'

'Let us hope it remains so, K – Captain Farrell,' I said.

One had to maintain formalities in the hearing of his own crew, especially as I had seen the looks in the eyes of some of his men: the jealousy and resentment of those who knew full well that their captain was drawn from the same social rank as they were, but had risen much faster, and at a much younger age, than any of them. We had discussed it at dinner in his great cabin, the previous afternoon, shortly after the shattered *Royal Sceptre* had left the fleet, taking with her Francis Gale and a bitterly complaining Phineas Musk, who'd seemed convinced that I would be killed as soon as I was out of his sight.

'You have the advantage of birth, Sir Matthew,' Kit had said. 'Even in our time on the *Happy Restoration*, the men respected you as the brother of an Earl, a man of birth to whom they would naturally defer, despite –'

He blushed, and took a sip of wine instead of completing his sentence. He still lifted his glass cautiously, as though he were not entirely sure of this unfamiliar drink and the refined manner in which commissioned sea-captains of the King were expected to drink it.

'Despite the fact that I knew less of the sea than the rats who plagued our orlop on that unhappy ship? You have the right of it, Captain Farrell.'

He smiled.

'And now, they respect you as a brave and famous commander, and a knight of the realm. Sir Matthew Quinton, who has the favour of Prince Rupert and whose brother is a friend of the King. Whereas as far as they're concerned, I'm just plain Kit Farrell, a mere tarpaulin from Wapping, an alehouse landlady's brat who just happens to have had more luck than they have.'

'Nonsense. Oh, nonsense, man!' Kit rarely stooped to self-pity, but when he did, it irritated me beyond measure. 'The heroism you displayed in the late battle is a byword in the fleet, and seamen always respect a captain who knows his business. Besides, Kit, you're an example to them. They'll all be out there in their messes, or at their stations, thinking to themselves that if you can do it, then so can they.'

'If they don't mutiny and fillet me first, that is.'

'I'd worry about the Dutch rather more than about your own men, Captain Farrell.'

He frowned, as though still not entirely convinced, but then looked back at me, and his mind seemed to be more at ease.

'Amen to that, Sir Matthew, amen to that. Now tell me, in confidence – is this good wine or no? With ale, one sip is enough to tell me its origin and its quality. But wine… I fear I will never become a judge of it.'

I had not the heart to tell him it was a foul abomination, a glassful of Satan's piss masquerading as claret. For all I knew, his mother had supplied it, and the notion that she might have fleeced her own son would only have discontented him on the eve of battle.

The bad judge of wine was, however, an excellent judge of the movement of ships through water, as was clear that next morning, as our squadron moved steadily through the Dutch shoals.

'There goes the first marker buoy from the *Tyger*,' said Kit. 'So far, the Dane is proving his worth.'

'Lucky for van Heemskerck that he is,' I said. 'But our Dutch friend will still have much explaining to do if this expedition miscarries after all.'

The captured ship-master was piloting the flagship unerringly through the narrow deep water channel between the low, featureless islands, leaving buoys on either side to mark it for the return voyage. Our excellent Blaeu charts showed the buoys that should have been there, but the Dutch had cut them in haste in an attempt to deter our attack; a vain hope, with Sir Robert Holmes in command. The rest of the squadron followed the *Tyger*: first the *Dragon*, then ourselves, the Fifth Rates *Sweepstakes*, *Pembroke* and *Garland*, two more Fourths in the *Hampshire* and *Advice*, with the ketches and fireships interspersed between us, the longboats being towed, five or six behind each frigate. Once we were through, and into the open water behind the islands, the *Hampshire* and *Advice* came to an anchor, to guard the buoys in case the Dutch attempted to take them up in order to hinder our escape.

In that moment, however, there seemed very little prospect of the Dutch doing anything so aggressive. Indeed, there was no sight nor sound of the Dutch at all. We could now make out windmills and church towers on the two islands, Vlieland to our west and Terschelling to our east, but there were no signs of alarm: no warning beacons being lit, for instance, nor church bells rung.

'Perhaps the butterboxes are sleeping late,' said Kit.

'Or perhaps they think we're one of their own squadrons,' I replied. 'After all, who would imagine the English daring to sail into their own private lake like this?'

But sailing into it we were, moving out into the calm waters of the Wadden Sea. And a sight to behold lay before our eyes as the *Tyger* and *Dragon*, ahead of us, turned slightly to the north-east, opening up the prospect dead ahead.

Kit and I peered through our telescopes, counting masts.

'One hundred and fifty at least,' I said.

'One hundred and seventy, I'd say, Sir Matthew.'

'I defer to your opinion, Captain Farrell – your eyesight was ever superior to mine. But such a number, moored so tightly together… not even a blind man could fail to hit such a target.'

And our admiral was no blind man, that was certain. Robin Holmes had a name as the most violent and aggressive sea-captain in England, if not the whole of Europe. Many blamed him for starting the entire war, due to his ferocious depredations of Dutch colonies on the coast of Africa, and Holmes did nothing to disabuse them. Indeed, he seemed inordinately proud of the label. So putting Sir Robert Holmes into the Wadden Sea on that morning, with such a vast fleet of rich and nearly defenceless hulls before him, was very much a case of putting a hungry fox into a crowded chicken coop.

* * *

The hungry fox was, indeed, in the mood for a hearty Dutch dinner. I joined him on the tiny quarterdeck of Prince Rupert's yacht, the *Fanfan*, having been rowed across from the *Black Prince*. In truth, it was not a quarterdeck at all, simply the space at the stern of the one upper deck; but naval tradition decreed that a man-of-war should have a quarterdeck, and that was doubly the case when she embarked such an eminence as the Rear-Admiral of the Red, whose banner of distinction flew from the masthead. Regardless of such niceties, though, a splendid and very busy sight was going on all around us. The squadron had lain to just inside the channel between the two islands, and men were disembarking from the frigates into longboats and ketches. Holmes had transferred his flag to this nimble little craft, specially loaned to him by the Prince, so that he could take part in close action in shallow waters. He was in high spirits, insisting that his company commanders join him in a toast to the success of the expedition.

'Well, Sir Matthew,' he said, 'how do you fancy a little fiery sport today?'

I smiled. 'I am at your command, Sir Robert.'

The other commanders vigorously nodded their agreement.

'Excellent. Then let's to it! Gentlemen, to the boats! Let's light a fire here that'll singe *Meinheer* de Witt's warty republican arse!'

Barely a turn of the glass later, the *Fanfan*, five fireships, and a dozen longboats were moving relentlessly across the calm waters of the Wadden Sea, directly for the great mass of merchant ships lying dead ahead of us. The flooding tide was with us, carrying us into the serried ranks while making it very difficult for any of the merchantmen to attempt to escape the anchorage. The men on the ships had evidently realised this, together with the imminence and scale of the threat they now faced. Crews were taking to their boats, rowing for the isle of Vlie or the mainland as though their lives depended upon it – which, of course, they did. And ashore, scores of men were moving hither and thither on the Vlie island, many carrying spades, which they were using to dig what would evidently become makeshift ditches and ramparts. I could even see some small cannon, presumably taken from some of the merchantmen, being moved into position. *Much good it will do them*, I thought.

I stood in the bow of my boat, sword drawn, as did all my fellow company commanders. I looked behind me, toward my men. This was a small but able crew, composed overwhelmingly of sailors from the *Tyger*. The business we were now about was a seaman's affair; the soldiers would play their parts later. In the bottom of the boat, our principal weapons lay upon a canvas tarpaulin, waiting to be brought into action. We carried several dozen *grenadoes*, and an equal number of the rather cruder fireballs, simply balls of cotton cloth enclosing a mixture of gunpowder, saltpetre, sulphur and resin. The men's eyes were eager, full of anticipation. After the summer's two hard fought and bloody battles, this would be a very different business.

'Sir Matthew!' cried the man on the tiller, pointing behind me, back toward the ranks of merchant ships.

Finally, it seemed, the Dutch were rallying to mount some sort of a defence. Two small frigates, of perhaps twenty-six or twenty-eight guns apiece, were moving out from behind the mass of hulls, bearing towards our little fleet.

'Steady as she goes!' I commanded.

The men behind me began to shout defiance at the oncoming frigates. They knew, as I did, that they posed little threat to us. True, if they somehow got in among our longboats, they would smash us to pieces in short order. But they would never do that: if needs be, we could simply turn to the west and outrun them by rowing for the shallow waters of the Vlie island, where they could not follow us, or retire to the north-east and the protection of our own, vastly more powerful, frigates. Above all, though, the Dutchmen had to contend with what lay between us and them. Our fireships.

The men in my boat cheered as the *Richard* and *Bryar* adjusted sail, put over their helms, and made directly for the two frigates. In that confined and crowded anchorage, there was almost no room for the Dutch ships to manoeuvre. In effect, they had committed themselves to what they knew to be a suicidal charge, and now their bluff was well and truly called.

The *Richard* struck home first, closing the nearer of the Dutchmen. A few desultory shots rang out from muskets in the frigate's forecastle, but the *Richard*'s crew knew what they were about. They grappled onto the bowsprit and the beakhead shrouds, pulling the two ships tightly together. The Dutch crew, knowing the game was up, abandoned ship by their boats. We cheered as we watched our men row away from the *Richard*, from which the first wisps of smoke were already rising. Within minutes, the fireship was ablaze, the flames licking over onto the bows of the Dutch frigate. As the fire spread onto the main deck, gunpowder cartridges began to explode, and loaded cannon fired themselves into empty air. The flames fired the sails, pieces of burning canvas breaking away to float upon the breeze before landing in the sea. Fire climbed the masts and licked out along the yards, turning them into giant blazing crucifixes. And still we cheered.

At first, the *Bryar*'s attack seemed to miscarry disastrously. The bow suddenly rose before falling again, and even from a fair distance across the water, I could plainly hear the loud shuddering that unmistakeably betrayed a ship running aground. But the crew of the Dutch frigate, having witnessed the fate that had befallen their consort, were already in their boats, rowing hard for safety. The *Bryar*'s captain needed no orders from the likes of Holmes or myself: his duty was clear. The fire-ship's longboat cast off, taking the great majority of the *Bryar*'s crew in her, steering a course directly for the Dutchman.

Nothing could have been simpler. They secured alongside the deserted Dutch frigate and went about their business briskly. From the prow of my boat, I could see clearly the fuses being laid to barrels of pitch and tar, and knew that other men would be doing the same with any flammable material they discovered between decks. In what seemed no more than a matter of moments, the second Dutch ship was ablaze, and the *Bryar*'s men were rowing back toward their own ship so that they could tow her off the sandbank.

'Well, my lads,' I cried to my men, 'the example's been given to us! What say you we light a few fires of our own, to warm the hearts of every man and woman in England?'

'Aye, Sir Matthew!' came the reply. 'Aye, by God!'

With that, we entered the serried ranks of the Dutch merchant fleet.

Chapter Five

'Make for the furthest line of ships!' I ordered.

'Aye, aye, Sir Matthew!'

We were passing between row after row of hulls, sometimes four or five deep, some lashed together, most at individual moorings. But I knew two things. First, there was no point starting with the nearest ships; the wind was south-westerly, so we needed to start setting fires at the far end of the fleet, then work back, so that the breeze would do much of our work for us. Second, the ships furthest away for us were the ones most likely to try and make a run for the open sea; and so it proved. We emerged from between two rows of flyboats to see Holmes signalling from the *Fanfan*, while beyond, what looked to be a Guineaman, three privateers, and five more flyboats, were putting on sail and starting to move away toward the south-east, into a narrow channel between the Vlie island itself and some small inlets that lay between it and the mainland.

I looked across toward the *Fanfan*. Holmes was pacing the deck, jumping up onto the wale, shaking his fist and screaming inaudible obscenities at the fleeing Dutchmen. But he was a good enough seaman to know the reality of the situation. Finally, he went back to the stern of the yacht, waved across to the water to me, raised his hands as if to say 'it matters not a jot', and pointed back towards the hulls behind us. Nine had got away, but that still left over one hundred and fifty ships to burn. And in one sense, it was good that some of the Dutch had escaped. They would carry the news to Amsterdam of what the English had done at the Vlie, and God willing, that news would bring the consequences we all hoped for. So we left the fleeing Dutchmen to their own devices, put over the helms of our boats, and made for the ranks of ships in the Vlie anchorage.

* * *

'Every ship to be fired!' I ordered, as I climbed aboard a Baltic flyboat laden with grain from Poland.

In truth, my order was nearly as redundant as the fireballs. Every seaman knew how to fire a ship, and how to extinguish such a fire: countless vessels were lost to accidental blazes, so fire was one of the most feared of all the many hazards of the sea-business. Thus it was simply a case of men doing what they were always specifically ordered not to do, such as igniting straw below decks, laying a powder fuse to a tar barrel, and so forth.

As we pushed off from the flyboat and the oarsmen took up their strokes, I saw the first flames spit from the upper deck of the ship. It is remarkable how quickly a hull burns; soon, the whole vessel was ablaze from stem to stern. The breeze carried the flames into the rigging and upperworks of the ship secured alongside it, and in short order, that, too, was a roaring conflagration. So onward, through the entire fleet. It was slow work, but with no resistance at all, it was easy work, too. My men moved from hull to hull, methodically setting fires wherever they would cause the most damage. I looked across to the other groups of ships in my view. On all of them, Englishmen were engaged in the same work, firing their fuses and fireballs, getting back into their longboats, and rowing to the next batch of vessels. We cut the cables of many of the Dutch ships – in some cases, their own crews had already done so – so that burning hulls drifted against others, firing them in turn. Some ships burned more readily and fulsomely than others, depending on the nature of the cargoes they carried, but burn they all did, sooner or later. By the early evening, the entire Vlie anchorage was a carpet of flame, the smells of burning wood and scores of cargoes, from spices to pinewood to saltfish, putting me in mind of a vast kitchen. Guinea ships, Turkey Company ships from Smyrna and Scanderoon, Russia traders from Archangel, Balticmen from Danzig and Riga, flyboats laden with French wines from La Rochelle or Bordeaux, timber cargoes from Norway – all of them blazed away, sending a vast pall of smoke into the air. Even on the quarterdeck of the *Black Prince*, at anchor in Schelling Road some considerable distance from seat of the fire, the heat warmed the faces of Kit Farrell and I as we watched the great merchant fleet perish. Against the setting sun, it looked like Hell itself.

'A fine day's work, Sir Matthew,' said Kit.

'Indeed, Captain Farrell. The Dutch hit in the only place where they truly feel pain – their pockets.'

'And would you say that in the hearing of your wife?'

I laughed. Until only very recently, Kit would never have dared to make such a quip at my expense. But in many respects, we were equals now, and he, who knew Cornelia very well, was finally starting to come to terms with the fact.

''Sakes no, Kit. Even if she were on the point of giving birth, she would beat me black and blue for insulting her countrymen so.'

Little did I realise how prescient both Kit's question and my mocking response to it would prove to be.

At length, with the flames still raging all across the Wadden Sea, we went below for a supper of salt beef and execrable claret. Kit then climbed back on deck to take the middle watch, while I retired to my pallet in his cabin. It would be an early start on the next morning, when we were to execute the second part of the attack.

* * *

I was aware of rain during the night, and unexpected motions of the *Black Prince*'s hull. I went back on deck just after dawn, to find Kit still at the quarterdeck rail and a vast pall of smoke hanging over the blackened and, in some cases, still burning hulls in the Vlie anchorage.

'Joy of the morning, Sir Matthew,' he said, 'although a night of precious little joy, I fear.'

'There was a squall?'

He nodded. 'Sir Robert has sent fresh orders. The attack on Vlieland is cancelled – the rain ruined much of the arms and powder in the boats and ketches. So the entire attack is to be on Schelling alone.'

I frowned, but said nothing. The two small towns on Vlieland had grown rich from the countless ships that used their anchorage, and had warehouses and substantial merchants' houses galore. According to van Heemskerck, the VOC, the Dutch East India Company itself, stored enormous quantities of goods there, and the company's wealth was a byword throughout Europe. These were fit and proper targets for attack; but as Holmes well knew, that meant they were likely to be better defended, and he could not risk a humiliating retreat if we ran out of ammunition. But Schelling Island was a very different matter.

I still had those same doubts in my mind when I stood on the beach of that low, featureless island some three hours later. All around me, our eleven companies of soldiers and sailors were disembarking from their ketches and longboats, roughly two-thirds armed with muskets, one third with pikes.

'Well, Matt,' said Holmes, striding toward me from his own longboat, 'a fine day after all, eh, for invading Hogen-Mogen-land?'

'Fine enough, Sir Robert. But what is there to attack here, exactly?'

'What is there to attack?' He looked over his shoulder toward the squat church tower to the west, and the huddle of houses around it. 'Yonder is a Dutch town, on a Dutch island, with Dutch people in it.

What better for Englishmen to attack?'

I bowed my head. 'As you say, Sir Robert.'

And with that, he nodded toward the other company command-ers, who were forming into a little group further up the beach. We went over and joined them. Philip Howard eyed me suspiciously, no doubt resenting the fact that I, and not he, was second-in-command of this expedition, but I found warm smiles and greetings elsewhere in the group, who were mainly fellow sea-captains not then holding actual commands, like myself: the likes of Holmes' brother John, Tom Guy, and Dick Haddock, who would live so very long that he served every English ruler from Cromwell to the first George. Kit had not said a word when we parted on the *Black Prince*, but I knew he was frustrated, perhaps even discontented, at missing the attack. Yet we had to guard against the sudden arrival of a Dutch squadron, which meant that the frigates needed their captains, who needed to be ready for battle if necessary.

'So, gentlemen,' said Holmes, 'one company to remain here to secure our boats. Captain Hellyn, if you will.'

Hellyn, an old soldier, was crestfallen: there was no honour in act-ing as a mere sentry on a beach.

'Five companies with me, including my own. Then Jack –' he nodded at his brother, who smiled – 'Bellasyse, Hammond, Haddock. Five companies with Sir Matthew – your own, Sir Philip's, Captains Guy, Willshaw and Butler. My own force to surround the town in case any defenders attempt to surprise us. Sir Matthew, your force to go into the town and burn it. Any booty worth carrying is to be brought off, else it is to be destroyed. The same with cattle. No violence to be done to women, children or the lower sort of people, unless they resist, as stated in my orders from the Prince and the Duke. If we seize any of the better sort of inhabitants, they are to be taken aboard the ships, to be disposed of as we see fit. But, gentlemen, time forces our hands in all of this. I intend us to sail at or just after high water, praying the wind is still favourable. With the channel being so narrow, we dare not risk being trapped here by a contrary gale – the Dutch fleet down at Texel will know we are here by now, and I have no doubt they'll be sending a force against us. But, God willing, they won't get out of their sea-gate before we've done our business here. Questions?' I had many, but this was not the time to ask them, even if Holmes' tone had been more receptive to a response. 'Good. Well then, gentlemen, to the heads of your companies! God for England, Saint George and King Charles!'

'God save the King!' cried Howard in reply, and the rest of us echoed him.

'Oh, Matt,' said Holmes, casually, 'one thing I forgot to say. You can take our Dutch friend van Heemskerck with you. He knows the town and might be of use to you.'

'Does he know it as well as he knew the channels, Sir Robert?'

He looked at me in feigned astonishment.

'God in Heaven, Matt Quinton, I never thought I'd see the day you turned cynic!' He leaned toward me, and spoke more quietly. 'But a word of advice, Matt. Set a few men to be with him at all times. We can't have the King's prized defector being captured and hanged as a traitor. And we can't have him deciding it might be opportune to change his side back again, can we?'

Holmes strode away to oversee the formation of his little army. I shook my head, and stood stock still. I would have to both shepherd the Dutch turncoat and contend with Philip Howard, an ally of Albemarle, my sworn enemy. But worse, much worse, I was to be the commander responsible for burning the town. I thought of Veere in Zeeland, Cornelia's birthplace, where we had lived together contentedly before the Restoration. It was much bigger than the village before me, but containing no doubt the same kinds of people. Honest, God-fearing folk, loving parents, children, husbands and wives, all striving to make the best of their lives.

Lives that I was about to ruin.

But those were the orders from Sir Robert Holmes, who in turn took his orders from Prince Rupert and the Duke of Albemarle, who in turn took their orders from Charles the Second, by the Grace of God King of England, Scotland and Ireland, for whose throne my father had died, my brother had bled, and I had fought.

I turned, and began to walk across the beach toward the head of my own troops.

Chapter Six

As we approached the town of Brandaris from the east, along the beach, my misgivings increased. The only buildings that lay before us were small, single-floored houses with tall roofs, along with a modest church with a lofty tower, built so high to serve as a seamark. In the distance was the great square tower of the lighthouse that gave the town the name we English preferred for it (the Dutch calling it Westerschelling, which no Englishman can pronounce). There were no warehouses, full of goods from the rich trades, or even the produce of the whaling fleets or fisheries. Instead, there were modest gardens, well-maintained and productive despite the sandy soil, and even a few apple trees. Several small boats were drawn up on the beach below the church. This was no rich port; no great target at all. And there was no sign of any defenders. I thought of the villages I knew in Bedfordshire, on Quinton land, and imagined an invader entering their streets, terrifying the people and putting the houses to the torch.

Consumed by these thoughts, I had barely noticed that Sir Philip Howard was speaking to me. He was saying something about sending in scouts and starting to burn the nearest houses at once.

'No, Sir Philip,' I said, 'we will wait until we reach the western end of the town. With the wind as it is, fires laid there will spread eastward, and do much of our work for us. And it will give the townsfolk more time to save what they can and evacuate into the sand-dunes.'

To me, this seemed a common-sense stratagem: it was essentially what we had done to the shipping at the Vlie, namely using the wind to expedite our cause. But this was evidently some peculiar heresy in the world of soldiering. Sir Philip Howard seemed dumbstruck; he was evidently a man unaccustomed to being contradicted.

'Time to evacuate? These are enemies, Sir Matthew! Enemies of England!'

'Pensionary de Witt and his cabal are the enemies of England, Sir Philip. Admiral de Ruyter and his ships are the enemies of England. If these people were to put up armed resistance, they would be enemies of England, too. But I don't see any resistance, Sir Philip, nor any prospect of any.'

Howard's face was puce.

'With respect, Sir Matthew,' he said, impatiently, 'I have commanded His Grace of Albemarle's personal guard. I am a captain in the Life Guards. I am a commissioner of the militia for Yorkshire.'

I trust that I kept a straight face; but inwardly, I was groaning. Even at the age of twenty-six, I had already met far too many Sir Philip Howards.

'I do not doubt your soldierly credentials, Sir Philip. But if memory serves me right, you have never served in a land battle, have you?'

He blanched at that, then blustered.

'You're a damn fair few years younger than me, Quinton, so neither have you, by God!'

Some of the men were looking at us now, and whispering among themselves. Perhaps they hoped for drawn swords, a duel, and one knight of England or the other pouring out their life's blood into the sand of the Dutch Republic.

'I regret to have to disabuse you, sir,' I said, not a little proudly, 'but I was an Ensign in the King's Guard at the Battle of the Dunes in the year Fifty-Eight, on the right of the Spanish line, engaged against the Ironsides Cromwell sent to join the French army. I was badly wounded in that battle. And I hold a commission as a Major in the Lord Admiral's Marine Regiment.* Thus by right of experience, seniority, and blood spilled in the King's cause, I rather think I outrank you, Sir Philip.'

The shock and fury on Howard's face were unbridled. For a moment, just one brief moment, his right hand moved leftward, toward his sword hilt. But we both knew that I was right, and there was nothing he could do about it. Admittedly, my commission in the Marines had been but a ruse to give me sufficient rank to overawe a gaggle of recalcitrants and plotters at Plymouth earlier in the year; but whatever his personal feelings toward us, the Lord General of England, the Duke of Albemarle, would support the right of a major to command above a captain. And Howard knew it.

'That you do, Sir Matthew,' he said, bad grace sweating from every pore of his body. 'Your orders, then?'

* * *

We made our way through the empty streets of Brandaris, alert for any sign of resistance. I kept Lauris van Heemskerck within sight, but the Dutch renegade was silent. Was he reflecting on this, the true cost of his apostasy? Was he regretting what he had done? It was impossible to tell.

At last we reached the western edge of the little town. We could clearly see the cloud of smoke from the burned ships in the Vlie, off to the south-west. Now it was time for Terschelling island to burn, too.

'Captain Willshaw!' I cried. The eager young tarpaulin in question looked at me intently. 'Burn the boats and all the tackle along the shore. Sir Philip, you and your company to fire the houses on the

---

* See *Ensign Royal* and *The Battle of All The Ages*.

edge of the village. Captains Guy and Butler, your men and mine to fan out, firing the buildings on either side of the road, working back toward the east! But make sure to check there are no people hiding in the houses!'

So we began, groups of five or six men going into each house, setting fires, then moving on to the next.

There was no resistance; no sign of a living soul. But the houses were full of hastily abandoned goods, including clothes and bedding. The inhabitants must have fled inland in great haste, into the dunes and forest, long before we arrived, so my concern for them seemed to have been unnecessary. I prayed they had done so quickly enough to avoid Holmes, whose attitude to them would be rather less sympathetic than mine.

Despite the lack of opposition, Van Heemskerck stayed close to me. We were emerging from the church, a plain, whitewashed, Calvinist affair, when a man suddenly stepped out from behind a hay-rick, pointed at the renegade, and shouted *'Verrader!'*

Traitor.

The brave fellow was right, but his rightness, and his determination to proclaim it, cost him his life. One of the guards assigned to Van Heemskerck, one of Howard's men – a mere youth, nervous, unsure of the musket in his hands – took aim and fired, before I could utter a word to prevent it.

Others were raising their muskets, thinking the man's sudden appearance might presage a sudden attack.

'Hold your fire!' I commanded.

I went over to the fellow lying on the ground. Blood was oozing from the hole in his chest, and as I stooped down, he gave up his last breath. Thus I would never know how he was able to identify Lauris van Heemskerck. Perhaps he had served in the Dutch fleet in the previous campaign, or perhaps the traitor's face adorned cheap broadside pamphlets that had reached even this obscure corner of the United Provinces.

In any event, he was a young man, perhaps my age, and he was unarmed.

'Unfortunate,' said Van Heemskerck. 'But such petty tragedies are the hallmark of war.'

I stood, angry beyond measure, drew myself to my full height, and towered over the turncoat.

'Petty tragedies, Captain? Not petty for this man's parents. Nor his wife, nor his children.'

I glared at him, then at the soldier who had fired the fatal shot. But as I did so, I noticed something else, behind him. A movement at a window in an unburned house.

'Cover up this man's body,' I said to the soldiers. 'Lay it out with decency in the church, so his own people can bury him when they return.'

The order given, I went into the house.

It was dark inside: the shutters were closed, apart from the small gap that I had seen to widen for just a moment, and smoke from the burning houses was creeping between the slats. As my eyes became accustomed to the light, I saw simple furnishings, two books on a table, and an old woman, simply dressed in black and a white prayer cap, sitting upon a stool in the corner.

'Come to kill me too, Englishman?' she asked, in Dutch, seemingly addressing the question to herself rather than to me. 'Make it quick, then.'

'I have no quarrel with you,' I said, in the same language.

She was surprised at that. 'Not many of your kind speak our tongue,' she said.

'I speak it well enough to know you are not Frisian.'

'Zeeland,' she said, 'but not for many years now.' Zeeland – where Cornelia hailed from, and where I had lived. 'Would that I were still there, that I should not have seen this day.'

'Why did you not leave with the others?'

'They care not for me, nor I for them. I have lived here thirty years, yet still they see me as a stranger. So what do I have to live for? Shoot me, as you did Joachim the watchman. Or burn me, here in my house. It will not matter. No one will care.'

'You have no family?'

'None who live, or who care whether I live or die. So do it, Englishman. Take me out of this sinful world, that I may dwell eternally in the company of the Elect.'

'I am not your executioner, lady.'

'No? Were you and yours not so for poor Joachim, then?'

I had no answer. Instead, I averted my eyes, and looked at the two books on her table. A Bible, naturally. But the other was unfamiliar. I picked it up and studied the frontispiece. *The Martyrs' Mirror*, it was called. I knew it, or at least, I thought I had heard of it. Perhaps my uncle Tristram had spoken about it.

An uneasy thought.

'Lady,' I said, 'what sect do you belong to? You and the people of this place?'

'We follow the teachings of Menno of Friesland. Does that mean anything to you, Englishman? Obviously not, for if it did, you would not be doing what you are doing. But perhaps, being English, with a satyr for a king and a sewer for a court, you do not care.'

I knew two things, and two things only, about the Mennonite sect, one of the countless faiths – or heresies, depending upon one's point of view – that proliferated across Europe. One was that they were an offshoot of the Baptists, and thus held the unaccountable belief that only adults capable of making a conscious decision to do so could be received into the church. The other was that they utterly rejected war.

Suddenly, I felt nauseous. The room span, and I had to grip the table for support.

We were not simply burning a Dutch town. We were destroying a God-fearing community of pacifists.

The old woman was looking at me with utter contempt.

'God will damn you,' she said bitterly. 'He will damn you all. You as a man whose soul is now lost, your England as a realm of the reprobate.'

* * *

I became aware of a commotion in the street, and stepped outside to see the familiar form of Sir Robert Holmes striding toward me, his expression thunderous. I barely had time to issue an order to the two men nearest me to take the old Mennonite woman to safety at the edge of the village.

'Fuck and damnation, Matt!' bellowed Holmes. 'Why isn't this town in ashes by now? We need to be off with the tide, man!'

'Sir Robert – I thought it best to –'

'Wait for the wind to do its work? No time for niceties! All companies, spread out through the town! Fire everything, in the shortest order! Don't check inside – if anyone's stupid enough to be hiding in some of the houses, let the butterbox fuckwits burn! And loot, lads! Plunder like the Vikings of yore!'

I could see Philip Howard's smug face, and the arrogant, disdainful smile on his lips. I went up to Holmes, murmuring so that Albemarle's stooge would not hear what was said.

'Robin – the people here – they're Mennonites, man. Pacifists.'

He looked at me as though I had pissed into his ale.

'Excuse me, Sir Matthew – when, precisely, did a scion of the warrior Quintons become a simpering woman?' He looked down at his feet, rolling his eyes as he did so, and affected the Irish brogue that he would have spoken in childhood. 'Am I not on Dutch soil, Robin? Why, yes I am, Robin. Is this not a Dutch town, inhabited by Dutch people, Robin? Why, yes it is, Robin. And are we not at war with the Dutch, Robin? Why, indeed we are, Robin. All the better if the Dutch in question are from some fucking fanatical sect that believes all kinds of shit-headed heretical nonsense. *Pacifism*? Sweet Jesu, Matt, if man was meant to be *peaceful*, why the fuck did God give us swords and guns?'

There was no reasoning with Holmes in this mood. Worse, I knew he was right. Or at least, that the King and Prince Rupert would agree with him, which was very much the same thing.

So the burning of Brandaris was accelerated, the smoke rising from its blazing buildings to mix with that from the still-smouldering wrecks in the Vlie. The men needed no second bidding to obey the order to loot, thieving wine, beer, meat and clothing. A few lucky would-be Vikings found bags of coin, hastily but inadequately hidden by their owners, but such discoveries prompted several fist-fights in the streets and on the beach.

I watched it all with a heavy heart, but the worst was yet to come. The men I had detailed to take the old woman to safety returned after an unconscionable time, looking penitent. Had they ravaged her?

But the men's story seemed sincere enough. They had got her to the edge of the village and sat her down, but she promptly fell backward into the salt grass and died.

Fright?

Delayed shock?

A simple unwillingness to live any longer in a world that could perpetrate such horrors?

As we re-embarked into our boats on the beach and pushed off with the ebb, I could think only of the pointless deaths of the watchman and the old Mennonite woman, and of her last words to me.

God will damn you.

Chapter Seven

As the squadron returned to the fleet, every ship rejoiced even more fulsomely than it had done for my capture of the *Jeanne d'Arc*, the *Royal Charles* leading the way in firing off a salute that would not have disgraced the King's birthday. This time, though, as I stood at the quarterdeck rail of the *Black Prince* with Kit Farrell, I watched the celebration with mixed emotions, for I could not get the old Mennonite woman's words out of my head. Firing the merchant fleet in the Vlie was one matter: sea-trade was the life blood of the Dutch, and destroying it was a legitimate act of war. As Prince Rupert had said, the loss to the avaricious merchants of Amsterdam might be so great that 'Sir Robert Holmes, his bonfire', as it was already being called by the men at the foremast, would bring an end to the war itself. But burning a defenceless town, inhabited by people who would not fight for their homes out of religious principle – that was quite another thing, and where was the honour in it? I wished that Francis Gale was still with me, so that he could either confirm me in my misgivings or assure me that God truly would have wanted us to destroy Brandaris. Or, at least, to assure me that I was not damned as the old Mennonite woman said. But by now Francis would be ashore, perhaps paying his respects to my wife and brother, perhaps returning to the pastoral duties of his parish at Ravensden.

And there was another thought that came to me. Oh, people will say that it is ever the vanity of the old to claim such prescience – in other words, to claim that they somehow foresaw what was to come. London is full of knowing old sages who claim they knew the South Sea Bubble was going to happen: strange to say, they are always the ones who, by complete chance, had happened to invest in other stock, the fortunes of which they complained about loudly until the very moment that the bubble burst. But I can remember standing there, feeling the deck of the *Black Prince* sway beneath my feet, watching the smoke from the muzzles of the saluting guns of the flagship, and thinking: *will not England's enemies retaliate for this? Might they not inflict on us an even greater horror? What if they burned Dover, or Yarmouth?*

But I had no time to ponder such uneasy thoughts. A small ketch was racing toward us from the *Royal Charles*, and as it came under our lee, its skipper cried out that he bore urgent mails for Sir Matthew Quinton.

'It may not be so,' said Kit, as he sent a man down to obtain the papers from the ketch as it secured alongside.

He had served with me for more than long enough to know that urgent mail always prompted two thoughts in my mind, both equally dreadful to contemplate. One was for my wife: and in that summer of 1666, the plague of the previous year was not quite gone from London, and Cornelia was six months pregnant. Such concern would be the first thought of any husband receiving an unknown but urgent message. In my case, though, there was a second possibility, one that I had contemplated with horror since a certain day in June 1645, when I was five years old. My brother Charles Quinton, tenth Earl of Ravensden, who inherited the title and estate on that day, had never been entirely well, certainly not since he took three musketballs in an already fragile frame at the Battle of Worcester. And if the message stated that my brother was dead, then I was now the eleventh Earl, with all the responsibilities and significant debts that the rank conveyed, and my career at sea was almost certainly at an end.

So it was with a sense of relief that I recognised my brother's handwriting on the first of the two letters. Charles was not dead, but the script was very weak, and as I broke the seal, I wondered if my worst fears were fulfilled after all, that this was merely some sort of last message from brother to brother.

But it was not that. It was not that at all.

Join me at the House as soon as you may conveniently leave the fleet.
CP

No explanation as to why Charles wanted me to go at once to Ravensden House, our family's town property in the Strand. But then, my brother was always the most concise of men, both in what he said and what he wrote.

The signature, though, spoke volumes. Not *CQ*, Charles Quinton, nor *CR*, Charles Ravensden, but *CP*. Since the royal family's early days in exile, my brother had been one of the most important but most secret of King Charles' intelligencers, at the head of a network of agents who strove first to overthrow the cursed republic and return England's anointed sovereign to his throne, and then who, since the blessed Restoration, had worked to thwart the plots of those who sought once again to destroy their King. In that guise, my brother went by a secret code name: and that name was Lord Percival.

I opened the second letter. I recognised the writing on this, too, just as I recognised that on the enclosure it contained.

The enclosing letter read:

Sir Matthew,
It seems my efforts to keep you with the fleet have been to no avail. The FanFan is at your immediate disposal to carry you into the River. God speed, Matt.
Rupert

And so, finally, to the enclosure, addressed to the Prince, the wax seal bearing a very familiar insignia.

Cousin,

It is of the utmost consequence to our royal service that Sir Matthew Quinton attends the Earl of Ravensden at the earliest possible convenience. Therefore, we command you and His Grace of Albemarle to place the means of so doing at his immediate service.

Charles R

I stared at the three small pieces of paper. It was a little while, perhaps some minutes, before I was aware that Kit Farrell's gaze had been upon me the entire time.

'I take it, Sir Matthew,' he said, 'that I shall no longer be enjoying your company aboard the *Black Prince*.'

I breathed deeply, and looked over at him.

'My spirit will still be sailing with you, Captain Farrell. Take a rich Dutch East Indiaman for me, or another vast French prize. May fortune guide your helm, Kit.'

He drew his sword, and brought it up to his face in the age-old warriors' gesture of salute. Taken aback to receive this, the ultimate symbol of gentlemanly honour, from someone I still thought of as a brash young Wapping tar, it took me some moments to reach for my own sword and return the salute.

'God go with you, Sir Matthew,' he said.

* * *

The *FanFan* was a nimble little craft which cut the water better than anything I had ever sailed in, crewed by men who seemed convinced their master really was the devil incarnate, as Roundhead pamphleteers had claimed throughout the civil wars. But unlike the poor benighted citizens of Bolton, Liverpool, and all the other places Prince Rupert had devastated over twenty years before, his hand-picked crew seemed to take pride in his infernal reputation, grinning constantly to themselves – and at me – as they went about their business. By nightfall, we were at the Buoy of the Nore, where we laid to; but the brief August night meant we were underway again at dawn, not many hours later. Not even the *FanFan* could defy nature, though, and the ebb, together with the great meanders of the Thames that lay ahead, compelled us to moor at Gravesend, just off the blockhouse that defended the passage up to London. I went ashore and hired a sturdy-looking horse from an ostler whom the yacht's captain assured me was a reputable man. The road to London was already filling with coaches, carts, horsemen, pedlars, cripples, and all the other usual denizens of the highway. Although I made good progress between towns, weaving my horse between the slower travellers, the stalls lining the principal streets in Greenhithe, Dartford, Erith and Woolwich delayed me. At the last of these, I stole a glance toward the royal dockyard, where I could plainly see the masts of the *Royal Sceptre*. She had been taken into the dry dock, and, God willing, would be ready to go to sea again before the end of the summer's campaign – although whether Sir Matthew Quinton would still be in command of her was another matter altogether. The temptation to inspect my ship, and my men, was powerful, but the direct orders of my brother and my King were more powerful still. So it was, about the middle of the afternoon, that I rode into Southwark, passing St Thomas' Hospital as I made my way toward the tower of Saint Mary Overie, and thence onto the road approaching London Bridge.

I stopped just short of the southern gatehouse and the first of the houses that crowded both sides of the bridge, drinking in the sight before me. London – that giant ant-heap rising out of the Thames. A thousand noises and a score of different languages assailed my ears, but somehow, I managed to ignore them all, concentrating instead on the scene before my eyes. There, to the east, was the Tower, standing guard over the city as it had since William the Norman's day, as well as providing a final destination for the kingdom's traitors. In front of it, and down past Saint Katherine's toward Wapping, the shipping of the world filled the great tidal stream, lighters moving clumsily between the ships and carrying their cargoes to the wharves. To the west, a jumble of houses and churches stretched away toward the bend in the river that led to Whitehall Palace, hidden from view behind the buildings of Southwark. Skiffs and longboats thronged the river, carrying passengers up and down stream, and between the two banks. Towering over all was the vast bulk of Saint Paul's, like a great man-of-war surrounded by cock-boats. Truth be told, it was not a pretty cathedral: the loss of its spire, destroyed by fire in the early days of Queen Bess's reign, gave it a curious, truncated, even ugly, appearance. If it was a man-of-war, it was one that had lost its maintopmast. But it remained the single most potent symbol of London, and the city's countless people loved it for that.

I took in the view, and felt a sense of relief and homecoming. Dear, stinking, glorious, overcrowded, splendid London. Eternal London, that had stood for a millennium and a half, and would stand for evermore. I could claim otherwise, but this time I felt no shiver down my spine; the hairs on the back of my neck did not rise in foreboding. I had no sense, no sense whatsoever, that I was looking upon the prospect for the very last time, and that the London I knew and loved would soon be no more.

* * *

Ravensden House stood on the north side of the Strand, not far from the Temple Church. It was a curious structure that reflected the changing fortunes of the Quinton family over the previous two centuries. It was not some grand palace-in-all-but-name, like the nearby piles of Arundel House, Essex House, and the Queen's occasional residence at Somerset House. The frontage could easily have been taken for a relatively prosperous Tudor merchant's residence, the usual whitewashing cross-crossed by black timbers, with the upper floors overhanging each other and the street below. I knew, as most passers-by did not, that this was deceptive; behind the modest frontage was a rather larger and superficially grander Jacobean wing overlooking the remains of the house's gardens. But, once again, appearances deceived. My grandfather had been fleeced by his builders, and the shoddy workmanship in Earl Matthew's wing threatened the comfort, and, on occasion, the lives, of those who inhabited it, namely my wife and I.

The front door opened before me. Phineas Musk looked me up and down as though he were seeing me for the very first time, and then inclined his head in a gesture of respect so slight that a man less used to his ways might have missed it altogether.

'Sir Matthew,' said Phineas Musk. 'The Dutch still haven't done for you, then.'

Of course, most men of quality would have had such an impertinent servant whipped from there to Charing Cross. The thought had crossed my mind on many occasions, as I knew it had crossed that of my brother, Musk's nominal employer. But Phineas Musk was more than a servant, and I strongly suspected he always had been, even in my grandfather's and father's times.

'Musk,' I said. 'The plague hasn't done for you, either.'

'Expect you'll want to see her ladyship,' he said, as he allowed me to squeeze past him into the small, dark, oak-panelled space behind. 'She's out. Showing the French captain the sights of London. If they've run into the King in Saint James' park, the Lord alone knows when they'll be back.'

There was nothing remarkable about this, of course; Captain Ollivier was a commissioned officer of the King of France who had given his parole, so he was perfectly free to go where he pleased, taking with him the invisible prison of honour that he had erected around himself. Even so, I still felt a strange pang of unease. Honourable he might have been, but Captain Ollivier was still a Frenchman, and a markedly striking one at that…

I dismissed the unworthy thought. Cornelia was six months pregnant, after all, and had always been entirely loyal and loving to me, ever since we married at the age of no more than seventeen.

Entirely loyal.

'Lady Quinton is well, then?'

'Blooming, I think, is the term. The French captain makes her laugh more than I've seen in a long time.' *Entirely loyal.* 'Your brother, though – he's a different matter.'

'How ill is he?'

Musk averted his gaze. As a retainer of the Quinton family since his youth, he understood the different meanings behind my question.

'Doctors have no idea what's wrong with him,' said Musk, as we began to walk down the narrow, portrait-lined passageway that led to the stairs. 'But then, doctors are all idle cumberworlds, not one of them with the first idea of what they're doing, yet charging a galleon's worth of bullion for not doing it. But it's not a fever with the Earl, that's certain. A weakness of the body of some kind – he hasn't been out of his bed for three weeks. He's got a nurse with him, but she's like no nurse I've ever met before.'

I went upstairs alone, with Musk scuttling off to the other wing, talking to himself as he went. I paused outside the door of my brother's bedchamber, took a deep breath, knocked, and lifted the latch.

The window shutters were closed, only two or three candles were lit, and it took some moments for my eyes to adjust to the dimness of the light, such a contrast to the bright August afternoon outside. A woman was sitting on a stool in the corner of the room and bowed her head slightly, but otherwise, she remained still and silent. I saw what Musk meant. Nurses were invariably aged harridans, often gross and ugly, frequently bearing the marks of the various diseases they had caught from their patients. This one could not have been more different. About my age, fresh-faced, with tight brown curls tumbling over her cheeks and pronounced eyebrows, she could easily have been taken for a lady of the court, perhaps even a new object of attention for His Majesty's insatiable lusts, were it not for the simple smock she wore.

I was aware of another pair of eyes watching me, and moved toward the bed.

'Welcome home, Matt,' said Charles Quinton, Earl of Ravensden, his voice little more than a whisper.

My brother was always pale of complexion, but his thin face, framed by pillows, now looked like a death mask. His cheeks were drawn in, and there were great dark patches below his eyes.

I went over, bent down, and embraced him.

'My Lord,' I said.

'As you see, I am somewhat inconvenienced. Some form of wasting sickness, although every doctor I summon seems to disagree fundamentally in his diagnosis with the previous one. Whether it will do for me and make you Earl before the year is out – before this month is out, in truth – is in the hands of God, but it will make you a lord one way or another, Matt.'

'I – I don't follow you, brother –'

'You know the King and I would only summon you back from the fleet if it was a matter of the utmost importance. The truth is, Matt, there was no one else we could turn to. No one we could trust to such a degree. No one else who could take my place.'

'Take your place? Which place?'

'There is a great matter in hand. A secret matter that concerns the safety of England, and is known to only a very few people. The King, the Duke of York, Clarendon, Arlington – and then also to myself, as Lord Percival, and to one of our best agents, who goes by the name of Astraea. So there's the rub, brother. To thwart this deadly threat, Lord Percival must be active. Certainly he must be able to climb out of his bed. Therefore, another must become Lord Percival in my stead.'

He stared at me earnestly, and did not need to name his candidate.

I pulled back in astonishment. *Me?* Lord Percival? An intelligencer – a spymaster, even? I stared at Charles in disbelief. My head swam, my thoughts racing off in a hundred directions at once. The idea was impossible, preposterous.

I was aware of a slight movement behind me, and remembered the nurse. I turned to look at her, but she merely gave me a demure glance. I turned back to Charles. Perhaps he was fevered after all, to speak so unguardedly, of such secret things, in front of this lowly creature. Perhaps his mind was disordered, and he had simply forgotten she was there.

'Brother,' I said, 'should we be speaking of such things, here and now?'

The Earl took my meaning. He lifted his head from the pillow, and looked intently toward the quiet nurse upon the stool. In a feeble but determined voice, he said, 'Oh, I think we should, Matt. Would that not be so, My Lady Astraea?'

'It would be so, My Lord Percival. My two Lords Percival.'

The nurse stood, and inclined her head slightly in my direction.

Charles Quinton said, 'Matt, allow me to present this lady by her true name. Sir Matthew Quinton – Mistress Aphra Behn.'

Chapter Eight

'Of course, there have been plots galore ever since the King returned. Many more rumours of plots, and false alarms. You know this as well as any man, Matt – you have helped to scotch several of them.'

The Earl of Ravensden's voice was weak, but his judgement, his ability to sum up any situation, was as sharp as ever. I sat to the right of his bed, the mysterious Mistress Behn – Goodwife Behn, perhaps? Widow Behn? – to his left. Thus far she had said very little, and I wondered what it was about this young woman that made her so special to my brother, and to England's royal cause.

'But this year, the talk has multiplied tenfold. The sectaries whisper in their conventicles. The old Commonwealths-men creep out of their hiding places and speak of a new dawn. Much of it is to do with the date itself – 1666. The appearance of the number of the beast in the calendar was always going to excite the credulous. Oh, we expected to hear all the usual fantasies about the end of days, and tall tales of signs, wonders and portents. But it has been more than that, much more.' Charles Quinton paused, and breathed deeply several times. 'I'm sorry, Matt, I have to conserve my strength. Mistress Behn, please continue.'

'My Lord, here,' she said, 'and Lord Arlington and his agents, have worked wonders, Sir Matthew.' Her voice was soft, and strangely accented, but I thought there was something of a Kentish burr to it. In all events, it was pleasant to listen to, even as it expounded a catalogue of horror. 'Fortunately, we have informers nearly everywhere, in most of the dissenting congregations, even in many of the drinking dens frequented by old New Model troopers. Not all, it's true, but enough. So we know the whispers of the sectaries, even the Quakers. How they cry up the number of the beast, the significance of this year, and the great changes that are to come. The death of kings. Fire. Blood. Terror. The destruction of Babylon, of Sodom and Gomorrah.'

'Hardly the preserve of the discontented,' I said. 'My friend, our vicar, the Reverend Gale, has had his nose buried deep in the Book of Revelation for months, pondering its meaning. And I remember our uncle talking of all the predictions of doom that had been laid down for this year. Didn't he say old Mother Shipton predicted London would burn in the year Sixty-Six?'

Charles nodded silently, but smiled. Recollection of Tristram Quinton, the shambolic, brilliant, unlikely Master of Mauleverer College, Oxford, invariably made those who loved him smile. Regrettably, much of the rest of mankind greeted any mention of his name with scowls; or else, at worst, with sheer horror. Even good Protestants had sometimes been known to cross themselves as he passed by.

'All the almanacs for this year prophesy calamities beyond belief, that's true,' said Aphra Behn. 'But then, of course, they always do. Who would buy an almanac that claimed a year would see nought but crops being harvested and planted, the sun shining, rain falling, babies being born, the old dying, and men and women swiving?'

She looked at me frankly, but I glanced away at once. I was not accustomed to women who spoke so brazenly of the act of hymen.

'The seamen,' I said, 'make much of the fact that there have been both solar and lunar eclipses these last few months, and several comets in the last year and a half. True, your English seaman is a superstitious and credulous creature at the best of times, but the heavens have been strangely active, that's for certain. I've witnessed it myself.'

'And all of that has encouraged the discontented,' said Aphra Behn. 'There was the Rathbone plot back in the spring, for instance.'

'I heard of it,' I said, 'but only at second hand. I was busy paying off the *Cressy* after our Gothenburg convoy, and then engaged in manning the *Royal Sceptre*.'

Colonel John Rathbone, an officer of the old republican army, had conspired with others to restore the old killjoy Commonwealth; by no means the first such plot since the King's blessed Restoration.

'God be praised, we discovered Rathbone's conspiracy in ample time,' she said. 'He and seven other ringleaders were executed, many hundreds arrested. But they are only a drop in the ocean, of course. There are still thousands of sectaries and old rebels hiding throughout the length and breadth of the land, and especially so here, in London. They cry up how much better things were in the old Commonwealth days, waiting for their chance to come. All they need is a leader – and a sign.'

Throughout our discourse, Charles had listened silently, recovering his breath. Now, though, he raised himself again.

'These last few months,' he said, 'since Rathbone's execution, there has been especially worrying talk. The same tale, coming from several places at once, from reputable sources. It tells of some great act that will be committed on or around the third day of September. A date England knows well, of course. A date *I* know well.'

I nodded. Oliver Cromwell, that walking curse, had died on the third of September, eight years earlier; and on the same day, seven years before that, my brother had very nearly lost his life fighting against the future Lord Protector in the Battle of Worcester.

'We do not know the nature of this act,' said Aphra Behn. 'Lord Arlington thinks it might be a plot to kill the King or the Duke of

York, or both, but then, regicide is always an aim in all these plots, as it was in Rathbone's. And he planned to strike on the third of September. The most auspicious date, in the most auspicious year.'

'Two names are always spoken of in connection with this mysterious act,' said Charles. 'The first is Mene Tekel. A common choice of name for these sorts of people, but a potent one.'

That it was, for I knew my Book of Daniel as well as any man. The story of Belshazzar's feast, in the great, corrupt, ancient city of Babylon. The disembodied hand inscribing words into the stonework.

Mene, mene, tekel, upharsin.

The writing on the wall.

'But,' said Aphra Behn, 'the rumours say that our Mene Tekel is merely preparing the way for an even greater figure – the real threat to the King and the realm. Just as I am Astraea and My Lord, here, is Lord Percival, so this person, this new Messiah to Mene Tekel's John the Baptist, has an alias to conceal his identity. He is called the "Precious Man".'

'*The Precious Man*?' Despite myself, I could not resist scoffing at the notion. 'It is hardly a name to strike terror into hearts, Mistress.'

'Perhaps not, Matt,' said the Earl. 'Except that, thanks to Lady Astraea here, we think we know who he and Mene Tekel are. Tell the story, Mistress Behn. Weave the words for my brother.'

I did not grasp, then, what Charles meant by Aphra Behn weaving words; but I realised at once that she told a tale well, and held a listener's attention. But that might have been just as much to do with the softness of her voice, and the fetching way in which she tilted her head as she spoke.

'Over twenty years ago, Sir Matthew, when you and I were little more than babes-in-arms, the whole of Europe was at war. Protestants and Catholics had been slaughtering each other in Germany for years. France and the Dutch were at war with Spain, the Swedes at war with the Empire.' *Dear God, a woman – aye, a woman! – who knew of such things, and spoke of them so confidently.* 'And then, of course, these isles of Britain, almost the only lands that had stood apart from the carnage, were suddenly plunged into civil war. All those wars, all those armies – so there were opportunities galore for young men from many lands to come together, to fight, and to discover countless new ways of killing people.'

'Mercenaries,' I said, with contempt for those who fought for money rather than honour.

'As you say, Sir Matthew. Several groups of men developed particular reputations,' she said. 'Among them, four men, two Dutch, a Frenchman, and an Englishman, who came together by chance in some foreign regiment or other during some obscure campaign beyond the Rhine, and discovered they had a common interest. A common passion, perhaps. They became more and more expert in their chosen field, until their reputation was known from Muscovy to Portugal. They revelled in it. They even gave themselves a name: the Four Horsemen of the Apocalypse.'

'The Four Horsemen of the Apocalypse,' I repeated, shaking my head. 'The Writing on the Wall. The Precious Man. We're not dealing with notably modest souls, then. But, Mistress, this chosen field of theirs – what was it?'

'Fire,' said Charles, before Aphra Behn could answer. 'Explosives. Gunpowder. They became experts in inventing new ways of bringing down great walls, of firing impregnable fortresses. Burning entire towns, come to that. Master gunners and officers of ordnance, brought up on the same hoary old manuals and the same methods of instruction, were hidebound by traditional thinking. Not these men. As their successes multiplied, so their value increased. They became highly sought after.'

'But then, of course,' said Aphra Behn, 'during the course of ten years or so, all the wars ended. Peace returned to Europe. It seems that one of the Horsemen, the Frenchman, was already dead by then, or so it was said, and their leader was repentant of all the death and devastation they had caused. He was one of the Dutchmen – Anton Schermer by name, by far the most skilled and inventive of them. He persuaded the other two survivors, an Englishman named Shadrach Goodman and the second Dutchman, de Wildt, to go with him to start a new life in a distant land, to set up as honest farmers. They went to Surinam, in the Americas. But Goodman soon tired of it, and returned to England. When the present war began, de Wildt went home, too, and took service in the Dutch fleet as a mere master gunner, having lost his money in Surinam. Where Schermer is, no man seems to know.'

It was extraordinary to hear a woman speak of such things, in such a way. I wanted to know more of this Mistress Behn; wanted to know her better.

'I do not see,' I said, 'how these men are connected to the great plot that is meant to come to fruition next month. And what could just three men do? What sort of fire – or explosion, come to that – could possibly cause so much harm to England?'

'As to that,' said Charles, 'there are many possibilities. Parliament is not sitting, of course, and probably will not sit until November, so we need not fear an attempt to surpass old Fawkes. And as you know better than I, the fleet will not have come in from sea by the beginning of September, so they can hardly scheme to burn it at anchor, as you recently did at the Vlie. But burning all the trade in the Thames, below London Bridge, might be a different matter – vengeance like for like, as it were. Whitehall Palace, too, could be a target – or the Tower arsenal, come to that, which Rathbone planned to seize. And if their associates succeed in killing the King, and perhaps the Duke of York too, at the same time…'

I nodded. Our uncle Tristram had taught both of us enough history to know that monarchs often fell victim to random murderers. Both Kings Henri the Third and Fourth of France had perished in that way, as had the first William of Orange, while England's own Queen Elizabeth spent much of her reign fearful of the countless Jesuit daggers and pistols that were ready to despatch her, if only the opportunity arose. In that year of 1666, if both Charles and James Stuart fell, and the throne passed to an infant, would monarchy really be able to survive in England? And even if the old Commonwealths-men did not succeed in restoring their miserable, pedantic, holier-than-thou republic, who was to say that chaos and confusion in London might not lead the Dutch to invade and install a puppet king: the next closest male in blood to the King and Duke of York, namely William, Prince of Orange?

A Dutch King: it was inconceivable to me, then. Thank God my youthful self was spared a prophecy of our line of lumpen Germans.

'Goodman has become a leading figure among the sectaries and malcontents,' said Aphra Behn. 'There is good evidence to suppose that he, in fact, is Mene Tekel, and that he is seeking to reunite the remaining Horsemen. De Wildt is in England – his ship was taken during the Saint James day fight, and he is said to be in Chelsea College, where hundreds of Dutch prisoners are being held. We can be certain that Goodman will attempt to get him out.'

'And Schermer?' I asked. But even as I formed the words, I realised the answer. 'Schermer is the Precious Man?'

'We believe so,' said Charles. 'And that is why you need to become Lord Percival, Matt. As you see, I cannot move, and the task demands a man who can travel – and wield a sword, if necessary. De Wildt needs to be identified in Chelsea College and then imprisoned more closely. Goodman must be found and apprehended. We believe him to be in hiding in a notoriously disaffected port in Essex by the name of Leigh, where we have precious few loyal men, and no intelligence of his exact whereabouts. And if Schermer is in England, perhaps hidden away with Goodman, you must find him and take him. Or kill him, if needs be.'

'But My Lord, how will I find these men when I know so little about them – not even what they look like?'

Charles and Aphra Behn smiled.

'That is why the King chose to recall My Lady Astraea from her current mission in Antwerp,' said the Earl.

'I lived in Surinam for over a year, before the war,' said Aphra. 'It is where my career as an intelligencer began. It is a huge country, Sir Matthew, but the colonies were relatively small, and I travelled extensively in the governor's retinue.' I wondered exactly what role in such a retinue might be performed by a nubile young woman in her early twenties, but thought better of it. 'So I have met these men, you see. I know their faces. I can identify them.'

'So it all depends on you, Matt,' said Charles. 'Will you play my part for me, and help Mistress Behn here hunt down these men before they can cause God knows what havoc in this land?'

I looked from one to the other. Of course, my brother already knew what my answer would be. After all, I was a Quinton.

'Lord Percival is at the service of his King and his brother,' I said.

Chapter Nine

The next morning, Aphra Behn, Phineas Musk and I set out westward in the state coach of the Earls of Ravensden, bound for Chelsea College along the road that ran from Westminster through Tothill Fields and the open country beyond. Musk, who had often assisted Charles in his role as Lord Percival, had been admitted to the secret purpose of the mission and to Mistress Behn's true identity the previous evening, shortly before 'Lady Astraea' and I supped at Ravensden House with my wife Cornelia and Captain Ollivier.

This did not go well.

It might have passed off rather more smoothly if Francis Gale had been there, able to amuse and divert the company with his stock of anecdotes, but he had been summoned back to Bedfordshire by my mother, the Dowager Countess. There was some talk of the arch-dissenter Bunyan being released from Bedford Gaol, and she wished Francis to second her in ensuring that no such calamity occurred (my mother detested dissenters more than head lice). As it was, Captain Ollivier related tales that ranged from the splendours and scandals of the French court to the customs of the naked savages of the Carribee. There was a little too much repetition of the word 'naked' for my liking, and rather too many knowing glances toward my wife. For her part, Cornelia seemed to take an instant dislike to Mistress Behn, who traded stories with both Ollivier and I, calling upon her own recollections of Surinam just as I did upon my voyage to Guinea and the Gambia river, some years before.* My wife, who had never been anywhere more exotic than Rotterdam, listened intently to the Frenchman and dutifully to me, but she scowled and fidgeted throughout every one of Mistress Behn's discourses. She knew enough of my brother's secret life not to enquire too closely into why he should want me to work in harness with this person. But Cornelia was, at bottom, a woman, and a noticeably pregnant woman at that, who might well have wondered if her husband's attentions would stray toward this alluring and significantly less rotund new dish.

So there were glances. And sighs. And more glances.

'You are a widow, then, Mistress Behn?' asked Cornelia, glancing.

'My poor husband – he was German – fell victim to the plague,' said Aphra. 'We were married only a matter of months.'

'How tragic. How very tragic.' Cornelia sighed, and nibbled thoughtfully upon a piece of mutton, but sympathy was evidently not her principal emotion. 'And you say you wish to become a *writer*?'

'I do, Lady Quinton. Why should a woman not become a writer? If we can now act upon the stage, why should we not write for it?'

Cornelia could clearly think of dozens, if not hundreds, of reasons, but kept them to herself. Her own writings, even of household accounts, mangled the English language beyond all reasonable measure, and her native Dutch only a little less when she wrote in that, so the notion of a woman doing such a thing for a living was evidently quite beyond her comprehension.

'Not so strange, perhaps,' said Captain Ollivier mildly, flashing one of his smiles at Cornelia. 'Why, in France, we have the likes of Mademoiselle de Scudéry and Madame de Villedieu… '

---

* See *The Mountain of Gold*.

For once, Cornelia ignored him, cutting across Ollivier to address Aphra once again.

'And you hope the Earl will be your patron in the theatre, perhaps?'

Ollivier looked at me and raised his eyebrows, as if to say: *Is it usual for such anarchy to prevail in English households?*

'We have not discussed the matter,' said Aphra, 'but Charles' interest in the stage is of very long standing, and we are old friends. Who knows what the future might bring, Lady Quinton?'

The revelation that this strange creature was somehow an old friend of my brother came as news to both Cornelia and me. But I could see from my wife's face that her mind was already building an entire edifice of supposition upon that one simple fact, and although this edifice was probably preferable to the other – that Aphra and I were about to fall into bed together – it was only marginally so. Charles Quinton had already been tempted into marriage once, albeit very much against his inclinations. What was to say that, if he lived and prospered, he might not return to the matrimonial altar, this time with a bride entirely suited to him, who shared his twin worlds of intelligence and the theatre, rather than the murderous harlot he had wed before?* And if Aphra Behn became the new Countess of Ravensden, she would immediately displace Cornelia as mistress of this household.

Who knows what the future might bring?

* * *

Chelsea College was a large, square building, rather like an Oxford college, with a single quadrangle, a tower framing its gateway, and grounds stretching down to the Thames. It had been a pet scheme of that most curious King, James the First, who had wanted it to become a hothouse where great theologians and controversialists would be

---

* *The Mountain of Gold* and *The Blast That Tears The Skies*

trained to do intellectual battle with the rampant Jesuitical legions of the Pope. Regrettably, very few had shared his enthusiasm for the project, so the college soon withered. My uncle Tristram once told me that he and John Thurloe inspected it during the days of the Rump Parliament, with a view to it becoming a training college for intelligencers – a school for spies, in other words. That, and all the other projects for making some new use of it, came to naught, so in due course it was demolished, and the present hospital for retired soldiers was erected on its site. But back then, in the year Sixty-Six, its thick walls and large rooms made it an ideal prison for some of the thousands of Dutch prisoners we had taken during the war, others of whom were lodged in the likes of Leeds and Portchester Castles.

'De Wildt, you say,' said the Keeper, as he led us along the loggia on the east side of the quadrangle. 'There is no man of that name on our musters, Sir Matthew.'

'He will have adopted an alias,' I said, parroting the words Aphra had spoken to me in the coach. 'But our intelligence out of Holland states that he was aboard the *Tholen*.'

'Ah,' said the Keeper, 'the *Tholen*. Forgive me, Sir Matthew, but was it not your ship that captured her?'

'That it was,' said Musk, on my behalf. 'After a damned hard fight.'

This was not strictly true; the *Tholen* had been severely damaged before we came upon her and forced her surrender. Nevertheless, she had been the *Royal Sceptre*'s prize, and Phineas Musk was not a man to shirk from taking credit for anything at all.

The Keeper summoned half a dozen of his turnkeys to our backs: large, vicious-looking rogues with a range of cudgels and blades at their belts. Then he led us into a high, square, poorly-lit room that must once have been some sort of lecture theatre, and we were thrust at once into a circle of Hell.

The stench assailed us even before we stepped through the door. There must have been three hundred men in the room, all of them unwashed and wearing the clothes in which they had been captured, some weeks earlier. The single toilet seemed to be a bucket in the corner, which had overflowed some hours previously. Men were shouting and arguing in Dutch, but those nearest to us fell silent as we entered. Several dozen pairs of eyes fell upon Aphra, and the mouths beneath them broke into leers.

'Should have drowned the lot of them when we had the chance,' said Musk.

I could hear obscenities galore, all of them about Aphra and what they proposed to do with her, but also other remarks.

'Not the usual time for a muster. What's going on?'

'Isn't that the *goddeloze staartman* English captain that took us?'

'Tighten up, lads.'

What the crew of the *Tholen* did not know was that I spoke Dutch with a considerable degree of fluency, thanks to my wife and the time we had spent living in her home town of Veere before the King's Restoration. Admittedly, my fluency did not stretch to understanding why the Dutch might elect to describe an Englishman as *goddeloze staartman* – a godless tailed man – but I was not alone in that.

'That group of men, in the far corner,' I said to Aphra. 'Let's make towards them, then work back from there.'

'He's not in these front ranks,' she said. 'I'd swear upon it.'

The Keeper and his turnkeys formed up in front of and at the sides of us, leading us like an arrowhead into the heart of the throng. A few prisoners pressed forward menacingly, but were swiftly cudgelled back into place. All the while as we advanced, Aphra scanned faces methodically, her head moving from side to side, ignoring the obscene gestures and lewd catcalls from the prisoners. We made directly for the group that had shuffled closer to each other, and seemed to have something to hide.

'I don't like their mood,' said the Keeper. 'Don't like it at all.'

'Too many of them for my liking,' said Musk, 'and far too few of us.'

'They wouldn't dare attempt anything,' said the Keeper. 'They'll have no prospect of an exchange if they do.'

But he did not sound as though he was convincing even himself. Ranks of prisoners were closing in behind us, growling menacingly, talking of rushing us and overpowering the turnkeys. Time to surprise them.

'My friends!' I shouted, in Dutch. Aphra looked at me in surprise. 'Fellow mariners! I am Sir Matthew Quinton, a friend of your former captain, Pieter de Mauregnault!' This news, and my fluency in their language, stopped both the advance and the murmuring. 'We seek one man, a gunner. An old man, perhaps fifty or more. His name is de Wildt, although he may have adopted another. Double allowance for a month for the man who shows him to us!'

The murmuring began again, but quieter this time, to prevent me hearing it. No man stepped forward. And still the group straight in front of us kept tightly together, like Romans guarding a bridge.

The Keeper was increasingly nervous, and now took matters into his own hands.

'Make way, there!' he cried, and beckoned two of his turnkeys forward.

The phalanx stood firm. Cudgels were raised in warning. Still no movement.

'Fuck this – begging your pardon, mistress,' said Musk, pushing his way to the front and then throwing himself, head first, at the nearest Dutchman. Taken by surprise and winded, the fellow fell back, making a gap in the line.

And revealing the dead body on the floor, lying in a pool of blood.

'Christ,' said the Keeper, 'it's Jackson, the turnkey who lets in the slop-boy!'

'Goodman,' said Aphra. 'Mene Tekel. It must have been. He's freed de Wildt. We're too late!'

There was a cry in the crowd. 'Nothing to lose now, boys! Kill the

English!' The guard at the door shouted for the alarm bell to be rung. And the mob came at us.

I drew my sword and waved it from side to side in front of me, slowly clearing a path for us toward the door. This tactic kept a dozen of them at bay, but I knew it was only a matter of time before someone plucked up the courage to charge. Or they might work round behind us, but for the time being the Keeper and his turnkeys were guarding that flank, cudgelling and stabbing at any man who came close enough. Musk was in his element, punching any stomach or chin that strayed within reach of his fists. But the most astonishing sight was that of Aphra Behn. From somewhere within her skirts, she had produced a vicious pin, several inches long and nearly thick enough to be classed as a dagger. With it, she lunged expertly at any man near her, showing at once no fear and a very fine grasp of strategy. She was evidently well-versed in this kind of combat, as the Dutchman who took a vicious stab through the left shoulder swiftly discovered.

At last, two prisoners charged me, one with fists alone, one with a rough, bloodied blade that he must have somehow concealed from his gaolers – perhaps the very weapon that had killed Jackson. I lunged at the bladesman, forcing him back, then cut sharply into the side of the other fellow, slicing open his flesh below the ribs. He screamed and fell away, just as the bladesman came at me again, his grip reversed, stabbing high and hard for my head. I had the advantage of reach, though, and thrust straight for the heart. I felt my sword enter the body, saw the blood spill out over his shirt, saw the look of death-horror in his eyes, withdrew the bloodied blade, and took guard again, menacing any other man who thought to be so brave.

The Dutch were still shouting defiance and obscenities, but now there were new sounds: the familiar sounds of soldierly boots running on flagstones, and cries of 'For God and the King!' The first red-coated soldier ran into the room, followed by a crowd of his fellows, brandishing muskets and halberds. The prisoners fell back, and the soldiers made a path for us through to the door.

Later, in the Keeper's quarters in the gate tower, we took wine and recovered ourselves.

'Don't usually take on so many at once with the other Lord Percival,' said Musk. 'Hope that's not going to be your way, Sir Matthew – taking on the sort of odds that Phineas Musk finds daunting. Can't be doing with that, at my age.'

'I'll try to bear it in mind, Musk,' I said. 'But Mistress Behn, if I may venture such an enquiry – when did you learn to fight in such a manner?'

She did not hear me at first, being distracted by a tear in her sleeve that she seemed to find particularly distressing.

'Mm? Oh, your brother gave me some lessons, in Flanders before the Restoration. And in Surinam, well, a woman had to be resourceful.' She looked up, and gave me her full attention once again. 'But I did not realise you spoke Dutch, Sir Matthew – and like a Dutchman, too.'

'My wife and her brother would disagree with you, Mistress.'

Indeed they would. Captain Cornelis van der Eide of the Zeeland Admiralty took a particular delight in correcting me on minor points of Dutch grammar and pronunciation.

'No matter. It puts me in mind of a way in which we might pursue Goodman into his lair. It will involve some play-acting, Sir Matthew, and a little script of my devising. Your brother, the Earl, is always willing to play such roles. Is the new Lord Percival, I wonder?'

* * *

We parted at Ravensden House, Mistress Behn to work on her 'little script', I to report to my brother. But I very nearly failed to make it alive to his room. In the entrance hall, I was assailed by a furious Cornelia, her face scarlet and sodden from copious tears.

'*Schurk*!' she cried. 'Villain!'

'My love…'

She struck me hard on the left cheek. Reeling from the shock, I managed to grab hold of her hands before she could strike again.

'*Moordenaar! Leugenaar!* Murderer! Liar!'

'Cornelia, *in hemelsnaam*! For heaven's sake, what's the matter, woman?'

She struggled to escape my grip, but I held her firmly. She looked around wildly, as though seeking an exit or a weapon, but finally held my gaze. Her eyes were blazing with anger.

'Terschelling,' she said, almost spitting out the word. 'You lied to me about Terschelling.'

I could think of no reply, because, in truth, she was right. I had kept my explanation to her of 'Holmes' Bonfire' as brief and general as I possibly could. It was hardly a story to recount with pride or honour, even if one's wife was not Dutch.

'People *died*, Matthew. People were killed. Innocent people. Peaceful people.'

'We are at war,' I said, without conviction, for her words simply echoed my own doubts about what we had done.

'Oh, and do I not know that? Do I not know it every time I venture out of the door, and see the hostile looks on faces, and hear the catcalls of children? England is at war with the Dutch, I am Dutch, *ergo* I am an enemy of England. I know that. I live in England's capital, so I accept that. I accept that you must fight the navy in which my brother fights. You are both warriors, it is what warriors do – I am no cloistered nun, husband, shut away from such worldly affairs, and I know it is what you both *must* do. But to kill and burn on the soil of my country – to bring my own father – the father of your own wife – to the brink of ruin…'

'Your *father*?'

She blinked away more tears. 'A letter came from him today. He

91

had five cargoes at the Vlie. *Five*. All burned by you and your friends, husband. His credit is ruined. He does not know you helped to command the attack, but he tells of the fate of the poor Mennonites, and demands God's righteous judgement upon the devils who perpetrated such a crime.'

I was struck dumb. I had never been close to my father-in-law, Cornelis van der Eide the elder, a dour Calvinistic merchant of Veere. But he had taken me in when I was a penniless, wounded exile, and he had consented to my marrying his daughter, whom he might have bestowed on any sea-captain of the Zeeland Admiralty, or any rich burgher of Rotterdam. The beautiful, spirited daughter with whom I had fallen passionately in love, and who had loved me passionately in return, without really believing that my King would ever return to his throne, that she might one day be Lady Quinton, perhaps set fair to be Countess of Ravensden. He had given her the Calvinist faith, and thus the fatalistic acceptance of predestination, that enabled her to accept – in truth, to accept far better than I – all the long years when we tried, and failed, to have a child, a boy, the heir who would allow my family's inheritance to continue.

'I could not have known,' I said.

But even as I spoke them, I knew the words were utterly hollow, and Cornelia's cold, staring eyes showed that she knew it, too. *It is what warriors do.* We both knew it would not have mattered a jot if I had known that my father-in-law's ships were in the Vlie anchorage. I had my orders, I had my duty to my King and country, and I would have burned them all the same. After all, the ruining of merchants like Cornelis van der Eide the elder had been one of the explicit purposes that Prince Rupert and Robert Holmes had ordained for our expedition.

If anything, Cornelia's Calvinist faith should have told her all this. In her mind, what I did at Terschelling could only have been predestined by God; and if that was the case, she took out her anger on me chiefly because she could not take it out on He who was truly responsible.

'We are at war,' I repeated, the words coming out as barely a whisper.

Chapter Ten

A rare summer storm was darkening the late afternoon skies over Essex, as well it might. This, after all, was a county notorious as one of the principal seed-beds of rebellion during the late unhappy civil wars, and one that still contained countless ignorant souls disaffected with the rule of His Majesty the King. Admittedly, the same was true of my native Bedfordshire, but that was smaller, the people more placid. And Bedfordshire, for all its faults, contained rather fewer witches than Essex, despite the best efforts of the self-styled Witchfinder-General to exterminate them all during the late civil wars. A ruined castle lay just off to the south of the road we were taking, its tall, ivy-covered towers standing sentinel over the salt marshes below and the broad estuary of the Thames beyond. It was easy to imagine a coven within its dark walls, casting evil spells and incantations, benighting the prospects of the strange little party that now rode past.

We were on horseback, Musk, Aphra and I, and we were soaked to the skin despite the heavy cloaks we wore. But a coach would have been unsuitable for the play we were now acting out.

The port of Leigh appeared before us. For such a den of sin and treason, it seemed unremarkable enough: a village largely of timber-built, weather-boarded houses, nestling beneath a hill that fell down to the sea, with a fine old church standing amid trees, high above the main street below. Fishing craft and a number of coastal traders, including the broad hulls of several Newcastle colliers, sat on the mud of the tidal flats that flanked the creek. Therein lay the one obvious danger to our mission. Leigh was a port of some eminence, despite its small size and unprepossessing appearance. It had produced many Brethren, even Masters, of Trinity House, and many stout officers and men for the Navy, the Captain Dick Haddock who had taken part in Holmes' bonfire amongst them. So it was just possible that there might be a man in the town who knew me by sight: a pressed seaman, perhaps, who had served under me in the *Merhonour*, the *Cressy*, or the *Royal Sceptre*, during the two sea-campaigns of the war. But it was deeply unlikely, sufficiently so for it to be worth the risk. Until the fleet paid off in a month or thereabouts, all of the eligible mariners of Leigh were nearly certain to be at sea; and if there were any deserters in these parts, they were unlikely to linger long in a port which could be visited by a pressing tender at any time.

Of course, it was equally possible that Schermer, Goodman and de Wildt might spot and recognise Aphra before we had a chance to put our plan into effect. But she and Charles reasoned that they were unlikely to venture out too brazenly in public in the aftermath of the Rathbone plot and the recent escape of de Wildt from Chelsea College. Besides, the Aphra riding alongside me was a very different creature to the one who had been at Ravensden House – presumably different, too, to the young woman the Horsemen had known in Surinam. The long brown tresses had been cut off, and the remaining unfashionably short and straight hair dyed jet black. In high-necked, grey Puritanical garb and old-fashioned coif, riding sidesaddle, she looked every inch a demure, godly, and above all insignificant, goodwife.

We entered a middling-sized inn at the west end of the High Street. Musk took the landlord to one side and had a whispered conversation with him, during which a purse of coin exchanged hands. Of course, Musk was not playing a part: the role of the slightly dishonest rogue, engaged upon some marginally illegal scheme, had been his since birth.

He returned to where Aphra and I sat, close to the unseasonable coal fire that dried our sodden clothes.

'The best room in the house for you,' he said, so quietly that no others in the room could hear. 'The best room in the entire town, he says. A mattress in the garret for me. No doubt with fleas.'

'Excellent, Musk,' said Aphra. 'And our business?'

'He's sent word to a likely man. Says he'll be here by nightfall.'

'Good,' she said. 'Then let's dine, and while away the hours.'

We ate an acceptable ham broth, washed down by some Maldon ale. Musk and Mistress Behn talked of the wonders of the Americas, and of the relative merits of the inns of Antwerp. I remained entirely silent throughout. That, after all, was my part in this business, at least at this stage of it. Musk and Aphra Behn were both expert at this game; both had taken part in countless secret missions on behalf of my brother and others, and knew what they were about. But it was new to me, and I was utterly convinced that at any moment, one of the drinkers would point at me and shout, 'Ha! There's Sir Matthew Quinton, that notorious cavalier and malignant, pretending to be...'

A man walked up to our table and sat down upon the settle opposite us without introduction or ceremony. He was a rough-shaven, hard-faced fellow with warts on his hands, perhaps sixty or so. He had a cast in his right eye.

'Jack Crane, yonder, says you're interested in a passage.' His voice was a rasp, and although he spoke with the accent of those parts, there was a trace of something else, too: a touch of New England, perhaps, where many of the dissenting kind had once sought to establish the new Zion. 'A passage into Holland. That's a dangerous voyage to take in time of war.'

'We are prepared to pay well for it,' said Aphra.

'Reckon you would be, for what you're asking. So I've got to be asking myself, what business is afoot for such a fair lady as yourself to want something that might get us all hanged?'

'It concerns my husband, here.' She nodded toward me, and lowered her voice. 'He is a Dutchman. It is now – well, it has become difficult for him to remain in England.'

'And why might that be, then?'

'No need for you to know,' said Musk, playing the part of the ruffian bodyguard to perfection. 'Are you interested in the purse you've been offered or not?'

'If I'm risking my life, even for a weighty purse, I want to know what I'm risking it for.' He turned toward me. 'So what's your story, friend?'

'No English,' I said, in what I hoped was a passable imitation of my father-in-law uttering the only phrase of my language that he knew.

My father-in-law. The father of Cornelia, from whom I had parted in such bad grace.

'That right?' said the fellow. 'No English. Well, then.' He was silent for a moment, then looked up at me again, and began to speak in fluent and very rapid Dutch. 'So let's try the Netherlandish way shall we, if you're more comfortable with that? What's your story, friend? Why do you need to get out of England so damn fast, eh?'

'My name is Vandervoort,' I said in Dutch, hoping I had not displayed any hesitation in responding to a ploy clearly meant to catch me out, 'Adriaan Vandervoort. And I would rather not tell you my story, *meinheer*. All you need to know is that I have gold, and I can get more once I am landed in Holland.'

The fellow studied me closely. The mention of gold should have piqued his interest, but he seemed too interested in how I was speaking, rather than in what I was saying.

'You don't talk like any Dutchman I know,' he said, 'and I've been in and out of every harbour between Friesland and Zeeland for thirty years and more.'

'I am not from the coast. I am from Assen, in Drenthe, although I lived in Zeeland and Amsterdam for…'

'Drenthe? That's far inland, ain't it? Some sort of a bog. Poorest part of the entire republic, I heard.'

'All of that is true, unfortunately. And this is how we talk in Drenthe, the poor bog.'

He was silent, evidently sizing me up. Somehow, I managed to avoid looking at Aphra or Musk. But I was assessing the distance to where my sword and pistols lay, and estimating just how quickly I could reach them.

'All right, *Meinheer* Vandervoort, let's assume for the present that you're telling the truth. So what I want to know is, how does a Drenthe man like yourself come to be in England in the first place when our two countries are at war, and why does he then want to get out of it so quickly? Because I'll tell you this, friend. You telling me your story is your only chance of me agreeing to sail you across to Holland.'

And so I launched into the speech that had been written for me by Mistress Aphra Behn. How I wish I had preserved that piece of paper, given what befell her thereafter; Congreve or Vanbrugh would have paid a fortune for it.

'I serve the banking house of De Hondt,' I said, hoping I was acting with the degree of boastfulness and indiscretion that we had decided *Meinheer* Vandervoort ought to display. 'One of the most reputable in Amsterdam. On its behalf, I have carried out tasks in the likes of Vienna, Madrid and Paris. But this has been the most difficult mission of all, Mister–?' The fellow made no response, but simply nodded for me to continue. 'Of course, this war is a decided inconvenience to many in both our countries. To those with moneyed interests in both. You will know, I do not doubt, that many of my nation prosper here in England. We are not far from Colchester, which contains more

Dutchmen than my home town of Assen. We may be at war, but there are still countless Dutch in London, and elsewhere in these islands – why, sir, at this very moment, the mayors of your towns of Dublin and Limerick are Dutchmen.' This was an embellishment of my own; Cornelia had held forth on the matter at our awkward supper. 'It is important to many of these Dutchmen to continue to have contact with their brothers, cousins and bankers in the United Provinces. For monies to be able to continue to cross the North Sea in both directions, as it were, by means of discreet bills of exchange drawn upon neutral third parties. That has been my part, sir. I have lately been to Ireland, and Bristol, and London, and was bound for Colchester.'

'Nothing untoward in any of that,' said the fellow, grudgingly. 'But why do you need to leave England so fast, then, before you get to all your Dutch friends in Colchester?'

Aphra feigned alarm, and put her hand on my arm.

'You do not need to know all,' she said to our visitor in English. 'You know now that my husband can afford to pay you well for sailing us to Holland. Will you take the voyage, or should we seek some other man who will?'

'I thank you, mistress,' said the fellow, 'but this is a matter between me, here, and your husband, there.' He turned back to me, and resumed in Dutch. 'So, friend, your answer? Why do you need to get out of England, eh?'

I exchanged glances with Aphra, who was a more accomplished actor than I. It was easy to see why she had proved so useful to my brother, in his role as Lord Percival.

'You will know,' I said, 'that the Dutch are not only in England to trade. Lord Arlington, your King's great minister of state, is married to a Dutch lady. Lord Ossory, one of your King's favourites, is married to that lady's sister.'

'Not my King,' said the fellow, although he had raised an eyebrow at the mention of Arlington. As well he might: at that very moment, the King's principal spymaster might be poring over this villain's name on one of his many lists of malcontents.

'My apologies, sir. I, too, am no lover of kings. My bank is staunch for the True Freedom, and the cause of Grand Pensionary de Witt, and against…'

'Yes, yes… But Arlington and Ossory, and their wives? What of them?' I feigned reluctance.

'Sir, it is a matter of confidence…'

'If you want me to get you out of England, friend, you'll share that confidence. And if you've got Arlington after you, I think you'll need to leave this shore as swiftly as possible.'

I gave a show of considering the matter intently, casting glances at Aphra and Musk (who was lost in a bottle of modest wine), and sighing deeply.

'Very well,' I said.

* * *

'Do you think he believes it?' I asked.

Aphra seemed more interested in inspecting the small, low-timbered room we had been allotted. If it truly was the best room in Leigh, then the place evidently received precious few visitors.

'It is an irresistible story, Sir Matthew. Mark my words, he believes it, which is why he has promised to find us a ship within five tides. And, God willing, it will draw out Schermer, Goodman and de Wildt, too. A Dutch banker, able to find them limitless credit on the Amsterdam bourse? A Dutch banker with damning evidence against Arlington and Ossory? Yes, they will believe it all, and they will come to us.'

I was yet to be convinced, although my still-anonymous companion of earlier in the evening had seemed impressed enough by the web Aphra Behn had spun. A tale of scandalously large debts being run up by Ladies Arlington and Ossory at a card table presided over by the Queen, debts that could only be paid off by recourse to assets the two ladies still held in their native Netherlands, sounded utterly implausible to me. But then, I knew the two ladies in question – indeed, Aemilia, Countess of Ossory, was a friend of my wife – and knew them to be dutiful, modest, matrons of virtue. I knew the Queen, too: an insignificant, innocuous creature whose only mark to date upon the history of England had been, not the appropriate, necessary, and politically providential production of a Prince of Wales, but instead the introduction of tea-drinking.

But as Aphra had said, it would all seem very different through the suspicious eyes of the ever-febrile malcontents. To men like the creature to whom I had spoken that evening, Ladies Arlington and Ossory were unknown quantities, notable only and hated only because they were married to two of the leading lights in the notoriously debauched court and government of the licentious, Popishly-inclined whoremaster Charles Stuart. The very fact that they were wed to two such reprobates would make it possible to believe anything of them. Arlington, of course, was especially hated for his part in driving forward the persecution of those who regarded themselves as the pure, godly body of the divinely elected; or rather, as we cavaliers knew them to be, deluded, canting hypocrites. As for the poor, blameless Queen: she was, of course, a Catholic, and thus by the inexorable logic of the disaffected, she must therefore be one of the principal agents in England of Popery and the Jesuits, who spent day and night conspiring how to slit the throats of all true Englishmen and burn their children upon spits.

Whereupon, presumably, they would be basted with tea.

Whether Mistress Behn's assumptions were correct, and whether her script really would flush out the surviving Horsemen of the Apocalypse, remained to be seen. In the meantime, we had effectively made ourselves prisoners of our enemies, in a place full of hostile and rebellious spirits, with our proposed method of extracting ourselves depending upon...

'One bed,' said Aphra, diverting me from my thoughts by suddenly looking up at me in a smiling, questioning way that I found markedly disconcerting. 'And we are supposed to be a married couple. How do you propose to negotiate that matter, Sir Matthew?'

Chapter Eleven

I blushed.

'I shall make up a bed upon the floor, Mistress. I – I am accustomed to sleeping upon decks, when there is a prospect of battle.'

'Is there a prospect of battle tonight, Sir Matthew?'

She tilted her head, and smiled innocently. She took a step toward me.

'I am a married man,' I said, my throat suddenly as dry as glasspaper.

'So is the King. Such an upstanding model of marital constancy to us all. But you, too, Sir Matthew, are an upstanding fellow, I see.'

Another step. She was close enough for me to catch the first hint of her scent.

'I am a married man,' I repeated, for I could not think what else to say.

'And you have *never* been unfaithful to your wife? My God, Sir Matthew, for a man of your rank, you will be unique in England if that is the case.'

Part of me wanted to scream *I have never been unfaithful to my wife*, but the other, rather larger, part knew that for the lie it was. Admittedly, I had never been unfaithful to Cornelia in England. In all, since our marriage, I had slept with five other women, but all of them had been abroad – one, indeed, at sea – and all of them after inordinate periods of absence from the wife for whom I loved and longed. I had deluded myself by applying my satyr-like uncle Tristram's dubious logic, namely that Protestant marriages were deemed invalid by the Papists and the Mahometans, so fornication in any land under the sway of those faiths (that is, the great majority of the known world) could not possibly be adultery. But there were no possible legal or moral grounds that could permit an extension of this principle to Essex.

She was very close now. Very close indeed.

She was utterly beautiful. And, since I had learned Cornelia was pregnant, I had not – we had not…

The likes of Robin Holmes and, God help me, the King of England, would have been shocked by my restraint and prudishness, had they known of it. But I could not suppress my memories of childhood escapes to the mill and the smithy, and overhearing what the good-wives of the local villages said to their lusty boys and their wenches: of how *doing it* to a wife with child damaged babies in the womb, made them soft in the head, and other such nonsense that the brother of an Earl, even one barely breeched, should have dismissed as arrant superstition and foolery.

Superstition and foolery that, twenty years later, made Sir Matthew Quinton reluctant to lay a hand on the wife who might be carrying the future Earl of Ravensden, despite that wife being eager enough. For some reason I had a sudden image of Captain Ollivier, and felt my heart chill, just as another part of me warmed unbearably.

I gripped Aphra's shoulders. I could still have pushed her away, still proclaimed my constancy to my wife, still been faithful. If I had only shared Cornelia's steadfast belief in predestination, I could have argued –

Argued what?

For predestination was the most elusive of masters. Perhaps it was predestined that I should reject the advances of this skirted would-be

Shakespeare. Or perhaps it was predestined that I should take her bodily, there and then.

Who knew?

As it was, I looked into Astraea's eyes, and saw dark, bottomless pools of lust. My hands slipped from her shoulders, down to her breasts.

She sighed.

'You are brazen, Mistress Behn,' I said, at last.

She slipped her hands inside my shirt.

'Ours is not an age that values chastity and modesty in women, Sir Matthew,' she said.

I kissed her, and her tongue responded enthusiastically. We moved to the bed, our hands moving urgently over each other's bodies, pulling off clothing. And then we gave ourselves over to sin – to warm, moist, blissful, guilty, predestined sin.

* * *

I slept little, and rose before dawn. She was still asleep, her bare arms lying free above the blanket, a peaceful smile on her lips.

I walked down to the foreshore, breathing in the smells of the sea and the mud. It was starting to get light in the east, where the fleet was still at sea. A fleet I should still have been with, seeking out Dutch or French men-of-war. In the creeks within the marshes, and at the wharves within the villlage, fishermen were already at work, preparing their boats and their nets prior to setting out. A large merchant hull, a prize fly-boat by the looks of her, was newly hauled up high on the beach, so high that it would surely only be possible to float her off upon a spring tide. A sheet of canvas covering a patch of hull below the waterline suggested that she had been holed, and been run ashore for repairs. A young man, some three or four years younger than I, stood next to the ship, upon the mud of the estuary, looking up at the piece of canvas. He saw me, and nodded in silent greeting. A member of the carpenter's crew, contemplating the day's work ahead. Or so any observer would have assumed.

The sun came up, and bathed me in new-born guilt. I felt pain in my bones, in my head, in my blood. I had slept with Aphra Behn. I had betrayed Cornelia. I had sinned against my marriage vows. In England. *In Essex.* What, in God's name, had I done? What if I had made her with child? She had assured me it would not be so, but women's assurances upon that issue had been found wanting by mankind since the beginning of time. What if a bastard child lived, and the legitimate child, the heir to Ravensden that my wife might be carrying, perished? I thought of the old Mennonite woman's curse. What sort of retribution – what might befall Cornelia, our child, if it was ever destined to be born and to live, our very world?

'Give you joy of the morning, *Meinheer* Vandervoort,' said a familiar voice behind me, in English. 'You are about markedly early, this day.'

Lost in my thoughts, consumed by guilt, I spun around with a start, and the words of an English reply framed in my mouth –

Only to come out, by some miracle, in Dutch.

'Your pardon, *Meinheer*, I do not understand you.'

He repeated his previous words, this time in Dutch.

'As are you, my friend,' I replied.

'Sallows,' said the fellow. 'Daniel Sallows. If I know your true name and business, *Meinheer*, there's no good reason for you not to know mine, now is there?'

A gesture of fellowship. But we both knew that his first addressing me in English had been one more attempt to catch me out.

'And how goes your business, *Meinheer* Sallows? Will our ship be here in five tides, as you promised? The day after tomorrow?'

'That it will. You have my word on it, *Meinheer* Vandervoort, and I'm ever a man true to his word. But there are other men, also true to their words, who are keen to talk with you.'

I feigned alarm.

'That was not part of our agreement.'

'It's a part of it now. Oh, these men won't delay your sailing, *Meinheer*. But they have propositions to put to you. It will be to your advantage to listen to them. Tonight, at eleven. At the church. And to display their *bona fides*, they won't insist on you coming alone. Bring your man, if you wish, as a safeguard.'

'I do not like it.'

Sallows stepped closer.

'*Meinheer*, if you want to get out of England, you'll be at the church tonight. Leigh is mainly true to the Old Cause, but even a place like this has its share of malignants, and not a few who'd inform on you to one of the Essex Justices if they were to receive an anonymous information. And if you were to be arrested by a constable or the militia, *Meinheer*, how long do you think it would be before you were taken up to London? I'd reckon Lord Arlington would be very interested in your story, especially as it concerns his wife. Wouldn't you agree?'

'Very well, *Meinheer* Sallows, it shall be as you say. Eleven at the church.'

* * *

We walked out later that morning, looking for all the world like ordinary travellers taking a tour of inspection of the village. Aphra looked every inch the demure Puritan maid, and Musk dawdled dutifully a couple of paces behind us. I struggled to make conversation. I feared that any words I uttered would betray to the whole world – worse, would betray to Phineas Musk – the guilt of my adultery with this woman. As it was, I could have sworn I saw a knowing, condemning look in Musk's eyes. I tried to chide myself. That, after all, was surely nothing more than the way in which Musk always looked upon the world. Yet it also seemed as though the gulls, swooping above us while searching for rotten fish to devour, were shrieking 'Sinner!'

We proceeded past the strand and the jumble of meanly-built, lath-and-plaster houses clustered around the street and the foreshore. Many of the mariners may have been away at sea, but there were still many fishermen at work on their nets and the hulls of upturned boats pulled up onto the shore. These were curious affairs, double ended, with pointed sterns and a wet well in the middle of the boat where the catch could be kept alive. I wished to learn more of these 'peter boats', as I later discovered they were called; but I was a monoglot Dutch banker, not a captain of the Navy Royal, so I had to feign ignorance of everything I saw and heard.

Finally we were well out of earshot of any bystanders, climbing the steep path that led uphill, from the main street of Leigh to its parish church. This, dedicated to Saint Clement, stood near a substantial old stone-fronted, three-bayed house, which appeared to be empty. The graveyard was full of headstones for long-dead mariners; of the living, there was no sign.

'Good place for a secret meeting,' growled Musk from behind us.

We stopped and turned, pretending to take in the view. This was impressive. It was a fine, warm morning, with the Kent coast clearly in view, and several large merchant hulls outbound upon the newly-turned tide and south-westerly breeze. What appeared to be a Second or Third Rate lay at the Buoy of the Nore, presumably just come in from the fleet, but she was too far away to make out her identity. Victualling hoys, outward bound, were coming out of the Thames mouth. Closer at hand, several fishing smacks and cockle boats of Leigh lay at anchor in the roadstead. The flyboat was still aground a little further along the beach.

'High enough to give a good view in all directions,' said Musk. 'And it's out of the town, so easy to escape north, west or east if they need to. A fair choice as a meeting place for suspicious men.'

'It might not be them,' I said. 'There are disaffected creatures galore in these parts. All sorts of rebels and traitors who might want a Dutch banker to fund their conspiracies.'

'It's them,' said Aphra. 'Lesser men wouldn't scruple to come to us at the inn. Men who were less wary of being recognised.'

'But how can we confirm it?' I demanded. 'I can bring only Musk to the meeting – they'll be mightily suspicious if Vandervoort the banker turns up with his wife. And my Dutch might be good enough to fool Sallows, but I doubt if it'll bear more than a few seconds' listening by a native Dutchman such as Schermer, assuming he's there.'

Here, of course, was the difficulty: the great conundrum that no amount of thinking and talking on the parts of Charles Quinton, Aphra and myself had been able to resolve. If the Horsemen came to us at the inn, it might have been just possible to conceal Aphra, so that she could cast eyes on them and confirm their identities without them recognising her. But if we encountered them in any other way, in any other place, it was almost impossible to see how Lady Astraea could identify the Horsemen of the Apocalypse without giving away her own identity to them. If that happened, the elaborate trap that my brother had devised would come to naught.

'I shall think of a way,' said Aphra.

'We have only a few hours, Mistress,' I said.

'Then I shall think of a way quickly,' she said, smiling in that impudent, irresistible way of hers. 'In the meantime, let's go into the church. A little prayer might be efficacious.'

Musk glanced at me. I knew that look: it was his customary expression when he thought he was upon on a fool's errand.

* * *

Leigh churchyard looked very different by night. There was little light; none from the dark mass of the adjacent house, only a few dim candles and lanterns showing in windows in the village below, or on boats in the roadstead. Table tombs and headstones that had looked innocuous in daytime now appeared infinitely sinister, as though the Last Trump had just sounded and the skeletons were stirring beneath, about to break through the prisons of earth and stone placed above them. There was a strong easterly breeze, and the rustling of the trees heightened the effect.

Sallows stepped out of the castellated porch of the church.

'You've brought your wife,' he said. 'That wasn't what I said, *Meinheer.*'

Musk and Aphra Behn stood just behind me, the latter caped and hooded.

'If the men I am to talk to are English,' I replied, 'then it is likely English will be spoken by some, is it not?' Sallows nodded. Even now, he could hardly reveal that those I was meant to be meeting might be Dutch. 'So my wife can ensure that any translation from one tongue to the other conforms to what is actually said. A guarantee on both sides, *Meinheer* Sallows. A form of insurance, if you prefer.'

Even in the darkness, I could see Sallows frowning. On the one hand, I was stating all too clearly that I did not trust him to interpret correctly; but then, he could hardly have expected anything else.

'Yes,' he said, 'I expect that is very much what a banker would demand. It is no matter. Your wife may stay, *Meinheer.*'

Sallows lifted something on his lips, and blew two short blasts. A sailor's whistle.

Some moments passed; perhaps an entire minute. Then a dozen or so figures appeared from behind the west end of the church.

The ghosts of long dead monks.

The momentary thought chilled me, but passed at once. These were men, real, living men, though they were cowled as Aphra was. Men who did not want their faces seen. But why so many of them? We had been expecting one, two or three – no more.

'*Meinheer* Vandervoort,' said one of the cowled men, in Dutch; in the tones of a native speaker. 'A banker, I'm told.'

This was the moment of truth. I prayed to God that Cornelia and her brother had taught me well enough.

'That I am. Whom am I addressing?'

The fellow did not reply. Had even my first words betrayed me?

'Not your concern,' said the cowled man, at last. 'A fellow countryman of yours. That is all.'

Aphra sniffed loudly, as though she was troubled by hay fever. Our agreed signal for identifying this particular one of the Horsemen. Anton Schermer – the Precious Man.

The other hooded men fanned out around the churchyard, surrounding us. It was impossible to tell which, if any, of them were the other two Horsemen. It was also impossible for us to retreat.

'You seek passage to our country,' said Schermer. 'And you shall have it, on one condition. A surcharge, if you like, upon the terms you have agreed with Master Sallows, here.'

'This is robbery!'

'Not so. This is revenge – and as a Dutchman, it is revenge in which you should rejoice. Revenge for what the arms of the malignant reptile Charles Stuart lately inflicted at the Vlie and Terschelling. A simple charitable act on your part, *Meinheer*, to facilitate a suitable form of retribution, and a new dawn of freedom here in England.'

Careful, Matt –

'Of course,' I said, trying to say as little as possible. 'But what revenge?'

Schermer did not answer immediately.

'Your speech is very strange,' he said. 'Even for Assen. I have been to Assen, and the people I talked to did not speak like you.'

A deep breath – but before I could reply, one of the other hooded men, standing by a headstone to my left, stepped forward. I thought he was trying to get a closer look at me, or to see Aphra Behn's face beneath her own hood.

'Phineas Musk,' he said. 'You cheated me out of five guineas in Alsatia, you fucker, that time in Ram Alley. And you're a fucking King's man!'

'You're certain?' said another cowled figure.

Aphra coughed twice. So here was Shadrach Goodman, Mene Tekel himself.

'Works for Lord Ravensden, that's a friend of the Stuart whore-master!'

Here was the flaw in our grand plan. Something none of us had ever considered. We had prepared for the eventuality that someone in Leigh might know me by sight, or that one or more of the Horsemen might recognise Aphra Behn. But none of us – not even Charles, Earl of Ravensden, whose planning was normally so meticulous – had envisaged the possibility that someone might identify *Phineas Musk*.

What happened next was a blur. The hooded men drew weapons – daggers, swords, at least three pistols. Schermer drew a fine rapier.

'I thought you were no Dutchman,' he said, advancing towards me, Sallows at his side.

I drew the knife I had secreted at my belt, but otherwise, I had only one weapon; and that weapon was a single word. A single, shouted word.

'*Sceptres!*'

A musket shot shattered the silence of the Essex night. The ball struck a tomb a few inches ahead of Schermer, who suddenly crouched. I made for him, but Sallows interposed himself, brandishing his blade in my face. Another two musket shots, followed by the sound of men running on hard ground. I caught a glimpse of Musk wrestling with the creature who had recognised him, and of the other hooded men retreating, trying to get out of the churchyard, but having to fight their way through the men who were now pouring into it. My men.

I wanted Schermer, but could not reach him for Sallows. The Precious Man turned and ran.

'Bastard!' cried Sallows. 'Cavalier bastard!'

He lunged for me, but missed. Instead, he found himself staring down the barrel of the pistol brandished by the young man who now stood at my right flank. Ensign Lovell, the young man whose nod I had acknowledged alongside the beached flyboat that morning. The beached flyboat that had secretly held a score of the *Royal Sceptre*'s Marines within its hold.

'Good work, Ensign,' I said, as one of the Marines bound Sallows' arms behind his back.

'Too dark for good aiming, Sir Matthew,' said Lovell.

I could hear shouts, and the sounds of men running. Marines were in pursuit of rebels, but they knew the ground and Lovell's men did not. If the Horsemen alone had appeared, as we hoped they would, it would have been an easy matter for our men to surround the churchyard, or wherever else we might be able to lure them into the open, and secure all of them. But the Horsemen were no fools; the three who still lived had not survived years of ferocious war without learning how to take sensible precautions in such a situation as this.

Aphra Behn was pulling back the hoods of the prisoners, examining their faces intently.

'None of them,' she said. 'We have none of them.'

'Very well,' I replied. 'Ensign Lovell, search the town. Every house, every garret, every cellar.'

But I held out little hope.

Chapter Twelve

Dawn brought the certainty that we had failed. The search revealed nothing; wherever the Horsemen had hidden themselves for days and weeks, it was not in the village itself. The citizens of Leigh, outraged at the disturbance of their sleep and the invasion of their homes, stood in groups in the street and on the foreshore, complaining loudly of the illegality of what we had done. They were momentarily shocked and cowed by the reappearance from their hiding place in the flyboat of Lovell's Marines, now properly uniformed and fully armed, but it did not take long for their outrage to reassert itself. I then had to endure an uncomfortable meeting with a Justice of the Peace from nearby Benfleet, a portly fellow who evidently did not take kindly to having been woken in the small hours and forced to ride through the darkness.

'*Arbitrary beyond measure, Sir Matthew!*' cried Musk, doing a passable impression of the Justice as we rode back west, through the scrublands of coastal Essex. '*This is not France, Sir Matthew! We shall proceed to law, Sir Matthew!* I'd give him arbitrary – I'd hang him arbitrarily for being an arse.'

The Marines marched in yellow-uniformed file behind us, escorting their prisoners. For all Musk's bluster – much of it, I suspected, born of embarrassment at having been the unwitting cause of our near-demise – the scene must have had more than a hint of France about it.

'He was right, though,' I said. 'Soldiers bursting into the homes of innocent, God-fearing people – we saw enough of that in England, in Cromwell's time.'

'The means to an end, Matthew,' said Aphra. 'A pity we did not achieve the end, but I doubt if the King will condemn us for trying. And, as I recall, the Lord Lieutenant of Essex, who no doubt can mollify the magistrate, is a friend of your brother.'

He was, though the thought of him did little to ease my troubled mind. Aubrey, twentieth Earl of Oxford, the last of the De Veres, spent his every waking hour gloomily contemplating the extinction of one of the most ancient bloodlines in England: a state of affairs uncomfortably similar to my own.

'What did he want, do you think?' I asked. 'Schermer. The Precious Man. Retribution for Holmes' bonfire, and a new dawn of freedom of England. What would Vandervoort's money have paid for?'

'Whatever it is,' said Aphra, 'they have been planning it for a long time. Schermer and Goodman must have had their plan in place to get De Wildt out of Chelsea College before news of the bonfire reached England. Whatever they have in mind, revenge is only one part of it, and a newly added part. Their scheme is deeply laid – talk of Mene Tekel and the Precious Man began back in the spring, at the time of the Rathbone Plot.'

'For men like them, and for Rathbone, a new dawn of freedom would mean only one thing,' I said. 'The overthrow of the monarchy, the re-establishment of the Commonwealth. Their notion of freedom being every right-thinking Englishman's notion of slavery, as Cromwell's time proved.'

'One fewer target for them, though,' said Musk.

'Crave pardon, Musk?' I said.

'Rathbone and his crew planned to kill Monck, the Duke of

Albemarle. No need to do that now, as the fat, gouty old – very well, Sir Matthew, *His Grace* – he's at sea, so well out of the way.'

So he was. George Monck, who as Lord General of the army had secured London ahead of the Restoration of the King, and then kept it secure for him. Any conspirator worth his salt would surely attempt to carry out his plot before Albemarle returned from sea and resumed his iron if lumpen grip on the capital.

'What else did Rathbone seek to do, Musk?' said Aphra Behn. 'Neither Sir Matthew nor I were in London when it happened.'

'Not a bad plot, as these things go,' he said, 'and your brother and I have fair experience of such things, Sir Matthew. Kill the King – naturally – and Monck, then fire London to create panic and confusion. If it was me, I'd have put knives in the Duke of York, Clarendon and Arlington too, and any other lords or gentlemen I could get my hands on. A new Sicilian Vespers, or a second Saint Bartholomew's Day massacre if you prefer, only this time in Whitehall.'

'God help England if you ever turn rebel, Musk,' said Aphra.

'Not in a dozen lifetimes, Mistress,' he said. 'Anyhow, they planned to surround and disarm the Life Guards, get across the Tower moat in boats, scale the walls, then break open the arsenal and arm every old New Model trooper and canting conventicler within a dozen miles of London. Chances are, they'd have had an army of fifty thousand by dawn and your neck would soon have been on a block waiting for the axe to fall, Sir Matthew.'

'But such a plot would need money,' I said, ignoring the prospect of my beheading, and thinking aloud. 'Ready money, for bribes to the necessary parties, and then to establish the government of the new republic. Ah, of course! When it began, the old Commonwealth already had control of Parliament, which voted it money every step of the way it took. Any sudden revolution, like the one Rathbone plotted, would need credit until it could convene some sort of new Rump or Barebones Parliament, a puppet assembly of fanatics to give it a semblance of legality – and above all, to vote it taxes. That's why the Precious Man was so keen to meet *Meinheer* Vandervoort.'

'Bravo,' said Aphra. 'Now that truly is Lord Percival thinking and speaking.'

'Bit obvious, though,' said Musk, 'for these Horsemen to attempt exactly the same thing as Rathbone.'

'No,' I said, 'they'll have a different plan, that's for certain. But it'll still come back to the same thing, Musk. Money. They'll need money to erect their utopia, the new paradise of the godly saints upon earth. Perhaps they can get it from another source, but the fact that they were so keen to get it from *Meinheer* Vandervoort suggest they don't have it yet. That being so, all they can do is destroy, to wreak havoc – to avenge what Holmes and I did at the Vlie and Terschelling.'

A strange, unwelcome thought then came to me: that my very own, recently ruined father-in-law might have been a likely candidate to supply the Horsemen with funds.

'Or else,' said Musk, 'maybe we've given them such an almighty fright that they've turned tail and gone off to find a different war. One with plenty of walls they can blow up and towns they can fire.'

'Remember, Musk, I know these men,' said Aphra. 'They'll seek to complete what they have started. Nothing is more certain.'

'Then we must find some other way to stop them,' I said.

***

The Horsemen had eluded us, but at least we had Sallows. The other men we had captured in Leigh churchyard were clearly ignorant fellows, brought along only to provide strength in numbers. I was content to release them to the local magistrate as a sop. But Sallows was too valuable; he was the one chance we had of finding the trail of the Horsemen once again. Knowing the treacherous reputation of such vile dens of rebellion as Rainham and Barking, we went by way of the road closest to the river whenever possible, and put up overnight at Tilbury blockhouse, where the garrison, augmented by Lovell's Marines, ensured there would be no attempt to rescue the villain before he could tell us anything of value.

Not that Sallows was talking. I had threatened him with the gallows. Aphra Behn had attempted to bribe him. But the man seemed an inveterate fanatic, one of those whose eyes were fixed firmly on the life to come, the eternal and markedly dour rule of the Saints, as they called themselves. The certainty of predestination made men insufferable, but it also made them difficult to break.

'One hour,' said Musk.

'Beg your pardon, Musk?'

'One hour, Sir Matthew. That's all I'd need with him. Lord Percival – the real Lord Percival – would know that, and grant me that.'

I forced myself to glance at Aphra – something I had tried to avoid doing – and she nodded grimly.

'And what will you do to him in that hour, Musk?'

His round face was unreadable.

'Best not to ask questions like that, Sir Matthew. Best to be well out of earshot, too.'

I averted my eyes, and thought hard upon the issue. But in truth, it was not so difficult a decision. God alone knew what monstrous crime the Horsemen might inflict – how many innocents might die, for instance. I also knew full well what Sallows and his kind would do to the likes of me and mine, if they ever held power in the land once again. Above all, I knew exactly what my brother would say, and I was there, in that room, in that fortress, merely as his substitute. His mouthpiece.

'Very well, Musk,' I said, my throat dry. 'Go to it.'

In the event, it did not take an hour. It did not quite take fifty minutes, during which interval Aphra and I at first discussed the remarkably dry and hot weather, albeit in a somewhat intermittent fashion, until she somehow wheedled out of me tales of my days in the likes of Naples, Sicily and Venice, when I commanded in the Middle Sea, even of my visit to Madrid in my youth. She had a way of getting men to talk, whether they wanted to or not; of getting men to do many things, whether they wanted to or not. And above all, she had a way of getting men to forget, if only for a few precious minutes, those otherwise nearly unbearable burdens called sin and guilt. Of getting men to forget that they had wives.

When Musk returned, he was in exactly the same unperturbed state as before, with no sign of his having been about any business of any kind whatsoever.

'He doesn't know where they are, and what they're planning. I'd stake my life on that.' Then it had to be true. Phineas Musk rarely staked his life, even in jest. 'But he's seen papers of theirs that mention a ship. A Swedish ship, with one Peterson as skipper. Lying at Saint Katherine's, he says, hard by the wharf for Corsellis' brewhouse, the Hartshorn.'

I knew the Hartshorn; it was close by the Navy's victualling yard, in East Smithfield, which I had often had cause to visit. But it was close by something else, too.

'Adjacent to the Tower,' I said. 'Rathbone planned to seize the Tower. Anyone seeking control of London must surely possess it, or destroy it.'

'Then, Sir Matthew,' said Aphra, 'surely Saint Katherine's is where we should go?'

I mustered as good a grace, and as positive an air, as I could manage.

'Indeed so, My Lady Astraea. That is precisely where we should go.'

Chapter Thirteen

A hunting party.

Myself, in the guise of Lord Percival, in turn in the guise of a buff-coated rogue, my face greased to darken my complexion; Phineas Musk, in the guise of Phineas Musk, clad in an extraordinarily gaudy scarlet coat; and a half-dozen of my brother's chosen men, led by one Marker, though I doubted that was his real name. A stout, ugly fellow with stooped shoulders, he claimed to have fought at Lansdowne, Cheriton, and God knew where else, but was markedly vague when it came to which side he might have been on.

And, of course, we had Aphra Behn. Once again, though, the Lady Astraea had transformed herself. Gone was the demure Puritaness who had been in Leigh-on-Sea with her Dutch banker husband; gone, too, was the Earl of Ravensden's nurse, and the coquettish, finely-dressed lady of the court who had supped at Ravensden House. In their stead was a gaudy harlot, rouged beyond measure, her breasts very nearly spilling out over her gaudy satin dress. A drunken whore, unwilling to let go off the arm of her latest master, the evident leader of the dangerous-looking gang, on whom she was lavishing the crudest attentions.

That being Phineas Musk.

I could not fault the lady's logic. A tall man and a beautiful woman, walking arm in arm through some of the roughest streets in London, would be bound to attract attention. But a doxy on the arm of such an ugly villain as Phineas Musk: any observer would reason that here was a high-and-mighty gang-mastering apple-squire, some sort of Grand Turk of the dockland rogues, out upon dark business of the night with his latest strumpet and his bodyguard. In other words, the sort of scene that, in this part of London, was as common as horse dung.

Thankfully, Cornelia had not witnessed Aphra's latest incarnation: God alone knew what she would have made of such brazen attire. We had dressed for our parts at Killigrew's theatre, where the Lady Astraea seemed to know everyone. I avoided Ravensden House, convincing myself that my decision to do so was due entirely to shortage of time and the urgency of our mission. Instead, I sent Musk there, to communicate our scheme to my brother. He returned to say that my wife was well, but silent; and silence was not the usual mark of Cornelia Quinton.

Our party walked through East Smithfield, the great walls of the Tower looming over us. Past the victualling yard, down the narrow, curving lane that ran down to Saint Katherine's dock. This was a pitiful affair compared to, say, the great wet dock at Deptford: just a narrow tidal channel completely overshadowed by the buildings around it, one of which was the great church of Saint Katherine's Hospital, another the Hartshorn Brewhouse. The streets were quiet, perhaps because anyone who sighted our little army determined at once to give us as wide a berth as possible. As we approached the water's edge, though, the bustle increased. Even at that time of night, bales were being taken off the coasters packed into the dock, men swearing and shouting as they struggled with ropes, cranes swinging cargoes onto the wharves. It was an oppressively hot night, and the twin stenches of hops and tidal ooze struggled for supremacy. There was even more of the latter than should have been expected at low tide; the long drought of that summer had turned even the mighty Thames into a shadow of its usual self.

Out in the river, ships were tied together so tightly that they almost entirely blocked any view of the south bank, although it was just possible to see lantern-light from some of the uppermost floors of the buildings around Pickled Herring Stairs on the Horselydown bank, and the very top of Saint John's church tower.

By the entrance to the dock, a small gaggle of watermen stood apart, puffing upon their pipes and engaging in desultory conversation. They fell silent at our approach. Bad custom we might have looked, but there was always the possibility that appearances deceived. Nine fares bound for Greenwich, or even only as far as London Bridge, might make it a very profitable night for one of these men.

'Ho, lads,' said Musk, revelling in his role as a dockland Archduke, 'we're for passage to one of the ships, yonder. Skipper's got some special entertainment for us.'

The watermen looked at each other. At last, one of them, a fellow with a huge grey beard that might have been fashionable in the old Queen's time, spoke up.

'Too short a passage, this time of the night.'

Phineas Musk looked around, lazily.

'Half a guinea for the passage,' he said. 'More than you'd get for rowing from here to Henley. And there'd be your bonus, of course.'

'Bonus?'

'We wouldn't burn your boat, cut you up, and throw you into the river. You'd return home alive, which I'd call a bonus, myself. So is it still too short a passage, friend?'

The waterman looked at his friends, but they, in turn, were looking at the gang standing behind Musk's back, myself included, weighing the odds. Their expressions indicated that they did not consider these to be good.

'Which ship?' said the waterman, conceding defeat.

'The *Milkmaid* of Stockholm. You know it?'

'Peterson's ship. That's it, yonder, the one closest to the Hartshorn's wharf.'

'Well, then, it's your lucky night, friend. A short and easy row, half a guinea, and you continue to breathe. What could be better, eh?'

* * *

The *Milkmaid* was a middling-sized flyboat with a high stern, probably Dutch-built, as so many Baltic traders were. Her watch on deck, a lad of no more than fourteen, shone a lantern at us as we approached, then called out something in a tongue that must have been Swedish. As the waterman brought us alongside the hull, a sharp-faced, crop-haired fellow of forty or more appeared at the ship's rail.

'What's your business?' he demanded, in good English. 'I had the customs aboard this noontime, the prize officers in the afternoon. The ship's clear – a confirmed neutral. Property of the Lord Hagerstierna.'

'We're not the customs,' said Musk. 'Nor from the prize commissioners, nor the Admiralty court, and we don't give a jot for any Lord Hags Turner. Throw down a ladder, Skipper Peterson!'

The Swede stared at us in silence. A boatful of armed men, approaching a laden merchantman at this time of the night – it was obvious what he would be thinking. But the chances were that most of his men were ashore, drunk in some riverside taphouse or other; and even if they were not, ships like this saved money by sailing with crews so small that probably not even the *Milkmaid*'s full complement could have put up much resistance against us. Unless, of course, the Horsemen were aboard, with an armed retinue of their own.

But if they were, they did nothing to stop Marker, who suddenly emerged from the darkness behind Peterson and put a knife to his ear. Marker, who had scuttled up the *Milkmaid*'s anchor cable with another of his men, the waterman having brought us in from that direction specifically for that purpose. Marker's companion now appeared at the rail, his right hand tight across the watch on deck's mouth to stop the lad screaming a warning.

A rope ladder came over the side, and we climbed up onto the deck.

'Pirates,' growled Peterson.

'On the Thames?' I said, mildly. 'I think not, Skipper. Lord Percival, rather, on behalf of the King of England. With credentials from your country's ambassador in this kingdom, the Lord Leijonbergh. Your Lord Hagerstierna should take up the matter with him, if he has objections.' The skipper scowled. 'You have guests aboard, Master Peterson? Passengers?'

The Swede was silent, but Marker pressed his blade against the skipper's cheek.

'Two passengers, below. No guests.'

I nodded to Musk. He and two more of Marker's men led the way forward to the forecastle, and then below, Aphra and I following behind.

The *Milkmaid*'s cabin for passengers was a tiny, stinking, damp space, so far forward that it must have been intolerable in a heavy sea. It was lit by one lantern, swinging from a hook on a beam. Directly beneath it, a fellow of about my age, fat-cheeked with matted, greasy black hair, was sitting on a stool, staring intently at something in his left hand, poking it with the thin metal object in his right, humming a tune I did not recognise. A second man, much older, was behind him, stretched out on a pallet on the deck, snoring loudly.

I turned to look at Aphra. She studied the two faces intently, then shook her head.

At that moment, the man on the stool finally registered our presence. He let out a cry that was more animal than human, dropped what had been in his left hand, and retreated, limping a little as he did so, against the bulkhead, to cower there. The object he had been holding broke as it struck the deck: a watch, but one that would not tell the time again. Some of its workings spilled out onto the timber planking.

The noises woke the man on the pallet, who sprang up, pulling out a blade from his breeches.

But he did not attack us. He seemed to weigh the odds, then turned at once to go to his companion, who was crying like an infant.

'It's all right, Robert,' he said, in French. '*C'est bon.*'

'*L'horloge est casseé,*' said Robert, over and over, between sobs. 'It's broken.'

'Don't worry, *mon cher ami*, you'll make better ones. That one was never going to work properly.'

'*Qui sont-ils?*' demanded Robert, pointing at us. 'Who are they? I don't like them.'

There was no threat here, that much was clear. I beckoned to Aphra and Marker's men to return above deck, leaving Musk and I alone with the simple-minded watchmaker and his friend.

'We are searching for other men,' I said in French. 'You are the only passengers on this ship?'

'We are,' said the older man. 'Bound from Stockholm for Rouen, whence we both hail. The ship was stopped at sea by your English fleet and sent in here for examination, in case it was running contraband to France.'

A common story: my own commands during this war had sent in supposedly neutral hulls galore, some of which were genuine, most of which were Frenchmen or Dutchmen pretending to be neutrals.

'Why are you still aboard the ship?' I asked. 'Surely you would be more comfortable ashore?'

'London is an expensive city,' said the older Frenchman, shrugging. 'Who knows how long we might be here before your Admiralty judges finally decide we can continue our voyage? Besides, my poor friend here… it is easier if he does not encounter too many people.'

'A simpleton, and yet a watchmaker?'

'A very fine watchmaker. *N'est-ce pas, Robert?* Isn't that so?' The poor fellow nodded, but continued to sob. 'Not so very strange, sir.

Doesn't the Lord God often take away one faculty from a man, but compensate by giving him an extra measure of another? Poor Robert's wits may be feeble, but he is an outstanding craftsman. Trained by his father, one of the best watchmakers in Rouen. All of his family follow the trade, *monsieur*. They are a quite renowned dynasty in Normandy.'

There was clearly little point in remaining there, frightening the harmless watchmaker. Perhaps the Horsemen had not yet come to the *Milkmaid*; perhaps they were long gone; perhaps the information Musk had extracted from Sallows was false.

'You have papers?' I said.

Lord Percival, the representative of King Charles himself, had to maintain appearances, after all. We would search the ship to see if there was any trace of the men we sought. We would question Captain Peterson and his crew. But somehow, I already knew that our mission had failed.

'Of course,' said the Frenchman. 'We are Huguenots, sir, vouched for by the French Protestant churches in both Stockholm and Rouen, and by the noble Lord Hagerstierna himself.'

I barely heard him. I wanted nothing more than to be off this ship, and well out of my brother's damnable world of intelligencing. A world where nothing was what it seemed, where duplicity and deceit reigned supreme. A world which brought with it the temptations of Mistress Aphra Behn, and a flood tide of unbearable guilt. I prayed to be back at sea. There, at least, I knew exactly who the enemy was; and there, Sir Matthew Quinton did not need to be responsible for frightening poor, soft-headed innocents.

'Musk,' I said, turning on my heel, 'inspect their papers.'

With that, I returned to the upper deck, knowing that I would have to report our failure to my brother.

* * *

'There is nothing for it,' said Charles Quinton, sitting up in bed and seemingly a little better. The first rays of a late August dawn were piercing the gaps between the shutters. 'I'll set Musk to interrogate Sallows once again, of course. We'll have Marker and his men watch the ship and the adjacent quays. But unless the Horsemen make a mistake, or we obtain some other intelligence of them, there's precious little we can do. If they're in London, they'll just disappear into the throng – war or no war, there are Dutch enough in London.' I nodded. One of them, my own wife, was under the same roof at that very moment; another shared the bed of the King's secretary of state. 'At bottom, all we can do is pray that all the talk of a great apocalypse on the third of September is as much a fiction as all the fanatics' other wild plots and fierce talk.'

'There is no more to be done?' I said.

'None. You are a free man, Matt – you can relinquish the role of Lord Percival. I can give orders easily enough from this bed, and it is as good a place as any in which to worry.'

My feelings battled each other like Levantine galleys. Yes, there was relief that I could extricate myself from my brother's dark and secret world. But I felt that I had failed him; and if I had failed Charles Quinton, I had failed Charles Stuart, too. Nothing pains a Quinton more than a sense that he has failed his King and his country.

'What will you do, Sir Matthew?'

Aphra's question seemed innocent, but the expression in her eyes was not. It was very apparent what she would have had me do – there and then, too, if only my brother was not present.

And there, of course, was the other half of the Levantine galley battle, the other set of emotions battling their bloody way through my head and heart. If I remained in London, I would surely succumb to Mistress Behn's charms yet again. For there was a part of me that wanted nothing more than to succumb, to feel her warm, naked flesh against mine. But if I succumbed again, the odds of my fathering a child on Astraea would multiply. And if I succumbed again, in

London, Cornelia would find out, by some means or other. Since my return from Leigh, she had been cold and distant, still embittered by the supposed ruin of her father and my part in it. I knew she would be cold and distant again, when I went down to her after Lord Percival's conference concluded. But if she found out my adultery, God alone knew how matters would go.

I imagined her face, red and livid once again, her lips framing words of justified abuse – but it melted into the face of Aphra, beckoning upon a pillow – and back to Cornelia again, then the worst thought of all. *What if the baby is lost?*

No way out.

But there was, and the realisation of it came to me like a thunder-clap from Heaven itself.

'I am a King's captain,' I said, as calmly as I could manage. 'My duty is to return to my ship. At Woolwich.'

Chapter Fourteen

No captain takes delight in riding into a royal dockyard. For his ship to be there means, naturally, that it is not at sea; and in a war, not being at sea means no glory, no honour, no prize money. Then, too, having a ship in a dockyard means that its captain has to deal with the officials and workmen of the yard on a daily, perhaps an hourly, basis. Any seaman will tell you that God created dockyard-men on the same day that he created foxes, rats, slugs, tortoises, and all the other sly, idle or slow creatures of the world. But that day in late August, even though the gates of Woolwich yard were a few yards ahead of me and a torrential downpour was soaking me to the very bone, I felt nothing but joy. I was returning to the *Royal Sceptre*, to a world I knew, to a world where I was safe.

I was not running, and I was not hiding from Cornelia and Aphra. Not in the least.

I was doing my duty by my King, and my crew.

Although it must be said, whatever the former might have thought if he had known of my movements and the reasons for them, the latter was uniformly astonished.

'Sir Matthew!' exclaimed Lieutenant Julian Delacourt, who was standing at the head of the double dry dock, beneath the beakhead of the *Royal Sceptre*.

Heads peaked over rails, and out of gunports. Ali Reis, who seemed to be fitting new foremast shrouds, grinned and salaamed, despite the precariousness of his perch.

'Lieutenant,' I said. 'Everything is in order?'

'As in order as it can be, Sir Matthew. Our men are working double watches – they all want to be back at sea before the end of the campaign, especially if the French fleet comes into the Channel. I wish the same could be said of the dockyard shipwrights and caulkers.'

'Ah,' I said, 'then perhaps I should have a word with Identifiable?'

'That would be a blessing. He evidently considers me naught but a jumped-up schoolboy, and pretends not to understand a word Mister Urquhart says to him. But here he comes, Sir Matthew.'

A florid, bewigged, slightly stooped fellow in his mid-forties, grossly overdressed for a mere Master Shipwright of a royal dockyard, was bustling across the ground past the sawpits, from the direction of the officers' houses. Identifiable Pett, this: to be precise, Christopher Pett, by-named Identifiable because he was one of very few male members of his vast dynasty not to be named Phineas or Peter. The Petts had ruled the royal dockyards on the Thames and Medway for the best part of a century, devising methods of nepotism and corruption that made the Borgias seem like newborn lambs. Like all of his family, Identifiable Pett regarded Master Shipwrights as somewhere superior to archangels in the natural hierarchy of things, debatably on a par with the King. Commissioned captains of the Navy Royal, even if they were knights of the realm and heirs to earldoms, ranked alongside the likes of voles and squirrels.

There was about to be an argument; an argument of the screaming-until-blue-in-the-face kind. Anticipating this, the heads of more and more Sceptres were appearing from nooks and crannies all over the ship.

I realised I was grinning broadly. At that moment, I wanted nothing more than the opportunity to berate the Master Shipwright of Woolwich Dockyard in front of my entire ship's company and his entire workforce.

Preferably for at least half an hour.

* * *

By the standards of the other royal dockyards, Woolwich was tiny, the site constrained by the Kentish cliffs that reared up immediately behind it. Somehow, one double and one single dry dock had been fitted into the space available, along with the usual storehouses, workshops, and so forth. It lacked Chatham's size and grandeur, Deptford's convenience for London, and Portsmouth's impression of endless space on land and water. Worse, all three of those yards had substantial towns immediately adjacent to them, where at least half-respectable rooms in half-decent inns could be found. Not so at Woolwich, which had no inn worthy of the name; travellers invariably stopped overnight at Gravesend or Deptford instead. I had the offer of a bed in the house of the master-attendant of the dockyard, it being an invariable rule of the Navy that the master-shipwright and master-attendant of any yard hated each other beyond reason. So as far as Thomas Clements was concerned, any enemy of Identifiable Pett was a friend of his. But Clements was a flatulent drunk, and a tarpaulin of the meanest sort – barely literate, his notion of genteel conversation was to hold forth on his new scheme for reordering the scuttles on Third Rates. So it was that I found myself in the best room of the Crown and Anchor, a damp, fetid space that would have been considered unsatisfactory even for Ravensden Abbey's poultry.

After a few days of discomfort, of nocturnal insects, and of berating Identifiable Pett and his shipwrights, I was doubting the wisdom of my abrupt departure from London. My own men still worked like demons, determined to get the ship back to sea; but on the last morning in August, some two hours after work had commenced in the dockyard, I stood upon the quarterdeck of the *Royal Sceptre*, looked at the scene around me, and knew it was all in vain. True, the hull was substantially repaired. I had been to sea in ships in infinitely worse condition. Men were repainting the gunports in good cheer, confident that they would soon be snapping open once again to unleash hell upon the Dutch and French. But with the best will in the world, our prospects were grim. Between the *Sceptre* and the river beyond was the *Arms of Sluys,* a Dutch prize taken in the previous war. For us to get back to sea, she would have to be taken out of the dock first. Those last few days, I had all but memorised the tide tables for Woolwich Reach; and I had an estimate in my head of the number of tides it would take to get both the *Arms of Sluys* and ourselves clear of the dock. And God alone knew how many more tides before the gunwharf could get all our cannon back aboard. Two days, perhaps more, to get down to the Buoy of the Nore. And the fleet might well begin to come in to pay off at the end of September; certainly no later than the middle of October. I looked out over the larboard quarter-gallery, toward the river and the distant sea, and knew in my heart that the campaign was over for the *Royal Sceptre* and her captain.

I turned, and saw a curious sight down in the ship's waist: Julian Delacourt, sitting on an empty gun carriage, staring intently at a piece of paper in his hand. He was ever a cheerful, smiling fellow, but his expression seemed infinitely sad. I went down to him.

'Joy of the morning, Lieutenant,' I said.

He looked up from the letter, met my eyes, looked down again, then back up once more.

'What is the matter, Mister Delacourt?' I demanded.

He shook his head.

'Sir Matthew – that – that is no longer my name.'

With that, the tears came to his eyes.

I understood. As the heir to a title myself, I understood all too well. I bowed my head.

'My condolences upon the death of your father, My Lord Carrignavar,' I said.

We spent the rest of the day in one after the other of Woolwich's mean alehouses, attracting not a little attention from the low-bred rabble who frequented them. But Julian, now the fifth Baron Carrignavar, had much to forget: a ruinous castle upon a blasted Irish headland, obstreperous Catholic tenants, decayed, unproductive and mightily encumbered lands, a half-dozen sisters in need of marrying off.

'I shall write to the Duke of York,' I said. 'I should imagine there will be no difficulty in you being granted permanent leave.'

He looked up from his pewter pot of ale.

'Begging pardon, Sir Matthew, but no. With your permission, I'll remain with the ship – for as long as there's a one in a thousand chance of us being able to get her back to sea, at any rate. God willing, I'll stay with the Navy until the war's end, too. The fields won't get any better if I'm there, least of all if I get back to them just for the start of winter. Our steward's an old rogue, but my sisters have his measure. And what I've experienced, these last weeks – the Saint James Day fight, our battle with the *Jeanne d'Arc* – why, those are the memories of a lifetime, and perchance I can garner a few more of them before I settle down to a life of initialling rental ledgers, and other such excitements.'

'I know what you mean, My Lord. All too well.'

'Then let us be warriors of the King for us long as we can be, Sir Matthew, and the devil take whatever lies ahead of us.'

I raised my tankard.

'Amen to that, Lord Carrignavar. Amen indeed.'

The following morning, my head somewhat thick from toasting the newly-minted peer, I was down by the side of the dock, inspecting the *Sceptre*'s rudder.

'Oppressive for the time of day, this weather,' said a familiar voice behind me.

I turned.

'Francis,' I said. 'Great God, man. I hadn't expected to see you for many weeks.'

The Reverend Francis Gale nodded.

'Your mother has been assuaged, and the arch-dissenter Bunyan will continue to grace Bedford Gaol for some time to come. That being the case, it wasn't difficult to persuade her that it was more important for me to provide spiritual support to her two sons.'

'You've seen my brother?'

'I've come from Ravensden House this very morning, despite the ungodly hour at which the waterman wanted to set off so as to catch the ebb. The Earl is a little improved, I'm glad to say. His will not to die is perfectly remarkable.'

'Thanks be to God for that.' *Thanks be to God that I do not yet suffer the fate of Julian Carrignavar.* 'And my wife?'

'Lady Quinton's temper is somewhat improved. It seems her father's fortune has been rescued, at least in part, by the safe arrival of the Dutchmen's return fleet from the East Indies. He had invested quite significantly in some particularly rich cargoes.'

I breathed a sigh of relief. Very nearly treasonable though the thought might have been, I thanked God that my own fleet had failed in one of its principal objectives of the war, the capture of the fabulously rich *retoorvloot*. And I marvelled once again at the transience of the world of money which my father-in-law inhabited, where everything could be lost and regained, or the reverse, in a matter of days. So different to the wealth of the Quintons, which lay primarily in land that we had held for centuries: land so heavily mortgaged, or otherwise encumbered, or entirely uneconomic, that we might as well have been paupers upon the heath.

'I fear you've had a wasted journey, Francis, if you've come in expectation of the ship returning to the fleet.'

'Oh, I come with no such expectation, Sir Matthew. I've served in the Navy long enough to be a fair judge of how long it'll take a ship to get to sea.'

He looked around. Although a few scavelmen were down by the dock gates, and men were busy in the sawpits, there was as yet little activity in the rest of the yard. Most importantly, there was almost no activity on the *Arms of Sluys*; and Francis knew what that meant as well as I did.

'That being the case, I wondered if we could find some cleaner air. A walk, perhaps.'

I saw Identifiable Pett emerge from his door in the row of officers' houses, and consented at once to Francis' suggestion.

* * *

We walked east for about an hour, through quiet lanes flanked by fields. Although we were so close to the dockyard and the river, it could have been a scene from my native Bedfordshire, the landscape interrupted only by the occasional windmill or distant church tower. I talked of the state of the ship, and of the progress of the war. We spoke too of the progress of the wounded men, including Treninnick and Macferran, who had been sent up to Saint Bartholomew's hospital to expedite their recoveries. Francis talked of my mother's health, and my brother's, of the condition of the Ravensden estate, of the latest rumours about the war and the doings of the court. The Duke of York's new mistress, one Arabella Churchill, was said to be with child. There was a new plot to bring down the Duke's father-in-law, the Earl of Clarendon, the Lord Chancellor. And so forth – the normal conversation of two men who were not saying what they were thinking.

At length, we came to a thick wood. Through the trees, we could catch occasional glimpses of the river, snaking its way down through Erith Reach toward the Hope. A big Balticman or Levanter was trying to make headway downstream, struggling against the strong east wind.

Then, quite suddenly, we were in the midst of ruins. Ancient, thick walls appeared amongst the trees and undergrowth, as though all had grown up together and were part of some strange, primal jungle. High up in one of the walls, it was just possible to make out a Gothic window, its tracery almost overwhelmed by ivy.

'Lesnes Abbey,' said Francis. 'An Augustinian foundation. Good men, the Augustinians – most of them, at any rate. Knew some of them in Ireland, in the days when they thought there might be opportunity to refound some of their monasteries there. The days before Cromwell came.' He turned away, gazing into the distance, and was silent for some time; thoughts of Ireland, and Cromwell's terror there, still haunted the Reverend Gale. But then he turned back to me. 'Ravensden could have been like this, had not your ancestor bought it. But of course, it might still become like this, in its turn. All things fade and pass, Sir Matthew. *Sic transit gloria mundi.*'

A strange reflection, I thought. But curiosity overtook me, and I began to hack at brambles with my sword, the better to inspect the monastic ruins.

'You always intended us to come here,' I said.

'The place is known to me. I was at college with the present Vicar of Woolwich. He has invited me to give the sermon in his church this Sunday, the day after tomorrow.' Francis drew a deep breath. 'I have been contemplating which text to take, and crave your advice, Sir Matthew. I am torn between One Corinthians Seven, Verse One, and Proverbs Six, Verse Thirty-Two.'

I stopped my hacking, my sword suddenly unbearably heavy in my hand. Slowly, I turned to face him.

One Corinthians Seven, Verse One. *It is good for a man not to touch a woman.*

Proverbs Six, Verse Thirty-Two. *But whoso committeth adultery with a woman lacketh understanding: he that doeth it destroyeth his own soul.*

I stared at Francis Gale, but his face was unreadable.

'How?' I said. But even as I uttered the word, I knew the answer. 'Musk. It could only be Musk. I was certain he could not know. Very nearly certain.'

'There is no secret concerning the House of Quinton that Phineas Musk does not know, or thinks he knows,' he said. 'And Musk, in his own way, is a man of faith, although I am never entirely sure whether the faith in question does not additionally embrace Odin, Zeus, and Baal, as a kind of multiple spiritual insurance. But even if he were not, it's surprising how many men and women still seek to unburden their greatest secrets onto a priest, even a full century after England dispensed with the sacrament of confession.'

'I – I'm sorry, Francis…'

I was ashamed beyond all measure, and wanted nothing more than for the brambles to grow up around me, to suck me into themselves, to make me as one with the crumbling walls of Lesnes Abbey.

Francis raised a hand. 'I'm not judging you, Matthew. You know me, man – I'm no saint. I'll wager I've committed far more fornication than you ever have and probably ever will, so if either of us is going to burn in eternal hellfire for it, I rather suspect it'll me being prodded into the fiery pit, a long way ahead of you. And the examples presented to us by the King, the Duke of York, and every man of rank in this kingdom, hardly encourage chastity and abstinence.' He smiled. 'Besides, having seen the lady myself only recently, I certainly do not judge a man I envy.'

'Why, then?'

'Why bring you all this way, so that we could talk in complete confidence? Only this. Think upon it well, my friend. Your brother might or might not survive this latest illness of his, but we both know he cannot live more than – what, a few years at best? Your Uncle Tristram is an old man, close to sixty, and he has no children. At any rate, no legitimate children, like our Sovereign Lord. No, the only thing that stands between Ravensden Abbey and the fate of this Lesnes is you, Matthew Quinton. You and your Cornelia's unborn child, especially if it is a boy. I am the Vicar of Ravensden, and one day soon, you will be its Earl, and then, perhaps, your son after you. Do nothing to imperil all of that. I can forgive you. God can forgive you. But if your wife finds out that are committing adultery with Mistress Behn, we both know she will *never* forgive you. And what the consequences might be of that, only Our Father knows.'

My own thoughts, my own nightmares, articulated better than I ever could. The thoughts and nightmares that had plagued me ever since I sinned with Aphra Behn. I looked up at the nearly-lost window, and thought of the long-dead monks who would have trodden the very ground where I stood.

'But Musk? What's to stop him telling Cornelia? He loves her as the daughter he never had, would do anything to protect her.'

'As I said, Musk knows everything about the House of Quinton. Everything – except, until, very recently, its greatest secret of all.' *But not even Francis knew that* – 'His principal loyalty, beyond his loyalty to himself, is to the rightful Earl of Ravensden. I simply convinced him that it was entirely possible you were already the rightful Earl.' He saw my look, which must have been incredulous beyond measure. 'Musk isn't the only one who has felt the need to confess, these last few weeks. I think all this wild talk of the end of days has prompted much reflection in certain bosoms.'

'You mean my mother.'

'As you say, Sir Matthew. Your mother felt the need to unburden herself of her – her dealings, one might say – with the late King and Martyr, Charles of blessed memory. Now, shall we return to the dockyard, do you think?'

I barely remember the walk back, so shattered were my senses. All the while, I was recalling a conversation the previous summer, in a room in Salisbury, whither the entire court had decamped to avoid the plague in London.* A conversation between myself, my brother, and the King of England. Charles Quinton and Charles Stuart, *who might have been half brothers* – for as I had only just learned, my mother was briefly the mistress of King Charles the First, and there

---

* *The Blast That Tears The Skies*

was no certainty that the martyred King had not been the real father of the tenth Earl of Ravensden. But if that dark legend was true, my elder brother could not be the Earl. That title belonged to the only undoubtedly legitimate son of James Quinton, ninth Earl, and the Countess Anne, and had rightfully belonged to him since the age of five, when James Quinton fell in battle on Naseby field.

In other words, to me.

As we walked back down the hill toward the dockyard, past Woolwich Church where Francis Gale was to deliver his sermon on adultery, I remembered the words I had spoken to King Charles the Second, that day in Salisbury.

'Majesty, there is no certainty that Charles and I did not share the same father. My mother's opinion is but that – it is not fact. And faces can disappear in families for generations, then suddenly reappear in a newborn. So we also have no certainty that Charles does not resemble some long dead Quinton whose portrait was never made. This being so, it seems to me that Charles is as likely to be the rightful Earl of Ravensden as I am. And this being so, then Earl of Ravensden he should remain.'

For the past year, I had tried to forget the dark secret of the Quinton family; or at least, to bury it so deeply that there was no prospect at all of it being resurrected. Both war at sea and, more recently, the role of Lord Percival and the charms of Mistress Behn had diverted me from such thoughts. But it was time to cut through all that, and to remember what truly mattered: the honour, and the future, of the House of Quinton.

I was still thinking such thoughts when we walked through the dockyard gate, and I was assailed at once by a creature I recognised: one of Marker's men. He handed me an urgent note from my brother, although the handwriting was actually that of Aphra Behn.

Matt, return to Ravensden House at once. A party of men has gone aboard the ship, and shows every sign of remaining there. Our friends, God willing. We strike tomorrow tonight.

Chapter Fifteen

This time, we approached the *Milkmaid* differently, not relying on the vagaries of Thames watermen. A small hoy, coming downstream from the Custom House wharf, the dark bulk of the Tower to larboard, a few lights still showing in the Dutch potters' workshops of Horselydown to starboard, the shadow of St Mary Rotherhithe just visible far ahead, where the river bent northward; it was a scene that stretch of the Thames witnessed a hundred times every day and night. Francis Gale stood with me in the forecastle, the choice between remaining in Woolwich to deliver a sermon and joining a dangerous expedition to arrest or kill traitorous mercenaries having taken him the best part of the blinking of an eye. Like the rest of our party, we two were clad in black. A little way away stood Phineas Musk, who had been uncharacteristically silent since joining us. He was eyeing me, but it was too dark for me to judge his expression. Astern of us, Marker and his men. And up on the poop deck, for all the world like the ship's captain, stood Aphra Behn, dressed in man's garb.

The hoy struggled to make headway against the warm easterly breeze. Or, at least, that was how it would have seemed to the lookouts on the twenty or so hulls moored together off Saint Katherine's Dock. The *Milkmaid* was now in the middle of the pack, others having secured around her since I was last here. If she had a watch-on-deck, or even if one or more of the Horsemen were on deck watching our approach, they would have seen nothing untoward in the hoy seeming to admit defeat at the hands of the wind, securing for the night to the outermost and westernmost vessel in the pack.

What they did not know, of course, was that this ship, a Sunderland collier, had been purchased by the Crown on the previous day. That its master and crew had been replaced by three more of Lord Percival's men, whose one task was to ensure that no other vessel secured alongside the collier's free quarter.

The hoy was significantly lower than the collier, unladen and thus riding high in the water. Thus it would have been impossible for any man on the *Milkmaid* to see me signal to my men to assemble in the waist.

'Pistols only to be fired on my command,' I said. 'Otherwise, we use blades. The Horsemen to be taken alive if possible – the Lady Astraea, here, to call out their names as she sees them. Any other man on that ship is of no consequence, so if you have to kill any of them, don't hesitate. In the name of the King, may God be with each of you.'

One of the stern windows of the collier opened, and a rope was thrown down to the deck of the hoy. I took hold of it, and began to haul myself up. Two of my brother's men, part of the watch on the collier, hauled me into what had been the skipper's cabin, and then did the same for each of our party. Francis, who had been a strong and agile man in his youth, accomplished the ascent with little difficulty; but Musk struggled, nearly losing his grip and falling on two occasions, and was wheezing markedly when he was finally pulled through the window. Mistress Behn, though, climbed the rope like a cat, her male breeches accentuating the curves of her thighs and arse. *Get thee behind me, Satan.*

Up, onto the deck of the collier, staying low so as to keep out of sight, beneath her wale. She was higher in the water than the next ship inboard of her, a small Danziger with grain for the Hartshorn. And beyond the Danziger, a little higher in the water than she, was the *Milkmaid.*

I went forward, bending as low as I could. Down onto the beakhead of the collier, each of our party following me, each keeping out of sight beneath the wale. Marker handed me a grappling hook, and I threw it. *Dear God, let it not strike metal.*

The hook held in the bowsprit shrouds of the Danziger. I swung myself across, then moved silently across to her larboard side, looking up at the wales of the *Milkmaid.* No sign of any lookout; if Peterson had posted one, he would probably be at the stern, higher up, with a better view. That was the custom of the sea. That was common sense. And, God willing, it would prove the downfall of the Horsemen of the Apocalypse.

Marker followed me into the tangle of cordage in the bows of the Danziger, then Francis Gale, then each of our party in turn.

I breathed deeply, took hold of the grappling hook once again, and secured to the shrouds of the *Milkmaid.* I offered up a silent prayer, and swung myself across onto the Swedish ship.

* * *

Men talking. Low voices, impossible to make out what they were saying. Perhaps speaking in Dutch. But they were close, very close. In the waist of the ship, probably.

Carefully, slowly, I pulled myself up, and peered over the wale of the *Milkmaid.* Nine or ten men, one holding a lantern, looking down at a small pile on the deck. A small pile of – what? Round objects. Impossible to see. Too little light. Were the Horsemen among them? But there were only three Horsemen. Were the rest from Peterson's crew? Goodman's men? Disaffected and treacherous rogues, perhaps even old New Model Army troopers? If the latter, they would be able to give a good account of themselves in a fight.

The odds were too equal for comfort. More equal than I had expected.

I beckoned for Aphra to come forward. She moved up beside me, so close that I could hear her breathing, could smell her scent. Her arm brushed against mine.

'The portly one, by the mainmast,' she whispered, 'is De Wildt. The one with the eyepatch is Schermer. The one bending down, Goodman.'

I dropped down beneath the cover of the wale once again. I thought quickly. My plan for a silent attack was based on the assumption that there were fewer men than this – perhaps only the three Horsemen – and that they would be below decks, as the French passengers had been. (And were they still aboard? God in Heaven, let us not kill innocent men, especially not the poor, simple watchmaker.)

A new plan of attack, then. The very opposite of my first.

I whispered my orders to Marker, who relayed them back to the other men. As I had requested, Phineas Musk came forward to crouch alongside me, hard up against the bulkhead.

'The fat man by the mainmast, Musk.'

He raised himself slightly, so that he could peer over the top of the wale. He stooped back down again.

'Light's difficult, but the range is easy,' he said. 'And he's a big target.'

I nodded.

'Very well, Musk. In your own time.'

'As you say, My Lord.'

Well, then: Phineas Musk had evidently decided which story he believed, and where his loyalties lay.

He took out a flintlock pistol, already cocked and primed. He counted silently to three, then pulled himself up with his left arm, levelled his right, and fired. In that same moment, I sprang over the wale and onto the deck, sword in hand, screaming 'God save the King!'

De Wildt had fallen back against the mainmast, gripping his chest.

Even in the dim light of the one lantern, I could see his life's blood oozing out over his fingers.

The others were momentarily startled by the blast of the pistol, by my shout, and by the screams of Marker's men as they sprang onto the upper deck of the *Milkmaid*. But at least two of them were veterans, who had fought with some of the greatest armies in the history of the world. Goodman already had a pistol levelled at Musk, but one of Marker's men came between them as he fired. The top of the man's skull came off, brains and gore splattering Musk, who wiped it all away as if it were a light summer's sweat.

I wanted Schermer, the Precious Man. One fellow interposed himself, but he was no swordsman. A single thrust, and my rapier's point sliced through flesh and between ribs.

The intervention had given Schermer time to draw his own sword, and his stance told me at once that he knew how to use it. Expert in ordnance he might have been, but few men survived the Thirty Years' War unless they knew how to wield at least one kind of blade.

He backed toward the foot of the poop deck, turning slightly behind the mainmast to give himself more space. That gave me a moment to glance across. Francis Gale was clashing blades with Goodman, while Marker and his men dealt with the others. Musk was leading two men below to check if anyone else was lurking within the hull. There was no sign of Aphra, who must have obeyed my order to stay concealed, down in the beakhead.

Schermer attacked. Crude but fast. I parried, rocking back and to my left. Weight back onto the right. Counterattack. He defended well. We circled each other.

'Who are you?' he demanded, in guttural English. 'You are no banker from Assen, that much is certain.'

'I am Sir…' No. In that time and place, that was not who I was. 'I am Lord Percival. And you are no Precious Man, Schermer.'

'Lord Percival? He is a myth of the night. He does not exist.'

'He exists. You fight him. And he will kill you.'

'Not this night. This, of all nights. Goodman! With me!'

Schermer suddenly broke his guard and ran to his right, jumping up onto the *Milkmaid*'s wale, then down onto the deck of the Danziger beneath. Goodman broke off his fight with Francis Gale and did the same. I followed, with Francis a few moments behind me. The two surviving Horsemen turned to face us once again.

Forward. A rapid exchange of steel on steel, Schermer trying to strike for chest, me using my height to sway back, then to counter. To my left, Francis backing Goodman ever closer to the bows, the righteous wrath of God guiding his swordarm.

Schermer attacked again, cutting hard for my left flank. Parry. Counter. Steel on steel. But the Precious Man was also a much older man; and a man with a much shorter reach. He was tiring. He was at a disadvantage, and he knew it.

And then he saw a ghost.

She dropped onto the deck behind me, and Schermer saw her face. '*Eaffrey?*' he gasped. 'Eaffrey Johnson?'

I lunged forward, as much weight onto my right foot as I could risk. He made to parry, but, surprised by the sudden appearance of this apparition from his past, realised too late that my attack was a feint. Instead, I went right, past his guard, straight into his chest.

There was a splash. I turned to see Francis standing in the bows of the Danziger, looking down into the dark waters of the Thames. Mene Tekel had jumped.

Aphra and I knelt down over Anton Schermer.

'*Oostelijke wind,*' he said in Dutch. 'East wind.'

And with that, the Precious Man died.

* * *

Back on the *Milkmaid*, Marker and his men had the survivors chained below decks. Francis, Musk, Aphra and I stood on the deck, looking down at the pile of round objects that the Horsemen had been inspecting prior to our attack.

'Fireballs,' said Francis. 'Saw enough of them in the Irish wars. Crude. Surely too crude for such experts in fire-raising?'

I thought of what my brother had said of the Horsemen's potential targets: '*burning all the trade in the Thames, below London Bridge, might be a different matter – vengeance like for like, as it were. Whitehall Palace, too, could be a target – or the Tower arsenal, come to that*'.

There were surely not enough fireballs here to attack the Tower, the stoutest fortress in England. And if they had thought to start a blaze here, on the *Milkmaid*, they would burn only the twenty or so ships that were moored together off Saint Katherine's. Hardly an impressive revenge for Holmes's Bonfire. Hardly a fitting objective for the skills of the Horsemen of the Apocalypse.

But Phineas Musk was staring out toward the west.

'Look yonder, Sir Matthew,' he said, for once remembering how to address me with propriety in public.

I followed his eyes. Not far from the north end of London Bridge, behind the familiar outline of Saint Magnus Martyr, somewhere by where Fish Street cut across Thames Street, flames were spitting into the sky.

There was a fire in London.

Chapter Sixteen

The wise will tell you that it began in the bakery of Thomas Farriner in Pudding Lane. The wise will tell you that it was caused by the careless-ness of Farriner, or one of his apprentices, in not checking properly that all the fires in all the ovens were properly extinguished. That is what the wise will tell you; and perhaps they are right.

But as Phineas Musk, Francis Gale and I walked-ran, walked-ran, through the streets from the Tower wharf toward the seat of the fire, an hour or so before dawn on that fateful Sunday, I could think only of the dying words of Anton Schermer, the Precious Man.

Oostelijke wind.

Here, just west of the Tower, the narrow lanes that sloped steeply down to the river were lined with warehouses, and the workshops of those engaged in marine trades. Nearly every building was filled to the brim with canvas, pitch, tar, oil, brandy, or some such substance – all of it highly flammable. Even the ordinary houses were old, timber-built, and tinder-dry, after the long drought of the summer. In short, if an attacker spent many months selecting the ideal place in which to begin a fire that would cause as much damage as possible in London, it would be very difficult to settle upon a more perfect location than Pudding Lane. Quite apart from the contents and nature of the buildings, a blaze beginning there accommodated the vagaries of the weather, too. If the wind was westerly, a fire starting in this quarter of London would quickly blow toward the Tower itself, and the kingdom's principal ordnance store. But in the strong, dry, summer easterly, it would blow to the west instead, toward the heart of the City, toward…

Toward Ravensden House, and Cornelia. I had to get to her. Or else I had to extinguish the fire long before it threatened her. Such was the madness of the moment – the very notion that one man, one man called Matt Quinton, could somehow make a difference!

'Papists!' came the shout, very close by, forcing the wilder thoughts out of my mind. An ugly, florid fellow in a dirty shirt was pointing at the three of us. 'Jesuits! Look at the three of 'em, clad all in black! What else can they be? Firestarters! At 'em, lads!'

A small group of apprentices stood at the street corner, staring at the strengthening flames just to the west. Now they turned to look at us. We had blades, but they outnumbered us nearly four to one. Frightened women were eyeing us suspiciously, and I saw several of them mouthing the word 'Jesuits'.

The apprentices pulled out cudgels and knives, and began to advance toward us.

'Agents of the Pope and the Antichrist, boys!' cried their ringleader. 'Setting fires to slaughter honest English Protestants! Frenchmen! Papists! Stick 'em, lads! Send 'em to hellfire for their crimes!'

'Papists?' cried Francis, stepping forward into the light of the single lantern that illuminated the street. 'Frenchmen? Jesuits? Here stands the renowned Sir Matthew Quinton, captain of the King's ship *Royal Sceptre*. Brother to the Earl of Ravensden – grandson to the famous Earl that sailed with Drake and fought the Spanish Armada! And I am Reverend Gale, his chaplain, ordained in the true Protestant Church of England! God save the King!'

'God save the King!'

The gang's response was thin and uncertain, but then, London apprentices were renowned for their lack of love towards monarchs. Also, of course, for their profound lack of intelligence, allied to a propensity for drunken violence.

The fat man who had accused us of Popery slipped out of sight, down an unlit alleyway.

'Well, lads,' I shouted over the sound of collapsing walls and screaming women, 'why do you stand around and look on idly? Every good man should come with us to fight the fire!'

The apprentices stared at me as though I were the man in the moon. They glanced at each other, and down at their feet, but did not move.

'Cowardly shitheads,' snarled Phineas Musk, as we strode onward.

We cut down toward the river, working around the seat of the blaze, which seemed to be strengthening with every moment that passed. Even though several lines of buildings still stood between them and us, we could feel the heat from the flames. Clouds of smoke billowed from alleyways, depositing flakes of flame into the lanes and, worse, onto the roofs of the buildings that lined them. There were great cracks as the timber frame of building after building gave way, and the crashes of entire roofs falling in on themselves.

Aphra had left us as soon as we got ashore. She had not indicated where she was going, but I was glad she was gone. Not only to save me from further discomfort in her presence, but also because this was most certainly not a place for any woman to be.

At Saint Magnus Martyr, we turned north into the steep and narrow Fish Street. Here, all was chaos. Carts laden with furniture, clothes, chests and children blocked the road, their drivers swearing at each other as they tried to make some headway. Those making for London Bridge were blocking the way for those who were trying to work to the north or west. The householders of Fish Street itself were frantically throwing possessions into the streets from doors and the windows of upper floors, not caring if they landed in the sewer that ran across the cobbles. Crowds of people stood around, seemingly just watching events, inadvertently blocking even more of the limited space in the road.

I recognised Sir Thomas Bloodworth, the Lord Mayor, in the midst of a throng of citizens. Men and women were shouting at him, while others were trying to draw his attention to what was happening in the streets just to the east, where fires were now blazing from rooftops. He was raising his hands to try and pacify the mob. As we came nearer, I could hear his words.

'... under no circumstances will I permit buildings to be pulled down. I, the Lord Mayor of London, give you that assurance.'

I looked to the east. The fire had already advanced since we had first seen it from the *Milkmaid*. It had crept down to Thames Street; the yard and outbuildings of the Star Inn, on Fish Street Hill, were catching light. It was clear to me, even if it was not clear to the Lord Mayor of London, that only pulling down as many buildings as possible between Fish Street and the seat of the fire could prevent a greater conflagration.

'Sir Thomas!' I cried, pushing my way through the mob, making directly for the Lord Mayor.

He turned. We had met on several occasions; he was some sort of acquaintance of my uncle Tristram. But then, Tristram knew a significant number of the rich men of London, having attempted to persuade many of them to invest in one or other of his countless schemes and projects. I could not recall whether Bloodworth was one of those who had profited from my uncle's inexhaustible optimism, or the rather greater number that had not.

'Sir Matthew Quinton! By God, what brings you here?'

I sensed that informing the Lord Mayor, in the hearing of several score of angry, frightened Londoners, that I had just come from a pitched battle with a murderous gang of would-be arsonists, would not necessarily be conducive to the maintenance of public order.

'Late business at the Navy Office in Seething Lane,' I lied. 'But Sir

Thomas, surely we should be forming a firebreak, by pulling down houses, ahead of the flames?'

He scowled.

'Oh, no need for that, Sir Matthew. No need for that at all. This is no great matter, this blaze. Why, sir, I can remember the great fire in Thirty-Three, that burned down all the houses on the northern half of London Bridge. This is nothing to that, sir. Nothing at all. Why, as I have said to many this night, a woman could piss this out. Fish Street is broad enough to stop it, if it gets this far. Which I very much doubt. I'm for my bed, Sir Matthew, and by the morning, this will be out.'

'But the wind, Sir Thomas…'

'It will be out, I say. With no need to pull down houses.'

I stared at him, but he quickly looked away, averting his eyes from both the fire and my accusing gaze.

And then I knew. If Bloodworth were to order the destruction of houses on his own authority, he would become personally responsible for the charge of rebuilding them. Sir Thomas was a very wealthy man, a stalwart of the Vintners' livery and the East India Company, but he could see his fortune being burned to ashes by the flood of compensation claims that would assail him.

'With respect, Sir Thomas,' I said, 'there is one circumstance in which you would be compelled to demolish buildings. Is that not so, my Lord Mayor?'

He did not answer me. Instead, he turned and walked away, his shoulders slumped.

'One circumstance, Matthew?' said Francis.

'Within the boundaries of this city, only one authority can override that of the Lord Mayor,' I said. 'Francis, to Whitehall – the King must know of Bloodworth's craven pig-headedness. Musk, to Ravensden House. Prepare Lady Quinton. And make arrangements to move my brother, if necessary.'

Musk looked at me as though I had just ordered him to charge an entire army of Janissaries.

'Ravensden House? Begging pardon, Sir Matthew, but if you seriously think a fire all the way over here is going to get as far as all the way over there –'

'Would you question such an order if it came from an Earl of Ravensden, Musk?'

His expression provided an eloquent answer.

'No, Sir Matthew. As you say, Sir Matthew.'

They left me, walking north toward Cannon Street, disappearing into the mass of people trying to get away from the fire.

Musk was right, I thought. Surely my concerns for Cornelia and my brother were baseless. No matter how bad this fire became, it would never threaten Ravensden House. No fire in this part of London would ever get remotely close; no fire in the City ever had. And yet…

I suppressed the thought. For now, at least, my duty was here, where the fire was.

The air was thick with smoke. The familiar smells of tar and pitch told their own story: the warehouses down on Thames Street must be well ablaze. I could tell, too, that the fire had now spread down to the river wharves, and they were stacked high with coal, hay and timber. Overhead, the wind was carrying sparks and fragments of blazing canvas, paper, hemp, and God knew what else. Some landed in the street, some on men's hats and shoulders, but many – too many – now began to land on the roofs of the buildings in Fish Street itself.

I heard the shattering of glass, and a great gasp went up from the crowd to the south of me, towards London Bridge. I pushed my way through, and saw flames spitting from the eastern windows of Saint Margaret's Bridge Street. No hymns would be sung there, later that morning; no sermon expounded from the pulpit. A few yards further downhill, flames were already assailing the east wall of Saint Magnus

Martyr. Neither of the two saints in question showed the slightest sign of intervening to save the churches dedicated to them.

Still the breeze came from the east, strong, dry and relentless. Inn and shop signs swung manically in the gale, providing a constant counterpoint to the wind that roared through the narrow alleyways.

'Damn you to hell, Bloodworth,' I said to myself, turning on my heel and starting to run north-by-east, toward Eastcheap.

The fire needed to be stopped. To do that, buildings needed to come down, so that firebreaks could be opened up in front of the flames. But even if the Lord Mayor – or the King, by overruling him – gave order for it to be done, the Londoners were in no state to do it. In theory, fires were fought by the men of each neighbourhood, working together for the common good. At the very least there should be chains of men bringing up water in buckets from the river. But fate – or the scheme of some ingenious arsonist – had dictated that this blaze should have begun during the early hours of a Sunday morning, when many fewer folk than usual were about. And those who were about hardly constituted a likely army of firefighters. As I ran uphill, I looked at the carts thronging Fish Street, and into countless pairs of frightened eyes, and saw nothing but selfishness. Every man was for himself alone, determined only to get far enough away from the fire to be safe, to keep on living.

If there were to be any chance of stopping the fire, better men would have to fight it. And I knew exactly where to get them.

Chapter Seventeen

Dawn had not long broken when I left the Navy Office in Seething Lane, somewhat to the north and east of the seat of the fire. The principal officers of His Majesty's Navy had been nowhere to be found. I had just missed Mister Pepys, the Clerk of the Acts, who was gone to the Tower to watch the progress of the fire from its high walls. I took some breakfast ale and cheese at a tavern on Mark Lane, and when I next registered the existence of the world around me, my head was on the table, my opening eyes were blinking uncomprehendingly at a tankard of ale and a plate of cheese that were at the wrong angle, a serving wench was staring at me strangely, and it was the middle of the morning. But the memory of the crisis meant that I was properly awake within moments. I hurried back out, into the horror that was Sunday, the second day of September, 1666.

I could see the great pall of smoke, blowing westerly, as I struggled along Eastcheap, forcing my way through the crowds trying to make their way to the east, toward the safety of Spitalfields and the open country between Whitechapel and Stepney. As I passed it, Saint Clement's church was being besieged by two opposing armies: those who believed the ancient building would be beyond the reach of the fire, and were trying to cram their cartloads of goods into it for safety, against those who already had their goods inside, but were convinced the church was doomed and were endeavouring to get them out again. There were angry shouts, and fists were thrown. Of churchwardens or the aldermen of the Ward, who might have been able to keep some semblance of order, there was no sign at all.

The fire was beyond Fish Street now, creeping westward into Cannon Street. And yet, London lived on. Although, in the wards nearest to the seat of the fire, the church bells were muffled as alarms, those further away were sounding as they always did, summoning the parishioners to services where they could pray for the safety of the City. Even the great bells of Saint Paul's were ringing out confidently. Some makeshift fruit-and-vegetable stalls had been set up, the traders spotting the main chance presented by the unexpected and very large, if somewhat preoccupied, crowds. A few of the more respectable hawkers were out too, standing on street corners, selling copies of the latest *Gazette*. But there were rather more of the less respectable ones, selling the sort of crude woodcuts that featured rude verse about Lord Clarendon's arse or Lady Castlemaine's cunny. And, yes, there were the street prophets, too, their hands and eyes raised to heaven, proclaiming this fire to be God's righteous judgement upon the sins of England. I saw one being pelted with shit by jeering urchins.

I do not entirely recall what I proposed to do. I may have contemplated returning to Ravensden House, then dismissed the thought at once. The fire was no threat to it, no threat at all – and perhaps worrying about my safety might make Cornelia more tender toward me. I believe I next had some notion of making my way back down to the river, there to try and organise whatever watermen, scavelmen and the like that I could find into fire-fighting parties. I had turned into Martin Lane and was heading south, struggling through the press of carts and people heading in the opposite direction, when an aged, weeping, goodwife or widow, probably fifty or so, limped heavily from the door at my side, collided with me, and grabbed hold of my arm.

'God save us, sir – please, in Christ's name, help us – I know not what to do!'

'Calm yourself, goodwife! What's the matter here?'

'The fire, sir! It's already at the back end of Saint Martin Orgar – I have to get my family out, and no man here to help me! The apprentices all run off, an aged father to save! Pray help us, sir! Merciful God in heaven, please help us!'

I went with her into her house. It was a typical, narrow, old affair, the dark ground floor clearly a printing business of some sort. She had evidently been throwing as many of her possessions as she could into the handcart and sacks on the floor.

'Where are your children, goodwife? Why are they not here to help you?'

'Dead of the plague, sir. A son and his wife, a daughter and her husband. The five children they had between them. All gone a twelvemonth ago. And I not a goodwife but a widow, my husband Newman having been taken by a bloody flux the year the king came back. Me a cripple from a fall, the last autumn, and the printing business gone to wrack. My father spared it all, though, and he past seventy. Where's the justice in that, sir?'

'God's plan is ever a mystery, Widow Newman,' I said, realising how feeble the words sounded. Francis would have made them sound convincing. Or, at any rate, less unconvincing.

Up on the second floor of the house, a gaunt old man sat on the edge of a bed, incongruously dressed in a nightshirt covered by a buff jacket. A soldier's buff jacket. He looked at me with undisguised contempt.

'Ye're one of them,' he growled. 'I can tell by the look of ye. By the smell of ye. A malignant. A cavalier.'

'Now, father,' said the widow, 'this kindly gentleman will help us. Will lead us safe from the fire.'

But the old man kept his eyes on me. Eyes that brimmed over with hatred.

'Quartermaster I was, Orange Regiment of the London Trained Bands. Fought at Gloucester, and at Newbury too. Fought against the murdering tyrant Charles Stuart, that Englishmen might be free of kings and bishops. That's who I was. That's what I was. And I'll not take the charity of an ungodly malignant! Psalm One Hundred and Forty-Four. *Blessed be the Lord my strength which teacheth my hands to war, and my fingers to fight: My goodness, and my fortress; my high tower, and my deliverer; my shield, and he in whom I trust; who subdueth my people under me.*'

'Forgive him, sir,' said Widow Newman, no longer fearful only of the fire. 'He's old and confused. He knows not what he says.'

I nodded, but we both knew she lied, and the old man knew best of all. He was not confused in the slightest; far from it. If he had been just a few years younger, he would have been out with Rathbone – or with the Horsemen, come to that. He was the sort of fanatic the Quintons despised. But this Quinton would do his utmost to save the old man's life, regardless.

'And the chattels, sir? Everything I have, it is.'

'Carry what you can, if you must. But too much will slow you, and make it harder to get away.'

I turned toward the window, and noticed a curious sight. There was an alley directly opposite, and that gave a view down to Saint Laurence Pountney, a fair way to the west. The church was a long way from the leading edge of the fire, which had not reached this side of Martin Lane. Yet Saint Laurence was on fire.

I could hear screams in the street, and made out a few shouts:

'Laurence Church is ablaze!'

'How can it be?'

'It's the Papists! The French and Dutch are burning the whole city!'

I went back down to the old man, leaving the goodwife to gather what she could. I took hold of his arm, and lifted him from the bed.

'Reprobate!' he shouted, and spat in my face. 'Get your hands off me, cavalier pig!'

I wiped the spittle from my cheek.

'Your choice, quartermaster,' I said. 'You can let a cavalier pig help you to safety, or you can be burned to death by your own people.'

'My own people? You lie. This fire's the work of the Jesuits – I hear the cries in the street, and Molly spoke but an hour ago with a man who'd seen a mass-priest flinging a fireball into the Star Inn...'

'Enough!' I said, and pulled him to his feet, unwillingly and slow. 'I'll tell you the true tale of this fire, quartermaster, as we go along. And if you don't believe me by the time we reach Cannon Street, I'll bring you all the way back here again, and you can perish in Papist flames if you wish.'

* * *

It took an hour and more to get Widow Newman and her father to safety in the churchyard of Saint Mary Abchurch, just off the north side of Cannon Street. The streets were even more frantic than they had been, with frightened folk not knowing which way to flee before the sudden new conflagration at Pountney. And the old quartermaster, although little more than bones and shrivelled parchment-skin covering them, was a heavy weight to half-drag, half-carry even the relatively small distance to Abchurch. But I kept my promise. He joined the very small circle of those who knew the true story of the Horsemen of the Apocalypse, although, of course, he chose not to believe a word of it. And even if in due course he did come to believe it, no man would believe him if he told them.

'Lying malignant bastard,' he said, as I sat him down finally upon an old tombstone. ''Tis the Papists, for certain.'

'Ungrateful old fool,' said Widow Newman, who proceeded to thank me effusively. 'But forgive me, sir, I never asked your name.'

I looked the old quartermaster in the eye.

'Tell your friends,' I said. 'Tell all those who still think as you do that you were saved by Lord Percival.'

The ancient's eyes opened wide. It was as though he was looking upon a resurrected corpse. He knew the name Lord Percival, right enough. Perhaps it had been whispered fearfully in the conventicles he had attended, before infirmity had confined him to his room.

I essayed the most extravagant Cavalier bow I could manage, and left the Newman family to fend for themselves.

* * *

I returned to Cannon Street by the London Stone, the strange lump of limestone said to have been set into the ground by the Romans. Others said the Druids had sacrificed virgins upon it, long ago. Perhaps London needs a sacrifice or two now to save it, if only it can find some virgins, I thought, irreverently.

As I turned east, back towards the advancing fire, I heard a voice I knew.

'My Lord Mayor!'

I pushed my way through the oncoming crowd in time to see Mister Samuel Pepys, Clerk of the Acts to the Navy Board, approach Sir Thomas Bloodworth, who, sweating and dishevelled, a kerchief tied round his neck, no longer looked quite so confident that a woman could piss out the great fire.

'Sir Thomas!' cried Pepys. 'I come directly from His Majesty, at the Palace of Whitehall, whither I went this very morning by boat. I have the King's direct command to you, my Lord Mayor, to pull down houses! You are indemnified, Sir Thomas! You have royal authority!'

'Lord, Mister Pepys,' said Bloodworth, mopping his brow and shaking his head, 'what can I do? I am spent. People will not obey me. I *have* been pulling down houses; but the fire overtakes us faster than we can do it.'

I was still some way away from the two men, and was thus unable to suggest to the Lord Mayor that if he had pulled down houses during the night, when the fire was still confined to Pudding Lane and the alleys immediately around it, it might have been extinguished already. But then, hindsight makes for poor readings of the past, and even worse ones of the future.

Pepys whispered some words privately to Bloodworth. The Lord Mayor looked as though he had been struck by a musketball, shook his head vigorously, said something to Pepys, and then turned away.

Pepys saw me, and raised a hand in greeting. He was not so many years older than myself, but with a long face that made him look infinitely older. He always had about him an air of attempting to be very serious, in the hope he would therefore be taken very seriously.

'A terrible day, Sir Matthew.'

'Terrible indeed, Mister Pepys. Did you say you have come from Whitehall?'

'I have – I went there by boat, directly from the Tower, after I had satisfied myself of the fire's rate of progress.' Despite the circumstances, Samuel Pepys was evidently mightily pleased with himself; he liked nothing more than to be at the centre of affairs, conversing on equal terms with great men. 'Your friend, the Reverend Gale, was there, and we both reported to His Majesty. The King is appalled by Bloodworth's behaviour. As am I, in truth. This is no time for politics, Sir Matthew. No time at all.'

'Politics, Mister Pepys?'

'"I need more men," says Bloodworth to me. "I need soldiers." So I say to him, "The Duke of York has offered the Life Guards." An offer confirmed to me by My Lord Arlington, incidentally, before I left Whitehall. "Ah," blusters Bloodworth then, "perhaps we have enough men after all." Or some such words. Politics, Sir Matthew. Politics.'

Politics indeed – and perhaps the most dangerous and potent politics in all of England. After all, ordering royal troops into the City of London had been one of the principal causes of the great civil wars that had ravaged the islands of Britain for nearly ten year. The wars that had killed my father and maimed my brother. The City guarded its privileges, and its independence, more zealously than the priests of the Temple of Solomon had guarded the Ark of the Covenant. Every man, woman and child in London might be in imminent danger of being burned alive, but the Lord Mayor would rather call upon the assistance of Old Nick himself than agree to have the Royal Life Guards marching through Temple Bar.

'So then, Sir Matthew,' said Pepys, 'where are you bound now?'

'For the river, I think, to see if something can be done to establish more effective bucket relays, and set up fire hoses.'

'I wish you well, though I fear you will find your task a thankless one. I went through the Bridge by boat, from the Tower to Whitehall, and the water wheels at the foot of the bridge are burned – the wheels that should be pumping water up into the heart of the heart of the City.'

A firedrop fell on his shoulder, but he brushed it off as he would a fly.

'And you, Mister Pepys? Where are you bound?'

Pepys blushed a little. 'Returning home to the Navy Office. We have guests for dinner. In this wind, Seething Lane is surely quite safe from the blaze. And my wife was loathe to cancel.'

He left me; and I smiled, despite myself. Samuel Pepys was an odd little man, pompous, self-important, and no friend to gentleman captains like myself. But, for all that, I found it impossible to dislike the fellow. For one thing, he worked quite astonishingly hard, which was more than could be said for any of his colleagues. And there was even something about him that reminded me a little of my Uncle Tristram: an insatiable curiosity, perhaps, although Mister Pepys's tended to flow down rather more conventional channels than that of Doctor Tristram Quinton.

I made to turn down Bush Lane toward the river, but as I did so, I thought I heard something I could not have heard. There were the ominous but now-familiar sounds of the wind, of the flames roaring out of gutted buildings, of walls and roofs collapsing, of carts rumbling across the cobbles, of people shouting and crying. But there was a new sound; and it, too, was a familiar sound, although of rather longer pedigree among my memories. At first, I thought it a false hearing, a trick of the thundering fire. But there it was again, a little stronger. Unmistakeable. The sound of men singing. It was a song I had heard often enough, though usually on the cusp of battle, and there was only one body of men in London that day who could be singing it.

Yth yskynnys un myttyn mar ughel, ogh mar ughel,
Y vyrys orth an le adro hag orth an ebren tewl;
Yth esa hy ow cana yn myttyn oll adro,
Nyns yu bewnans avel araderor un mys me ytho…

A song of a lark, and of young love. Hardly appropriate, in the circumstances, but sung as lustily as a battle hymn. Which, for the men who sang it, was what it had become.

Down Cannon Street, with Martin Lanherne and Julian Carvell at their head, strode three score or more of the crew of the *Royal Sceptre*.

Chapter Eighteen

'Once Lieutenant Delac – My Lord Carrignavar, that is, got your order, Sir Matthew,' said Lanherne as we strode down Bush Lane toward Allhallows, 'he ordered us to make for the City with all possible exhibition. So we commandeered a dockyard lighter, and rowed it up to Tower wharf.'

'The Fire's not reached the Tower?'

'No, and God willing, it won't – the wind's so strong from the east, the fire's only inching that way. And men from Deptford and Woolwich yard were going there to help defend it, along with sailors off the other ships in dock. But all around Tower Street and Mary Hill is ablaze, down to the bridge. I saw many a town burn during the late wars, Sir Matthew, but this is the most hellish sight I've ever witnessed.'

We came to a lane just north of Thames Street. Like all the so-called thoroughfares in those parts, it was barely wide enough for a single cart to get down it. Narrow, timber-built, weather-boarded, pitch-coated houses rose on either side, each storey projecting further and further out over into the street; I knew many houses in London where the residents could open their uppermost windows, reach across, and shake the hands of their neighbours across the way. Breeches, shirts and smocks hung from ropes slung between the higher floors, blowing vigorously in the wind. They would have dried well overnight, right enough; dried just in time to be consumed by the flames.

The fire was already destroying a pair of houses at the far end of the lane, and what appeared to be a one-armed fellow, along with a half-dozen boys and old men, were struggling with fire-hooks attached to the next building.

'Ho, there!' I called. 'Who commands here?'

The one armed fellow turned toward me.

'Hutchins,' he said, 'constable of this ward. Who asks?'

'Quinton,' I replied, 'captain of His Majesty's ship the *Royal Sceptre*.'

The fellow's eyes nearly sprang from his head.

'Sir Matthew Quinton? Son to the Earl of Ravensden, that fell at Naseby?'

I was not accustomed to being addressed in such a way; most men identified me in terms of my brother or my grandfather. Many did not even know that my father had held the title, albeit for only one hundred and eighteen days. But the man's age, and his lost arm, told a story.

'You were on that field?'

'I was, Sir Matthew. Corporal in Colonel Radcliffe Gerrard's regiment, Sir Henry Bard's tertia.'

He stiffened proudly, as though coming to attention.

'Well then, Corporal Hutchins, it will be an honour to serve alongside you – although this is a very different kind of battle, I fear.'

The old man nodded. Lanherne stepped forward and shook his hand firmly, one veteran of the old Cavalier army to another.

'Everyone's gone, Sir Matthew,' said Hutchins. 'Fled west, or north. All except these few, here. If we could only get three or four houses down, and get a score of water-squirts up here – but there's not enough of us, and we're not strong enough –'

I gestured to Lanherne and Carvell, who ordered the Sceptres forward to take hold of the fire-hooks.

* * *

And so we began.

The fire-hooks were perhaps thirty feet long, and difficult to handle. Above all, they were difficult to fasten to the rings that should have been provided on the front of every house for exactly this purpose; years of neglect meant that some had rusted solid, others had disappeared altogether. Although, in my youth, I had seen houses pulled down during fires in Bedford, it was the first time I had ever pulled on a fire-hook myself. At first, it seemed incredible that a mere dozen or so men, pulling upon a long pole, could bring down a house of four or five storeys that had stood for scores of years, if not centuries. But with Carvell in front of me, George Polzeath behind, I heaved on the hook, felt the wall come away from the rest of the building, and stepped back swiftly as the entire house collapsed in a cloud of dust. When it cleared, all that remained of what had been a family's home was a pile of rubble and timber.

Dry timber, in which fire from the blazing buildings directly to the east was already taking hold. And I could see that flames were already kindling in the yard of the next house to the west.

'Next one, men!' I cried, somewhat unnecessarily.

We pushed the fire-hooks up, but one grappling ring came away from its fastening, leaving only one that we could attach to. We pulled, but this house was stouter than the one before. Timbers cracked, some plaster and pitch-board fell into the street, but with only one hook it was heavy going.

'On three! One, two, *three*!'

A corner of the uppermost storey fell, landing on one of Hutchins' men, who had been standing too close. The fellow writhed on the ground and screamed, and the constable leaned down to inspect him.

'Broken ribs, I'd say, Sir Matthew. Came across enough of them in my days in the King's army. Tom, Silas, get him up to the bonesetter by Saint Mary Bothaw.'

A baby's cry, from the uppermost floor of the house.

I had been about to order the Sceptres to heave once again on the fire-hook; had it not been for the short delay occasioned by the old man's injury, we would already have pulled on it, and brought down the entire building.

'I'll go, Sir Matthew,' said Carvell.

'No,' I said.

I do not know why I said it. Perhaps thoughts of babies, and all of my attendant feelings about Cornelia and Aphra, occupied some dark, hidden recess of my mind, and drove what I did now.

With Lanherne, Carvell and some of the other Sceptres shouting imprecations after me, I ran through the door.

Like so many buildings in that part of London, the ground floor was a workshop. A thatcher's, by the looks of it. Piles of bound thatch stood against the walls, with others strewn across the floor – presumably knocked over by the hastily departing thatcher and his family.

All but one of his family. The baby cried again, I ran to the stairs, and nearly fell as the bannister gave way. The house timbers were creaking ominously, and plaster was falling from the ceilings. Up – an unmade bed, chairs overturned – up again, the floors getting larger at every level. The uppermost storey, the beams cracking like a man-of-war's yards in a storm – and there was the child, red in the face and wrapped in rough cloth, lying in a wooden crib. God alone knew why the mother had abandoned it. Too many mouths to feed, perhaps, and a dark realisation that an infant lost in such a great fire would not cause too many questions to be asked?

I stepped forward to lift the baby, but as I did so, the wall in front of me fell away. I nearly overbalanced and fell into the street, which would have meant certain death. But years spent on the swaying decks of ships had given me excellent balance, and I managed to steady myself. Flames spat across the sky in front of me. I could just see the rooftops of the houses on London Bridge, thankfully safe from the flames. But there was the tower of Allhallows, ablaze.

I could hear shouts from my men in the street, and knew they were saying the house could not hold long. I snatched up the baby, which protested by unleashing a surprisingly mighty jet of spew over my arms, turned, and ran for the stairs, which still just clung to the walls. Down. A step gave way, my left foot went through, and I very nearly threw the baby to its death. I extricated myself, made it to the ground and out into the smoke-filled air. As I did so, the thatcher's house collapsed behind me.

* * *

Hutchins took the baby. He did not know the thatcher or his family; they had but lately arrived in the country, perhaps Walloons. I thought of Goodwife Newman, and all her lost grandchildren. If the thatcher and his wife did not want their baby back, then why should the goodwife not have a new grandchild to make up for the ones lost to the plague? I knew what her father, the old Roundhead quartermaster, would say to receiving such charity from Constable Hutchins, late of the King's army; but if the act, and the child, reconciled two old soldiers from opposing sides, and helped end the quarrels that had killed my father, then perhaps one tiny piece of good would come out of this dreadful fire.

We abandoned the attempt to save the lane. The fire was too strong, not only in the lane itself but also to the south and east of us, so we moved down to the river, to see what might be done there. But as Mister Pepys had said, it was a dreadful sight, made even more infernal by the terrible night-in-day created by the thick pall of smoke. Lighters, skiffs and all sorts of other craft were jostling for position alongside wharves, or even in the mud of the river bank, and then struggling across to the safety of the Southwark shore. Fistfights broke out as men squabbled with each other for a berth, and then for headway once they had laden. As we watched, one badly overloaded skiff overturned, tipping tables, bookcases, chests and their owner into the fetid waters of the Thames.

'Needs seamen to impose order, Sir Matthew,' said Lanherne.

'Yet if we attempted it, they'd tear us apart,' I said.

'What's that thing, yonder?' cried one of the men behind me.

I turned. It was Graydon, a Lancastrian who served as a caulker's mate. He was pointing east, toward a strange object on the foreshore, hard under London Bridge. At first sight, and thanks to the strangeness of the light, it looked like a beached whale, but that was impossible above the bridge. I gestured for the men to follow me, and we made our way along the bank, threading our way through those trying to heave their goods onto watercraft and the lines of men taking leather buckets to and from the water.

As we got nearer, it was clear that whatever lay on the mud was some sort of mechanical contraption. I had seen several great funerals, such as that for the King's late brother, the Duke of Gloucester, and the thing before us reminded me of the sorts of hearses used upon such occasions.

Or, in this case, an overturned hearse.

Its principal features were a great brass hydrant, mounted atop what appeared to be a large, square coffin. The whole sat on a wooden sleigh such as I had seen in Sweden. A pipe of brass protruded from the cylinder.

Men were all around it, pulling on ropes, trying to right it. But the great beast remained obstinately stuck in the mud.

'Who commands here?' I shouted.

'Parrett. Constable of Bridge Ward. Who asks?'

'Sir Matthew Quinton, of the King's Navy. Here present, some of my crew. What's this, and what's happened to it?'

Parrett shook his head. The man was very nearly in tears.

'This is the Clerkenwell fire engine,' he said. 'Brought all the way across the City, thirty men pulling it. God knows, Sir Matthew, we could have put out the entire blaze with this, if we could have got it to the seat of the fire in time. But the streets were so crowded – so many people, so many carts, all coming the opposite way to us – and then we could get no water supply without bringing it right down to the waterline.'

He turned away.

Lanherne and I looked at each other. No words were necessary: it was obvious what we were thinking. The famous Clerkenwell fire engine, the best and most powerful in London, could have done the work of hundreds of men, pumping a constant jet of water from the huge water reservoir mounted on the sled. It would certainly have been a better prospect than the hand-held water squirts, which could deliver barely a gallon each. But with the water supply in that part of the City cut by the loss to the fire of the great waterwheels under London Bridge, the only place where the engine's crew could obtain enough water for it was the river. A river so low after several months of drought that the engine would have to be manhandled far down the bank. And on that steeply sloping bank, the great device had overturned.

One thing was certain: the much-vaunted machine would play no part in combatting the Great Fire. I set the Sceptres to help those pulling on the ropes, but every man there knew it was a forlorn hope. Hauling over a First Rate for careening was an easier task than righting the Clerkenwell fire engine. Moreover, the tide was coming in, and after barely half an hour, we had to abandon the machine to the inexorable Thames.

* * *

'Sir Matthew!'

I was now with a small number of my men by College Hill and Cloak Lane, helping the Cutlers to remove whatever they could from their brand new but doomed livery hall. I had despatched Lanherne northward with another party, to see if anything could be done to save the church of Saint Antholin, and Carvell to the east, to help the parties fighting the blaze in Thames Street. But in my heart of hearts, I doubted that even if Rupert and Albemarle were to sail the entire fleet up to Deptford Reach at that very moment, and landed every one of the twenty thousand or so men aboard it, it would suffice to extinguish the fire.

'Sir Matthew!'

A dishevelled youth of thirteen or so was pushing his way through the crowd, shouting my name all the time. It was Youngest Barcock, my brother's new pageboy at Ravensden House, the latest scion of a prolific dynasty that provided generations of retainers for the Quintons in both Bedfordshire and London. But why had he sought me out, unless…

'What's afoot, lad?' I said.

'Lady Quinton, Sir Matthew, and the French captain!' He was gasping for breath, having evidently been running hard.

'What of them? In God's name, what's the matter?'

'God help us, Sir Matthew, the mob's set fair to hang them!'

Chapter Nineteen

In the fullness of time, Francis Gale told me exactly what had happened.

After waiting upon the King at Whitehall on Sunday morning, Francis attended a service at Saint Martin in the Fields, and then went on to Ravensden House. Cornelia was all for going out to view the fire, as was Captain Ollivier, who was keen to help with the efforts to extinguish it. Phineas Musk was unimpressed.

'Sir Matthew wouldn't want you going out,' he said to Cornelia. 'Too dangerous.'

'Oh, pish, Musk. Sir Matthew's opinion matters not a...' She caught herself. 'But how dangerous can it be? A street fire does not advance quickly enough to threaten lives, unless those in its path are very old or very stupid. I have witnessed enough, both in Veere and in Amsterdam.'

'And we can ensure Lady Quinton's safety,' said Ollivier.

'Musk is right,' said Francis. 'The streets are crowded, even this far west. Even if the fire itself poses no direct threat, the throng will present a heaven-sent opportunity to every cutpurse in London. And you must think of the child, Lady Quinton.'

Cornelia pouted. 'Think of the child. That is what my husband tells me. Nothing but "think of the child".'

And with that, she stormed off to her room, not deigning to join the rest of the party for dinner. Francis slept uneasily that night, alternating between looking out of his window toward the red waves in the east and praying for the fate of London. The following morning, though, he went down to find Cornelia dressed for an expedition, Captain Ollivier at her side.

'Tell them,' said Musk. 'Tell them again, Reverend. They won't listen to me.'

But Cornelia simply raised her hand.

'The Earl has given his permission,' she said.

Francis looked at Musk, who rolled his eyes, but nodded. And Francis, knowing the two people in question well enough, knew at once what had happened. Cornelia would have pestered my brother mercilessly, and Charles, desperate for peace and quiet, would have conceded. But then, the Earl of Ravensden always did have a soft spot for his sister-in-law.

'Then we will accompany you,' said Francis. 'Musk, myself, Youngest Barcock. Together, we should be sufficient to deter even an entire gang of footpads. But at the first sign of any trouble, My Lady, we turn and come back.'

'Of course,' said Cornelia. 'I am in your hands, Francis.'

And so, much against Francis's better judgement, they left the house and made their way east, along the Strand and into Fleet Street, down across the bridge over the Fleet River, then up the hill toward Lud Gate, the city wall, the flames and the smoke. The way was crowded with carts heading west, each piled high with possessions of all sorts. One contained a large spinet; another, a sick old woman on her bed. Men and women alike wept for the loss of their houses.

The trouble began when they were by the site of Paul's Cross, the old preaching place, which had been demolished by the Roundheads during the civil war. Standing in the shadow of Inigo Jones' great and still very new-looking west front of the cathedral, the site of the cross was still a favourite spot from which street-preachers harangued passers-by. The fellow standing there now, berating all and sundry, had the look and sound of an old soldier about him (or so said Francis, who was amply qualified to recognise the type): leathery features, a rough black tunic, and a rasping voice that might have expounded many a psalm in front of wartime camp fires.

'... and, I tell you, they seized another Frenchman, that was throwing fireballs into houses in Lombard Street!' The substantial mob gathered before him growled its disgust. 'They've searched the houses of Dutch weavers down in Spitalfields, and found fireballs aplenty! Even now, De Ruyter and Beaufort and their fleets are coming into the Thames, ready to invade! But they don't want you to know that, Clarendon and Arlington and all the rest of them! And why not? I'll tell ye why not, brothers and sisters! Because the Duke of York's in league with them – Clarendon's own son-in-law – and every man knows the Duke's inclined to Popery. He and King Louis will be celebrating mass in there, in Saint Paul's itself, before the year's out! This fire's no accident, I tell ye!'

'If Beaufort's sailing up the Thames, you can call me Charlemagne,' said Jean-Paul Ollivier to Cornelia. 'And the same if the French have really fired London.'

Francis looked at him in alarm. The Breton captain was a very large, very noticeable man with a loud voice and excellent English, and even his whisper to Cornelia carried to several people standing nearby.

'Frenchman! A French spy!' cried a young girl.

'Not so!' cried Francis, stepping forward. 'All's well here, my friends. These people are under my protection!'

'And who the fuck might you be?' demanded a brazen strumpet.

The mob began to press closer toward the little Ravensden party.

'Barcock,' murmured Musk, 'run and find Sir Matthew.'

'Where'll he be, Mister Musk?' said the pageboy.

'Wherever the fire's at its worst. Ask where the men who've come from the dockyards are – the crew of the *Royal Sceptre* – that's where he'll be. Now go, lad!'

The boy was small and nimble, and easily dashed through a gap in the crowd between two old crones.

'I'll tell you, goodwife,' said Francis Gale. 'I am the vicar of Ravensden, chaplain to that noble hero, Sir Matthew Quinton...'

'Priest!' cried the man at Paul's Cross. 'Laudian! We know you bells-and-smells Anglicans – one left-footed step from Rome!'

There were further growls.

'Start backing down towards Addle Hill,' whispered Musk. 'Narrower. Easier to hold them off if we have to.'

'Good people!' cried Cornelia. 'All is well here! I am the wife of Sir Matthew Quinton. We are loyal subjects, just as you are. Good Protestants all, as is the noble French captain here, who has given his parole!'

'Aye?' sneered the strumpet. 'Lady Quinton, is it? Dutch bitch, then! So, a Dutch bitch, a Frog swordsman, and a priest – for all we know, a Jesuit pretending to be a vicar. A pretty collection of rogues! Enemies of good honest English folk, the lot of them!'

'The Frenchman,' cried a clerkish-looking fellow, who certainly spoke like an educated man. 'Captain of the *Joan of Ark*, it said in the *Gazette*. So what's to say he's not out to avenge that mad bitch by doing to London what we did to her?'

Another growl of assent.

'The firestarters will have had leaders,' proclaimed the street-preacher, pointing directly at them. 'Machiavellis and Torquemadas, ordering where best to throw fireballs. What more likely than that we're looking at them?'

Cornelia, Ollivier and Francis followed Musk's lead and started to back into the entrance to Addle Hill, a narrow lane that led down to the river. And the mob began to advance.

* * *

'You men, with me!' I cried to the half-dozen Sceptres within earshot.

I wished my best men were closer, the likes of Carvell, Lanherne and Tremar, but those I had with me were good enough: three loyal Cornishmen, Tippett, Penwarn and Gover; a stout Suffolk veteran called Frostick; and Marsh and Sheldon, two sometime pressed men who had stayed with the ship and not deserted when they had the chance.

We ran past Great Saint Thomas Apostle, already ablaze at its eastern end, through Great Trinity Lane and down Distaff Lane. The roads were jammed, and in places we had to barge people aside, or even leap on top of carts, jumping off on the other side. Sparks and firedrops fell continuously. Although it was late morning, at times it seemed like the middle of the night, so thick was the smoke borne upon the still-relentless east wind. And all the while, I had one thought only: Cornelia. My wife, and my unborn child. The unborn heir to Ravensden. Oh dear God, let me be in time – let their fate not be retribution upon me…

We burst out into Addle Hill. I saw Cornelia and the others at once, slightly uphill from us, and called out. She ran into my arms, weeping, and Musk and Francis fell back to join us. But three or four had hold of Captain Ollivier. They were tearing at his fine coat, punching at his face and gut. And all the while, the rest of the mob continued to advance downhill, jeering, throwing dung, shouting insults against the Dutch and French for having fired London.

'Mad, the lot of them!' cried Musk. 'Rabid dogs who'll listen to no reason!'

I pushed Cornelia to Francis, and stepped forward, directly into the path of the mob.

'I am Sir Matthew Quinton,' I shouted. 'You know my name. You knew my grandfather's name. Matthew, Earl of Ravensden, who fought the Armada, who defeated the Spinola Galleys, who saved Queen Bess's throne. You know the Quintons are loyal to England. In the name of the King, I order you to release the French captain, there.

And the first man, woman or child who frightens my wife any longer will have to deal with me, and my sword.'

I drew the blade from its scabbard, and the Sceptres closed around me. But the mob was so crazed with bloodlust, it had the opposite effect to what I intended.

'Sir Matthew Quinton, is it?' cried a voice from the depths of the mob. I could just make out the scoundrel: a young man, in the dress of a student from one of the Temples, seemingly intent on rejecting everything he had ever learned about the law. 'Then if I recall my genealogies aright, your grandmother was a French Papist! Trust none of 'em! Malignants! Firestarters!'

Ollivier pushed forward, trying to free himself from the clutches of the louts who held him, but one of them pulled a knife and held it to the Frenchman's neck, drawing blood as Ollivier struggled. Someone in the crowd threw a loose cobble. Cornelia screamed, and I saw a bloody gash on her forehead. Francis took her in his arms and turned her, shielding her with his own body.

'Cavalier scum!' cried another voice, this time from the back of the crowd. 'Dutch, French, Papists! Rush 'em, boys! String 'em all up, this day, to avenge London!'

A growl of approbation – those at the front of the mob stepped toward me – I swung my sword, felt it tear cloth and pierce flesh, and a man screamed – red flames of rage and guilt burned my eyes – infuriated, one of the mob slung a noose over Ollivier's head, and another struck out at Francis with a cudgel, trying to hit Cornelia – I swung again, ready to thrust my sword for the kill.

None in the mob heeded the sound of approaching hooves upon cobbles, coming down Addle Hill behind them; men riding hither and thither upon horseback were legion as London burned, men fleeing the flames or barking orders to others.

But the mob heeded the roar of a musket fired into the air, right enough. Heads turned, my own included. Eyes took in a troop of red-coated dragoons, one of whom held the smoking weapon in his hand. A troop that rode behind a tall, dark, moustachioed man, dressed in a purple frock-coat and mounted upon a fine grey stallion.

'Good day to you, Sir Matthew,' said the man. 'You appear to be in a little difficulty.'

I inclined my head.

'No longer, thanks to your timely arrival, My Lord Craven.'

The mob was silent, and fell back respectfully at the mention of the name. Even those who did not know William, Earl of Craven, by sight, certainly knew him by reputation. He was a legend of England: a veteran soldier and the lover of a Queen, he had earned the undying respect of every man in London during the previous summer, when he stayed behind to maintain control in the plague-stricken capital after the King, the court, and virtually every man of rank deserted the pestilential city.

'Excellent,' he said, 'for we have more pressing business, this day. A city to save, in fact.' He turned in his saddle, and addressed the mob. 'You hear me, my friends? No more idling in the streets. No more seeking out phantom French and Dutch firestarters. And release the honourable captain, there. Release him *now*, you hear me?' The men holding Ollivier let him go, and the Frenchman came to us, holding a kerchief to the blood at his neck. Lord Craven nodded grimly, then turned to the mob again. 'Listen to me, good folk. Every woman here, attend to saving London's children. Every man here, with me, to fight the fire! I have the King's personal orders, direct from the Palace of Whitehall!'

'God save the King!' cried Musk.

Many of those in the mob, who moments before had been as republican and murderous as Noll Cromwell, now took up the loyal cry. A few cast ashamed sideways glances in our direction before slinking off, back up toward Saint Paul's. Most, though, stayed where they were, ready to obey Craven's commands.

'Musk, Captain Ollivier,' I said, 'pray take Lady Quinton back to Ravensden House, and this time, make sure she stays there.' Cornelia mumbled something, but kept her tearful eyes to the ground. Musk was cleaning the graze on her forehead, but thank God, it was evidently no more than that. 'You men,' I said to my six Sceptres, 'go with them, and guard the house. Francis, I leave the choice to you. You can either return to the house, or come with me, or go where you will.'

Francis smiled. 'Oh, I think I shall go with you, Sir Matthew. Perhaps my prayers and my wielding of a firebucket will tip the balance in favour of saving London.'

The Earl of Craven nodded. He bore a startling resemblance to Prince Rupert, which was somewhat unfortunate, as he had spent several decades as the lover of that prince's mother, the Winter Queen of Bohemia; not even the undoubted fact that the Earl was only eleven when the Prince was born could silence the credulous.

'Amen,' he said. 'Above all, pray for rain, Father. We are come to a sorry pass indeed if rain has forsaken England.'

Chapter Twenty

Whatever Sir Thomas Bloodworth thought about it – and the Lord Mayor was nowhere to be seen – houses aplenty were being pulled down in Dowgate and the streets thereabouts, that Monday afternoon. Once again, I pulled on many a fire-hook myself, grappling onto cross beams and bringing down walls and entire buildings. So did all the Sceptres around me, a sturdy party of thirty or so led by Julian Carvell, who had fallen back from the east. All the while, the heat scorched our faces, arms and chests, for few men now deigned to wear shirts before the inferno. And still the blaze advanced, leaping easily over the gaps we had made. The wind, howling like a thousand demons through the lanes and alleyways, was unremitting, and carried the fire westward, ever westward.

The livery halls were falling almost by the minute now. I witnessed Skinners' Hall go, then the Tallow Chandlers' next to it, prominent liverymen weeping copiously in the street as their ancient treasures burned. The Steelyard was gone, and with it all the London property of the once-mighty Hanseatic League. Churches galore went up, too. I led a party of Sceptres, dockyard men and plain citizens in trying to save Saint Michael Paternoster Royal, where the famous Lord Mayor Whittington was buried in a fine marble tomb. It was close to the river, so we could establish a bucket-chain along College Hill and Church Lane, but nothing availed. Flames spouted through the windows like satanic tongues, the roof blazed and then fell in, and the tower, ancient and probably already unstable, collapsed in a great cloud of smoke and masonry dust.

We retreated westward, along Thames Street, abandoning to their fate Saint James Garlickhythe, Saint Martin Vintry, and all the streets around those churches. Francis knew the vicar of Saint Nicholas Cole Abbey, so we made our way there, but the man was nowhere to be found. Even so, we climbed the tower, to get a better view of the fire's progress.

As I stepped out onto the roof, the full force of the easterly wind struck me. Then I saw the fire in all its terror and majesty, a great curtain of flame stretching south-west to north-east across the City, its folds billowing out before it, reaching inexorably toward the buildings in its path. Thames Street was ablaze on both sides, London Bridge glimpsed only occasionally through gaps in the flames. At least the fire did not seem to be threatening the buildings on the bridge, which could have spread it into Southwark. There, in the shadows of Saint Mary Overie and Winchester Palace, crowds were thronging the riverbank, watching the horror unfolding before them as the fire rushed relentlessly northward. Even as I watched, Saint Mary Aldermary on Bow Lane caught fire, its thin tower transformed into a finger of flame, pointing toward Heaven.

If the fire was not stopped soon, the very heart of London would be consumed before the day was out. And over all lay the great cloud of black smoke, often blotting out the blood-red sun, leaving only the countless glowing sparks and firedrops being borne westward to illuminate us.

'Genesis Nineteen, verses twenty-four and twenty-five,' said Francis.

I did not reply; I did not need to.

Then the Lord rained upon Sodom and upon Gomorrah brimstone and fire from the Lord out of heaven; and He overthrew those cities, and all the plain, and all the inhabitants of the cities, and that which grew upon the ground.

I stared at the great blaze: stared at it long enough to see what happens every time any man stares into his own grate, only writ large across the sky. I saw the faces of the dead, of those once loved, of enemies long killed, all of them dancing in the flames. I saw angels, their wings reaching out to enfold the city. I saw devils, conjuring up yet more of hell itself. I looked into the fire, and saw the visage of death.

'No,' I said, finally. 'Whatever sins we may have committed, London will stand. It has to stand. Perhaps the next building we pull down will be the one to halt the fire's advance, Francis. We have to believe that. We have to believe it.'

But as we descended the stairs of the tower – which would, itself, shortly fall victim to the flames – I knew how hollow my words sounded.

All of England will burn, I thought. *Everything will be consumed, and it will be God's righteous vengeance for what we did at the Vlie and Terschelling. For what you did, Matthew Quinton.* And even if I managed to put that thought out of my head, another, even more dreadful, one swiftly took its place. *Did the Horsemen somehow succeed after all?* Goodman was still at large, and what if the fire had resurrected the apparently dead fourth Horseman, like a phoenix from the ashes, to accelerate what his brothers had begun?

The Horsemen.

Experts in fire, yes. But experts in something else, too. And that was when the thought came to me.

How would the Horsemen have *stopped* a great fire, rather than starting one? The same way any seaman would have done. But I was no true seaman. So, when we emerged from the church, I called over Julian Carvell, who was. He and I talked, and then I sent a Sceptre to find me a pen, paper and ink. This did not prove difficult, given the number of hastily abandoned workshops and offices in the vicinity. Carvell's eyes nearly sprang from his head in astonishment as I addressed the letter:

His Majesty the King and His Royal Highness the Duke of York Palace of Whitehall

* * *

I was resting in the middle of the afternoon, in a lane a little to the west of Garlickhithe, taking some ale to quench my mighty thirst, when word came that the Royal Exchange was ablaze. That meant the post house would have gone, and Cornhill with all the shops that Cornelia loved so much, and Threadneedle Street. I looked at Francis Gale, as sooty and begrimed as myself, and he at me, but neither of us had any words left. The London we knew was being wiped from the map, street by street, stone by stone, and it seemed there was nothing any mortal being could do about it.

A lad was running up the lane toward us, shouting, but at first I could not hear him over the din of the fire and falling houses. What new horror could he be proclaiming? Had the flames reached the Tower? If so, was the vast powder arsenal about to explode? Or had the street prophecies been fulfilled, and the French and Dutch really were invading? Part of me prayed for the latter to be true. At least Frenchmen and Dutchmen were tangible enemies; foes who could be confronted, and defeated, unlike the inexorable flames.

'Looters!' The word was clear now. 'Looters at the wharf by Black Swan Alley! My father's business…'

I stood, and grabbed hold of the boy.

'Take us there,' I said.

Francis beckoned to the dozen or so Sceptres closest to us, led by Carvell and John Tremar.

Down we went, through the warren of alleyways toward the river, fighting our way through the carts and people trying to get west, the stench of burning tar and pitch getting stronger with every step we took. The wharf was no different to any of its neighbours: a narrow piece of land, fronted by rickety wooden pilings and a crane, warehouses stretching behind it, up toward Thames Street. Lighters and barges were crowded up against it. Vintners Hall stood behind and a little to the east of the wharf, its roof ablaze.

On the wharf, a man was being beaten into a bloody pulp by three rough-looking fellows. Behind them, a dozen or so of their kind were rolling barrels of wine out of the warehouse, then stacking them on the deck of a lighter.

'Father!' cried the boy.

I drew my sword and advanced. The three men drew daggers, and turned toward me. The lad ran to his father, who fell to the ground.

'Who the fuck are you?' demanded the largest robber. 'This place is ours, so fuck off and find your own.'

'Your place? I don't think so. And here and now, I am the King's justice.'

The other looters had left their barrels, and were forming into a tight formation behind their leader. They had cudgels and knives, and they looked like the sorts of fellows who had seen many a fight in their time.

'King's justice? Like we give a shit for the Papist whoremaster Charles Stuart? With me, boys!'

The gang charged. The leader came at my right side, abetted by a plague-scarred, pockmarked fellow on the left. They had to avoid the greater reach of my sword, but if one of them could get under my guard while the other kept my swordarm occupied.

Pock-Mark feinted low, and the leader attacked high, stabbing for my neck. But such an obvious move was meat and drink. I pivoted, threatening Pock-Mark and then bringing my sword back up to block the leader, whose dagger struck my blade.

To my left, Francis Gale was engaged in a ferocious fist-fight with a dusky fellow who might have been a Spaniard or an Italian. To my right, Julian Carvell was exchanging vicious knife-thrusts with a young, nimble, one-eyed creature. All over the wharf, Sceptres and looters battled each other, while fire raged above the nearby rooftops and flame-flakes fell on us at every moment.

Now Pock-Mark and the leader came at me together, both jabbing for my chest, stepping away from each other in the hope that I would leave a gap in my guard. But this exposed Pock-Mark's left flank, just for a moment – I lunged, below his knife-arm, piercing him in the ribs, below the heart. He screamed and backed away, clutching at the bloody wound. The leader pressed home his attack, and as I swung around, his knife sliced a gash across my right arm, a mere second after it would have done the same to my neck. I felt the pain, saw the blood flow, but had taken enough wounds in my life to know it would not hinder me. I cut for the leader's shoulder, but he ducked out of the way in time. In doing so, though, he showed me his left side. I shifted my weight and thrust for his head. My blade ripped through the flesh of his left cheek and took off his ear. The fellow grabbed at the wound, screaming pitifully. Then he turned and ran, his minions breaking off from their own battles to follow him.

Julian Carvell came up to me. He picked up one of the many bottles of wine scattered across the wharf, smashed the top off it, and poured it onto my wound. I gasped, for it stung hideously. Then he tore off the sleeve of his shirt, which he wrapped around my wound without a by-your-leave.

'Beggin' pardon, Sir Matthew,' he said, 'but you'll soon have as many scars as me.'

The pain from the wound was dreadful, but I could still move the arm freely. If necessary, I could still wield a sword, or take hold of a fire-hook.

Suddenly, flames erupted from the head of the alleyway just to the east of the wharf where we stood. The first swirls of smoke rose from the roof of the warehouse behind us.

'Back!' I cried. 'Fall back on Queenhithe, men!'

Francis Gale helped the beaten merchant to his feet. The man and his son turned, and looked at the abandoned barrels of wine littering the wharf, where they would shortly fall victim to the fire. It did not take a seer to divine what they were thinking.

* * *

That afternoon and early evening, we pulled down more houses, around Trinity Lane and thereabouts. But the fire was merciless. Queenhithe itself, the principal dock on that part of the river, was consumed, and all the buildings around it – countless houses, warehouses, the glorious old Three Cranes in Vintry where in happier times I had enjoyed many a meal and good companionship with my old, dear, dead friend, Vice-Admiral Sir William Berkeley. I watched as flames took hold on the roof of Baynard's Castle, the squat, ancient riverside fortress where so much of England's history had been written. There, Edward the Fourth was crowned, his brother Richard the Third proclaimed King, Bloody Mary proclaimed Queen. But not even the weighty armour of history can defend a building from a disaster such as this. Soon, all of the castle's multiple octagonal towers and narrow gables that fronted the river were ablaze, flames spouting forth like dragon's breath from its countless windows, sheets of fire issuing from its roof like infernal mainsails blowing in the gale from Satan's breath.

That is how Whitehall will burn, I thought. *That is what the destruction of Parliament will look like.*

Dispirited, the Sceptres and I made our way up Saint Peter's Hill. We slumped in front of an alehouse at the back of the Heralds' office, eating and drinking in silence, trying to recover our breath and our senses. I felt overwhelmingly tired, my arm was painful, and I was on the verge of sleep, when a loud voice stirred me.

'Make way, there! You men, out of the way!'

I looked up, and saw familiar red uniforms. Life Guards. Bloodworth must have allowed them into the City, or else he had been given no choice in the matter.

In the middle of the Life Guards was a face I knew. A proud-looking, hawk-faced man in his early thirties, wearing a soot-stained grey coat, looked intently from side to side. I stood. Francis Gale and the rest of the Sceptres followed my lead.

I bowed.

'Your Royal Highness,' I said.

The man looked at me uncertainly, then screwed up his eyes to look at me more closely.

'Quinton? Dear Lord in Heaven, is that really you, Sir Matthew?'

'My apologies, Highness. I have not had the occasion to clean or dress myself for an audience.'

It was intended as a jest, but I should have known better than to attempt such a thing with the notoriously serious man before me, who merely frowned.

'No. You have been busy, I see. Would that more men in this City had been as busy as you.'

James, Duke of York, Lord High Admiral of England, the King's brother and heir, was the opposite of his sibling in so many ways: fair rather than dark, dour rather than frivolous, stupid rather than intelligent. But he was a man of action, who had led our fleet heroically in battle the year before, so he had my respect and that of the Sceptres around me.

'It's all gone between here and the river, Highness. Queenhithe, Baynard's Castle – all of it.'

'I feared so, but wanted to see for myself. Your report makes that unnecessary, Sir Matthew.'

'We have to stop it, sir. You and His Majesty received my note?' He nodded. 'There is only one way. You are a seaman yourself, Your Royal Highness, you know it to be true.'

The Duke's thin lips creased, in what might have been taken for a smile. Few things visibly pleased this serious prince, but being counted a true seaman was one of them.

'If it were left to me, I would give the order this very minute,' he said. 'I said so to my brother the King, when we received your letter. But there are still many who baulk at it – who think of the amount of property that will be destroyed, and raise one legal nicety after another. They are still convinced that the wind will drop at any moment, and the river will rise. Seamen know differently, Sir Matthew, but the Privy Council of England and the Common Council of London contain precious few seamen, more's the pity. What's more, my brother has recalled the Duke of Albemarle from the fleet. Only he can save London, it seems. Only he can give the King his capital for a second time.' Now, there was no hint of a smile upon the face of the man who would, one day, be King James the Second. The Duke would surely have known of my fraught relationship with Albemarle. Did he, too, wonder why both his brother and the people of England had such unaccountable faith in the obese old turncoat? 'Until His Grace arrives, though, or His Majesty sees fit to adopt the stratagem you proposed, I have set up posts at Temple Bar, and then four more north and east of there. A hundred men to fight the fire at each, along with thirty soldiers. Advance posts at Aldersgate, Coleman Street, Cripplegate. All of them commanded by two or three gentlemen of good rank. God willing, we can halt the fire at those positions, if we can pull down enough properties in good time. And the Fleet River ought to be a natural barrier that the fire will not cross.'

I offered up a silent prayer that he was right. Ravensden House, with Cornelia and my brother, stood not far to the west of the Fleet River. But much still stood to the east of it, directly in the path of the blaze. One building above all. Occasional gaps in the pall of smoke made it possible to make out its tower, rearing proudly above every lesser building, every lower steeple. But I could also see the waves of flame just to the east, still blown upon the gale, still clawing their way west like the fingers of Beelzebub.

The Duke of York's eyes followed mine, round to the north.

'Paul's Church is doomed,' he said, flatly, 'unless a miracle saves it. And I do not think this is a time of miracles in London, Sir Matthew.'

'Perhaps not, Highness. But when the story is written of how London burned, let it not be said that men did not fight for it.'

'Amen to that. God go with you, Matt Quinton.'

I called the Sceptres together. Taking a respectful leave of the Duke of York, we made our way uphill, toward Saint Paul's Cathedral.

Chapter Twenty~One

All night, and into the morning, we pulled down houses along Watling Street and Distaff Lane, trying to create a large enough firebreak in front of the cathedral. Exhausted men snatched a few minutes of sleep when and where they could, often on the bare ground. And all the while, a stream of people and carts passed us, fleeing the ruins of the City and the vast bow of fire that still advanced across London, with no sign of abating. Some folk cried that they had already moved their goods two or three times, as each supposed place of safety, well to the west of the blaze, was engulfed in its turn as the relentless flames advanced. And now it was day-in-night, just as it had been night-in-day when the smoke blotted out the September sun. Midnight was as bright as any summer's noontime. It was hot, and breathing was difficult. I had been in western Africa, during my command of the *Seraph*, and I had served many months in the Mediterranean Sea, so I knew such conditions well enough. Several times that night, as my senses twisted around due to lack of sleep, I thought myself back off the coast of Algiers, or far up the Gambia River.

There were endless reports of the progress of the Fire, through the Monday and into Tuesday. The Guildhall had perished. Cheapside, the greatest highway in London, was ablaze, Lombard Street already gone. Bankers by the score were said to be ruined, and some men smiled at this. But only the very rich could now afford to hire carts in London. What had cost ten shillings three days before now fetched a price of fifty pounds, the carters seizing the opportunity of a lifetime with both avaricious hands. Although its eastward advance was much slower, into the teeth of the gale, the fire was said to be only two or three hundred yards short of the Tower, and that meant the Navy Office, the ordnance store, and the Smithfield victualling yard, were all under immediate threat. If they burned, our fleet could not keep the sea. I thought of ordering my men there, to do what we could in the east, but we would never be able to work our way through the stationary rivers of humanity trying to escape down every road, lane and alleyway heading north or west. And in my heart, I knew I had to stay within range of Ravensden House, in case the fire threatened it. Threatened my brother, my wife, and my unborn child.

And all the while, a constant backdrop, there were the shouts, at once angry and terrified.

'The French are landed at Dover! Beaufort is marching on London at this very minute!'

'Seize the Dutch! Hang every last one of 'em!'

'A Papist's throwing fireballs into an apothecary's in Leadenhall! Constables!'

'God's righteous judgement upon a sinful nation for bringing back the fornicator Charles Stuart.'

'I tell you, a dozen French Jesuits were seen in Pudding Lane as the fire began!'

'Don't trust the Life Guards – they answer to the Papist Duke of York!'

I tried to shut my mind to it all. Cornelia and Captain Ollivier had escaped the wrath of the mob, if only barely, but how many innocents were being assaulted – perhaps murdered – all across London, simply because they were born Dutch or French? And knowing the indiscriminate rage of the English all too well, I wondered how many

Germans and Swedes were being mistaken for Dutch, or Spaniards and Portuguese for French.

Instead, I applied myself to the handle of a water pump, directing a jet onto a blazing house at the Saint Maudlin's end of the Old Change. Martin Lanherne and a party of Sceptres were with me, Francis having gone to see if he could save something from Saint Margaret Moses on Pissing Lane, where his mother had been baptised, before the church was consumed by the flames. Every bone in my body ached. My right arm was numb with pain from the knife wound. I longed for sleep. Yet somehow, I kept myself working the pump, the only way by which I could drive out the images in my head. The fires of London, and of Brandaris, and of the ships in the Vlie, all merging into one, spreading across the map of Europe, then burning the entire world.

I was barely aware of the tall man at my shoulder, or of his companion, standing to his left.

'We will relieve you here, Sir Matthew Quinton,' said the tall man, whose dark face framed the most impossibly ugly nose. 'You look as though you could do with a pot of ale and a wash. And sleep. London will not burn any more or less quickly if the heir to Ravensden dozes for an hour.'

My mind was so far gone, I was hallucinating. That could be the only explanation for it. It was simply impossible for both the King of England and the Duke of York to be standing before me, stripped to their shirts, covered in dirt, faces blackened by soot, prising my hands from the handle, laying their own upon it, and beginning to pump as if possessed.

'Y- your Majesty – your Royal Highness –'

'Go, Matt,' said the King. 'Go and rest, in God's name, in the knowledge that we have agreed to execute your proposal to halt the fire.'

Lanherne led me away.

'Seems the two of them have been all over the City,' he said. 'Helping with the pumps and the water buckets, encouraging the firefighters, giving orders to pull down buildings. God save them both.'

Like almost every man of Cornwall, Martin Lanherne was a staunch royalist. In his case, the wounds he had taken in Grenville's famous western army bore ample testimony of his devotion to the cause of the Stuarts.

'But my place is still at the pump.'

'Not when you've had a royal order it isn't, Sir Matthew. Would you have me commit treason, rather than make sure you do as the King has commanded you?'

That was how I came to be sleeping on a pallet in a deserted coaching inn by Saint Augustine Watling Street. And that was where I was woken, after what seemed to be barely a moment's slumber, by Francis Gale.

'The fire's across the Fleet River, Matthew,' he said. 'Dorset House is ablaze. It's advancing on the Temple.'

I was on my feet in an instant. From the Temple, it was only a stone's throw to Ravensden House.

* * *

West through Paul's churchyard, where fire flakes were falling by the score; then through the throng clogging Ludgate, to behold the terrible sight beyond it. The fire was across the Fleet, all right, advancing much more quickly near the Thames, where there were still wharves and flammable cargoes aplenty to fuel it. Not only was Dorset House in flames: so, too, were Blackfriars, Bridewell prison, and Saint Bride's Church. It was only a matter of time before it crossed Water Lane into Whitefriars, which bordered the Temple; and Ravensden House was just beyond the Temple. But it was not only my family's London home that was under threat. If the east wind continued to blow, and the fire continued to rage unchecked through the Liberties beyond London's walls, then it would inevitably reach the King's palace at

Whitehall, and then to Westminster, where Parliament and the Abbey would surely burn. Old Fawkes was surely grinning in his grave.

At Ravensden House, all was confusion. That much, at least, was apparent from the scene in the entrance hall behind Phineas Musk: paintings, boxes and sacks piled up, ready to be moved; Youngest Barcock and Cornelia's maid scurrying hither and thither.

'She's packing,' said Musk. 'Like it's for an expedition to the Indies, and she has half a year to prepare for it.'

'And the Earl?'

'Won't move. Says there's plenty of time, and where would he go? If he was still as ill as he was, we could move him and he'd barely notice. But he's well enough to be a true Quinton.'

'That being?'

'Stubborn beyond measure, Sir Matthew. Begging pardon.'

I found my wife in our bedchamber, attempting, unaided, to manhandle the portrait of my father from the wall. I rushed forward and took the weight.

'Matthew!' she said, surprised, and took hold of my waist affectionately. I lifted the bandage around her head to examine the wound on her forehead: a vicious bruise was developing around the gash.

'You should not be doing this,' I said. 'You should have called for Musk, or Youngest Barcock.'

She ignored my words, stepped away, and just stared at me. I caught a glimpse of myself in the mirror by the side of our bed, and realised why. My skin and hair were blackened and burnt, my arm heavily bandaged. I looked as though I had been in a ten-hour fight with an Algerine corsair.

'And you should not be doing *that*, husband,' she said, coming back to me and taking me in her arms. 'You cannot save all of London as you saved me, Matthew Quinton. London would not be worth the losing of you.'

I wept then, long and hard. Wept for the fallen city and all that had perished in the flames, wept for my guilt and my sin, wept for our unborn child, wept for the dear, precious, fragile creature who was my wife.

* * *

At length, after many endearments, I left Cornelia and went to the Earl's chamber. My brother was propped up on his bed, evidently conversing in French with Captain Ollivier.

'My Lord,' I said. 'Captain.'

The Breton bowed his head.

'You will have much to discuss,' he said. 'I will leave you.'

'My thanks, Captain,' I said. 'I pray you, sir, assist Reverend Gale in watching over Lady Quinton. Make certain she does not overtask herself.'

'I will do my utmost, Sir Matthew, but your wife has a strong will. If she wishes to overtask herself, I fear there will be very little I or anyone else can do to prevent it.'

With that, he left Charles and I alone.

'More than fifty livery halls gone, Musk tells me,' said the Earl of Ravensden. 'Perhaps eighty churches or more, Saint Paul's set to follow them in short order. Countless thousands of homes burned, and heaven knows what a loss to the Exchequer. If it was the Horsemen, Matt, they could hardly have galloped more rampantly, or to better effect.'

'It could not have been…' I began, but I knew I could not even convince myself of the argument.

We had destroyed the Horsemen aboard the *Milkmaid*. But had we only come upon them *after* they undertook their business in Pudding Lane?

'It does not matter whether they did or not. Even here, up so high and behind shutters, I can hear the shouts in the street. As far as the common sort are concerned, Papists began the fire, and I doubt if anything will shift them from that belief – not even in the lifetime of your child-to-be, I suspect. Whereas you and I know that, if it was begun deliberately, but the Horsemen had no part in it, then it is much more likely to have been by a Dutchman, enraged by what you did to them.' This was discoimfiting. It came too close to the guilty thoughts of my own sin that I had harboured since we burned the Vlie. I turned my eyes to the floor. 'The people will want a scapegoat, and they will want a sacrifice. Cornelia and Captain Ollivier might have fitted the bill, had not you and My Lord Craven intervened. Perhaps, for all we know, they've already strung up a few poor French or Dutch. But Parliament will want an enquiry, have no doubt. I imagine Venner will be hot on the matter.' Our brother-in-law, Sir Venner Garvey, Member of Parliament for Rievaulx, was a former Roundhead of the most serpentine kind. 'And the people won't be silent until they've had a hanging or two – or, better still, a hanging, drawing and quartering for treason. Nothing like the sight of entrails to satisfy a mob's lust for vengeance.'

Charles paused, and took a series of long but broken breaths. I stepped toward him, to see if I could somehow make him more comfortable, but he raised his hand and continued.

'Which, of course, is as it should be. Better that than the alternative.'

'Alternative, brother?'

'If it festers, with no enquiry and no guilty party, or at least no scapegoat – then the people will do what they always do in such cases. They will blame the government. Half of England is convinced that the Duke of York is a secret Papist, the other half that the King is, too. And Kings and the City of London have rarely seen eye to eye, certainly in my lifetime. So we don't want a new-born phoenix of civil war rising out of the ashes of London, Matt. This fire must be proved beyond doubt to have been an accident, or be proved beyond doubt to be the work of someone who cannot possibly cast suspicion upon the King and the Duke.'

'Ah,' I said, 'I had not realised I was again in the presence of Lord Percival.' He smiled, then coughed long and hard. 'But before the noble lord considers such matters of state, he should ponder the more urgent matter in hand. Which is to say, the means of getting you out of this house before the fire consumes you.'

* * *

Francis Gale returned that afternoon, having spent long hours ministering to the thousands of fearful souls packed into Smithfield. Together with Musk, we strapped my brother onto a narrow pallet, manhandled him to the head of the stairs, and realised at once that it would be impossible to get him down the narrow stairway, with its many sharp turns. My grandfather had once considered a scheme to rebuild this end of the house, and to put in a broad, open staircase; but as with so many of his grand projects, it had never come to fruition.

'Leave me,' said Charles. 'I may be dead next week in any case, or next month. It will be no great loss if I leave the world a little early, consumed by flame.'

'By God's divine providence, very few seem to have died in this calamity,' said Francis. 'How will history make sense of it, if one of the only casualties of this great fire was the tenth Earl of Ravensden?'

'None will die here,' I said, 'least of all you, My Lord. Be thankful that your brother found himself a captain in the Navy Royal.'

I sent for the seamen I had despatched to defend Ravensden House, realising with some astonishment that I had done so only a day earlier. Time played strange tricks during the fire of London: each hour was at once a century and a minute, each day an eternity and a moment.

I told the men what I had in mind. They understood at once, and went off to search the kitchen, stables and other outbuildings. Within a half-hour they were back with an assortment of timbers and ropes, even an entire block from a ship's rigging, which somehow must have found its way to the house in my grandfather's day. By the end of a further half-hour, the window of the Earl's bedroom had been taken out, and a respectable, if miniature, pair of sheerlegs protruded from Ravensden House. We tested the device by lowering my sea-chest, which was significantly heavier than my brother; it reached the ground in the Strand without any mishap.

'I concede the point you have often made to me,' said Charles, as we attached the ropes to his pallet, 'that the English seaman is a fellow of infinite resource. And by that, brother, I include yourself.'

Musk and I went down to the street, and I barked orders as the Earl of Ravensden was swung out of the window, then lowered gently toward the ground.

'Steady, there! Give – give – give – hold! Too fast, men! Slower! Now – give – give – belay!'

Even with the flames burning well beyond the Fleet Conduit, and the road jammed with carts heading west, quite a crowd of onlookers formed around us to witness the curious spectacle of a peer of the realm being treated in such an undignified, but effective, manner.

Finally the pallet nestled comfortably on the cart that Phineas Musk had somehow obtained earlier that afternoon. I did not enquire how, exactly, he had managed to do so, for carts were more valuable than the jewels in the coronation crown, that day in London.

Charles Quinton looked a little pale, but otherwise none the worse for wear.

'I have flown,' he said. 'Tristram will be infinitely jealous.'

Cornelia emerged from the house, attended by her maid, and came over to me.

'You'll take no more risks, husband?' she said.

I do not know why she asked; she knew that was a promise I could never give.

'I will do my utmost to save the house,' I said. 'This is where you will give birth to our child, my love.'

'A child may be born in a ditch, just as well as in an Earl's house.

Or in a manger in a stable, as the case of Our Lord proved. What the child needs most is its father.'

I kissed her, and again wondered how I had ever been tempted to endanger this – to endanger *us* – for the charms of Aphra Behn.

As I moved away from Cornelia, I realised that Charles was staring at me: to be precise, giving me the look that only a very much older sibling can bestow upon a very much younger one.

'This talk of saving the house, Matt. Have you become a Bedlam-man, brother?'

'Crave pardon, brother?'

'Perhaps your wits have been unhinged by the roar of one too many broadsides?'

'My Lord – Charles – what do you…?'

'The house, Matt. Let us both pray to God in His heaven that the fire consumes this foul abomination, this putrid hovel that disgraces the name and honour of the Quintons. Let the flames devour it, and allow us to build a fine new townhouse, a fitting London home for your child. Don't waste your efforts – or your powder – on saving Ravensden House, brother.'

'But…'

I was astonished. Charles Quinton, the most guarded, the most uncommunicative of men, never betrayed the passions that lay within his gaunt, damaged frame. And he had always seemed so content within the strange, rambling warren we were now abandoning.

'Every Quinton hates it,' he said. 'Those who came before us have hated it. All of us, except Grandfather and, for some unaccountable reason, yourself. But let it go, Matt. Take your powder where it might do some good, where it might save some decent houses of honest folk, or a fine church, or something else worth saving. But not this, brother. If this is the last command I ever give you as your Earl, let it be this.'

I stared at him, dumbfounded, but finally nodded my assent.

Then, guarded by Frostick and Gover, and under the somewhat

dubious command of Phineas Musk, the cart set off for the quarters that a generous monarch had agreed to provide for the fugitive Quintons within Whitehall Palace. How long they might stay there remained to be seen: that depended upon whether the great fire stopped before Ravensden House, contrary to my brother's unambiguous wishes, or continued onward to threaten the palace.

* * *

Evening.

Francis Gale and I stood in the great hole where my brother's window had been, looking out upon the terrible spectacle. We could see clear down the Strand and Fleet Street, which now burned nearly as far as Shoe Lane, to the city walls and Ludgate Hill. There, at the top, was Saint Paul's, but now the roof of the east end and the entire Choir were ablaze, the flames pushing west, toward the tower. Everwhere, mighty sheets of fire turned the night sky into a hellish new day.

'Truly,' said Francis, at my side, 'we are beyond Genesis Nineteen now. Far beyond Sodom and Gomorrah. Alas, my friend, we have lived to witness the truth of Revelation Twenty.'

'The lake of fire,' I said. 'Is this the day of judgement, then, Francis?'

He did not answer me. We watched, spellbound and aghast, as the flames enveloped the cathedral, bursting out on the roof of the tower and the windows, spilling out into the transepts, finally overwhelming the west front, built only thirty years before. The roof collapsed, and parts of the aisle walls with it. I later heard, from those who witnessed it, that the lead on the roof had melted, flowing away in rivers down Ludgate Hill; great gargoyles and other stone ornaments were blown clear like cannonballs.

Then there came the strangest sound I ever heard in my life. A distant, discordant roar, like some giant beast of legend roaring at the enemies who sought to destroy it. A roar that turned, somehow, into a great chord of music, a requiem for old London, a *te deum* for a new. I realised that what I was hearing could only be the bells, shifted by – what? The movement of the beams from which they hung, or the falling of masonry against them? It was impossible to tell. But however it happened, they rang out the death toll of old Saint Paul's. Another bell, nearby: that of Saint Dunstan in the West, our own parish church, sounding nine o'clock. I realised with astonishment that it had taken little more than an hour for fire to consume the great cathedral that had stood for a thousand years.

Numbed by the sight before me, I almost missed the thing I should have noticed at once: the first thing any true seaman would have noted. I was not a true seaman; not yet, at any rate. But at last, a firedrop landing on the floor of the bedroom, where Francis hastily stamped upon it, dragged the seaman within me from his hiding place.

'The wind,' I said. 'It's veering southerly. It's easing. The wind's lessening, Francis.'

But it was lessening almost imperceptibly. Only a man who had stood upon many a quarterdeck trying to gauge whether there was, perhaps, just the faintest breath of fresh breeze to fill his sails, would have noticed it at all. The fire was still licking at the precincts of the Temple, and advancing along the north side of Fleet Street. Perhaps the change in the wind would save Whitehall and Westminster, but it still looked set fair to destroy Ravensden. Part of me yet wished to defy my brother, and do everything in my power to save the dear, ramshackle pile in which I stood. But honour and duty directed me otherwise. The Earl of Ravensden had commanded me to save something worthwhile; and, by God, that was exactly what I proposed to do.

Chapter Twenty-Two

Shortly after dawn, we laid our first barrels of gunpowder in the houses huddled directly under the city walls, just north of Newgate and Holborn Conduit. The powder had arrived in the small hours aboard a cart under the command of Carvell, brought from the Tower by way of Moorfields and Long Lane. This was guarded by a dozen heavily armed Sceptres. In the chaos of the fire, who could say that malevolent men would not regard the sudden availability in London of dozens of barrels of powder as an opportunity not to be missed?

I laid several trails myself, propping barrels against the wall or corner where it was likely to have the most effect, then pouring snaking lines of powder onto the hard, dry ground, before retiring to what the Sceptres considered a safe distance, lighting the fuse, watching the flame make its way – and then the explosion.

The irony was not lost on me: that I, who had done my utmost to prevent the Horsemen blowing up London, should now be responsible for blasting whole swathes of it to kingdom come.

Each house died differently. Most collapsed in on themselves; others blew up like miniature volcanoes, fireballs blasting from their roofs, their wooden beams blowing outward in all directions. A moment after each blast, Sceptres ran into the smoking piles of rubble in order to stamp out any minor fires caused by the explosions. And so we proceeded down entire rows of houses, east towards Aldersgate, determined to preserve from the flames the precious prize that stood just to the north of us: Saint Bartholomew's Hospital, and all the poor, sick folk it contained. Among them, Macferran, Treninnick, and fifteen more of the crew of the *Royal Sceptre*.

The sounds of other explosions, further away to the east, told their own story. All along the northern flank of the great fire, houses were being blown up to the scheme originally proposed by the seamen, notably Julian Carvell. It was a stratagem that did not depend solely on the judicious deployment of barrels of gunpowder: for now one of the greatest strengths of the English mariner became apparent. Barely had the smoke, dust, and wreckage settled at every blown-up house than the Sceptres were leaping into the ruins, stamping out embers, grabbing hold of shattered timbers and any other flammable materials, and dragging them away at once, well beyond the reach of the flames. Then on to the next building to lay the next barrel and repeat the process.

Thus was demonstrated yet again a truth I had witnessed countless times during my service in King Charles's Navy: there is no goodwife anywhere in the kingdom who is as fastidiously – no, as obsessively – tidy as a naval seaman.

Carvell had explained it to me in simple terms, when we first discussed it.

'Problem is, Sir Matthew, the London men, they're just tearing down the houses and leaving the piles of wood where they lie, so the fire carries on regardless. What we should be doing is blowing up buildings, several at a time – that's the only way to build a firebreak big enough, quickly enough. But clear away at once. Get rid of the wreckage, especially the wood. Leave empty ground, a wasteland the fire can't cross. Only way, Sir Matthew. Only way.'

And that, God be thanked, was the policy that the King had finally approved, regardless of what Sir Thomas Bloodworth, the

Common Council, and the outraged property owners of London thought about it.

What effect the seamen's efforts were having, God knew; but it was certain that, as Wednesday morning passed, the wind was continuing to blow only from the south, and to fall off. I stole an occasional glance toward the west. The sheets of flame were still roaring, but no longer seemed to be advancing. Had Ravensden House and the Temple been spared after all?

I had little time for such thoughts. We were out of powder, and pulling down houses in the old way, grappling with firehooks. At last, it seemed as though there was some reward for our efforts.

'It ain't gaining northward, Sir Matthew,' said Carvell. 'Flames ain't so high, all around. Bart's and our men – they'll be safe enough, God willing.'

I had no breath with which to reply, but it was true. What had been a vast, unbroken curtain of flame, enveloping the whole of London, now had large gaps in it. And with every hour that passed, the wind died down a little more.

News began to come in, shouted along the lanes and streets by running urchins. The fire had not got beyond Cripplegate. It was halted at the foot of Seething Lane, so the Navy Office was safe. Leadenhall and the Tower still stood. And in the west, the flames had licked the walls of the Temple, but not consumed it. There was no longer any danger to Whitehall or Westminster.

A little after noon, the Duke of York strode up. Begrimed and sweating, clad in a torn shirt and dirty breeches, the heir to three kingdoms looked like the meanest pauper. He was accompanied only by two Life Guards.

'The worst is over, Sir Matthew, God willing,' he said. 'All over the city, the fire's advance is halted. And you have stopped it reaching Bartholomew's.'

'I pray so, Highness.'

'It is time to abandon your firehooks, men,' he said, addressing the Sceptres around me. 'Take up swords, and muskets. You still have your commission in my Marine regiment to give you authority, Sir Matthew.'

'Highness?'

'Control – that is what is needed in London now. People are still proclaiming that the French and Dutch are at the gates. Foreigners by the score are being assaulted, and the guards and trained bands are having to rescue them from the noose all over the City. Now, when we are vulnerable, is when the disaffected are most likely to strike. So we need good, loyal, armed men on the streets.'

'As you say, Your Highness. And you, Sir? What of you?'

'I go to join my brother, at Pye Corner. The flames are quite extinguished there, and all the way down to Holborn Bridge. We will inspect the area, then give thanks to God for the deliverance of what is left of London. I think it is time at last for prayers of thanksgiving.'

With that, the Duke left us, striding across the still smouldering rubble from the houses beneath the city wall. He was ever more religious than his brother, despite being, if anything, even less monogamous, which was something of a feat; and we were still a few years short of that most dreadful calamity for England, when the intensity of the Duke's faith, allied to his capacity for blind stupidity, led him to the conclusion that the only true channel for that unbending, black-and-white spirituality of his led inexorably towards Rome.

Carvell was already standing by the cart that had brought the gunpowder. He lifted out a large canvas bag that contained a formidable array of weapons.

'You seem eager to be a-soldiering, Mister Carvell,' I said.

'Better to be annoying rebels and dissenting scum, Sir Matthew, than blowing up the homes of honest Londoners. That's how I see it, at any rate.'

I took hold of a cutlass in my left hand, my right being still hampered by the knife wound I had taken from the looter. Fortunately, I had been trained to use a sword by my uncle Tristram, a left-handed man, and thus felt nearly as comfortable with this less familiar dispensation. I waved and slashed several times to get the feel for the weapon's weight.

'I think I concur with you, Mister Carvell. Better by far.'

* * *

We were moving down Cock Lane toward Holborn Conduit, hunting for looters in the unburned eastern half of the street and working towards the Earl of Craven and his soldiers, advancing from the other end, when I heard my name being called.

'Sir Matthew!'

I turned, and found myself looking at Aphra Behn, clad in man's garb once again, attended by Marker and two other of my brother's men.

'Mistress Behn? What brings you here?'

I had not seen her since the night aboard the *Milkmaid*, the night when the fire broke out in Pudding Lane. Sunday morning, in other words, and it was now Wednesday afternoon. But it felt as though an eternity had passed, and for most of the intervening time, I had not given a thought to the Lady Astraea, and the dire, conflicting thoughts she inspired.

'And joy of the afternoon to you too, Sir Matthew,' she said, smiling. I made no reply. 'Ah… business, then, if you insist. Mene Tekel – Shadrach Goodman. After he escaped from the ship, I reasoned he was likely to remain in London, to exploit the chaos caused by the fire. So I set some of our informers among the conventiclers to be alert for any talk of him – those we could find, who had not run from the City. But in a way, the fire helped. People were moving hither and thither across London, and moving rapidly. Word could spread very quickly.'

'You found him?'

'We had intelligence of him – leading the mob pursuing the King's

French firework maker, then inciting homeless men in Moorfields to kill the Lord Mayor. It was said he was hiding out in Alsatia or Sharp Island, in those lawless alleys south of Fleet Street. Not too far from your house, come to that. I finally caught sight of him from a distance, this very morning, just behind us in Smithfield, but there was such a throng of people that we could not get to him... Matthew? What's the matter? You look as though you've seen a dead man walking.'

I had. One thought repeated itself in my head, over and over again. My brother's words. *If their associates succeed in killing the King, and perhaps the Duke of York too, at the same time...*

'My Lord Craven!' I shouted.

'Sir Matthew?' He glanced quizzically at Aphra, but there was no time to waste on introductions.

'My Lord, where is the King? And his brother, the Duke?'

'Gone together to Great Bartholomew's, at the Duke's insistence, to pray privately and offer up thanks to God for the ending of the great fire.'

No time for explanations. I turned on my heel and began to run.

* * *

Through Smithfield, leaping over families sitting on the ground, brushing past the makeshift tents. Running toward Cloth Fair and the gatehouse that led into the churchyard of Great Saint Bartholomew's. A group of Life Guards idling by the gate, lifted their weapons as they caught sight of me.

'Sir Matthew Quinton!' I cried.

An officer recognised me, and ordered the men to lower their arms. He shouted something after me as I ran past.

Into the church, its vast tiers of Norman arches stretching toward heaven, blood-red light streaming through the high clerestory windows in the east end, casting strange, flickering crimson shapes onto the walls. It took a moment for my eyes to become accustomed to the near darkness. But there, at the high altar, knelt two men, deep in prayer and oblivious to the third figure, stepping out of the shadows toward them, a pistol in each of his hands.

'*Sic semper tyrannis,*' said Shadrach Goodman. The King and Duke of York stood at once, and turned to face Mene Tekel. 'In the name of the godly people of England, and the wronged innocents of Terschelling island, I sentence you, Charles Stuart, and you, James Stuart, to death.'

He raised his pistols, levelling them at the royal brothers.

'Goodman!' I shouted.

His head turned sharply towards me, but he kept the pistols steady.

'You,' he said. 'Lord Percival himself.'

'You're finished, man!' I said.

'Undoubtedly. But in a few moments, I will be singing alleluias with all my godly brethren in Heaven, these two whoremasters will be burning in Hell, and England will be set fair to become a Godfearing Commonwealth once again.'

I stepped forward. But I had no firearm, only a cutlass, and would never reach Goodman before he fired. Nor would the dozen or so Life Guards who had formed up behind me. Even those who had muskets levelled and primed dared not fire at Goodman for fear of hitting the King or the Duke, almost directly behind him.

Aphra stepped out from the north transept. There must be another way into the church, somewhere on that side. She had a small pistol in her hand, which she raised and fired.

And missed.

Goodman spun round to face her, but before he could fire, the King reached into his left sleeve, took out something that glinted momentarily in the red firelight, and flung it at Goodman, striking him hard in his right shoulder. I ran forward. The Horseman staggered, but he still held his pistols, and now he turned, trying to level them once again at the royal brothers. Charles Stuart broke to his right,

James to his left. Goodman fired the pistol in his left hand, but the ball found only the reredos behind the altar. Before he could aim again, I was upon him, sweeping my cutlass down, with my left hand, into the side of his head, driving deep into his skull. Blood poured down the lifeless body of Mene Tekel, onto my arm, and down onto the floor of the church. The blood-red firelight streaming down from the windows high above swathed him in the scarlet of death.

The King and Duke of York walked over and inspected the corpse, the Duke reciting aloud the words of the second Book of Samuel.

'The Lord is my rock, and my fortress, and my deliverer; The God of my rock; in him will I trust: he is my shield, and the horn of my salvation, my high tower, and my refuge, my saviour; thou savest me from violence…'

The King, meanwhile, turned to me.

'Well, Matt Quinton,' said Charles Stuart, 'I have quite lost track of the balance in the mutual debt of honour between my family and yours. But the King will not forget this service.'

He stooped, and pulled his small, thin blade from Goodman's shoulder, while the Duke of York continued to recite the words of the Bible.

'An old trick taught me by a Sicilian mercenary I encountered in the civil wars,' said the King, nonchalantly. 'In a nutshell, that one should always have something up your sleeve. Quite literally. Let us be thankful that the fanatics cannot resist speechifying. He could have come up behind us and shot us in the backs of our heads as we knelt at the altar – that is certainly what I would have done. But oh no, he has to deliver his little sermon, and thus undoes himself.'

Charles Stuart's voice was steady, but I could see that his hands were trembling. The Duke of York, his prayer finished, laid a hand upon his brother's arm.

'Now,' said the King, ignoring him, 'who is this fearless Amazon, pray?'

Charles and James Stuart both turned toward Aphra, who curtsied deeply. As she rose, the light of the flames through the clerestory windows illuminated her face, making it even more striking. I knew at once that the royal brothers were smitten; and, as I introduced her, so, too, was I.

Again.

Chapter Twenty-Three

That evening I went to Moorfields, hoping to find Francis. That noble soul had gone there to minister to the displaced, of whom there were countless more than at Smithfield. The huge, open space was filled with makeshift shelters, which stretched away up the roads toward Highgate, further than the eye could see. Everywhere, babies were crying, women weeping, and increasingly drunk men railing ever more loudly against the French, Dutch and Papists. The stench was overwhelming.

'That London has come to this,' said Carvell.

'Amen,' I said, for I could think of nothing else to say.

We found Francis in the south-eastern corner of the fields, hard under the tower of Allhallows-in-the-Wall, which had been saved from the fire by the ancient City defence immediately behind it. He was closing the eyes of an old man, newly dead.

'A jeweller of Hatton Garden,' he said. 'Proud of supplying emeralds to Anne of Denmark, back in King James' time.' Francis stood, and sighed. 'The mortality returns will say he died of old age. But his heart was broken, so it was the fire that killed him, right enough.'

We spoke a little of what we had both done during the day, but I thought it neither the time nor the place to tell Francis of the attempted killing of the King, nor my part in preventing it. There would be ample opportunity for the exchange of further confidences in the fullness of time.

The great confusion began about ten. First there were shouts in the distance, then a drunken fellow ran through the crowd of exhausted, desperate people, down one of the tortuous paths between the tents and shelters.

'The Temple's ablaze again! The fire's been started anew by the Papists! The French army's in the City, fifty thousand strong! There's a regiment of them at the foot of Coleman Street, marching for the Moorgate!'

From all around came similar shouts. The French were literally yards away. They would kill the men, rape the women, and plunder the precious possessions of both.

Then the screams started. A great wail of terror, the sound rising to heaven like the lamentations of the Israelites.

'This is madness,' I said to Francis. 'A French army can't materialise out of thin air. There's been no intelligence of a landing!'

'Hysteria,' said the Reverend Gale, buckling on his markedly unclerical sword. 'I saw many a case of it during the civil wars. Men swearing blind they'd seen entire armies of Irish papists slaughtering honest folk in the next town up the road. Many a town was abandoned or burned due to panic and false rumours.'

There was no time to give any real thought to the notion that a new fire had indeed broken out at the Temple, perhaps threatening Ravensden House. For the shouts and rumours racing through the thousands packed into Moorfields were having their effect. People were picking up their sacks and infants and fleeing northward, trampling down the shelters of others, not caring if anyone was underfoot. A great mass of humanity pressed toward the exits from the fields, especially northward toward the new burying-ground in Bunhill Fen, screaming that the enemy was at hand.

'Dear Lord,' said Francis, 'hundreds will be crushed – thousands!'

Yet there was a second tide of people, too, moving in precisely the opposite direction. The flood moving northward consisted principally of women, children and the old, but the one that marched purposefully toward London Wall and the Moorgate contained only men. Young men. Angry men.

'Arm! Arm!' was their cry. 'Avenge London! Save our womenfolk from ravishment! Fuck the Frogs and the Butterboxes!'

Fights were breaking out among the crowd. It was turning into a riot.

'Sceptres!' I cried. Julian Carvell and the other dozen men of my ship looked at me expectantly. 'Form line!'

The men fanned out, blocking the way from that corner of the fields toward Moorgate. There are few sights more terrifying than that of a body of English seamen intent on a fight, and the men advancing to do battle with an imaginary French army – or to slaughter every innocent foreigner they came across – halted abruptly, the men at the back careering into those at the front.

'We are men of the King's ship *Royal Sceptre*,' I shouted. 'We have fought the French. We have captured a great French ship, the *Jeanne d'Arc*, which even now lies as a prize in the Medway river.' There was murmuring now. Many would have heard of our battle, which had been reported in the *Gazette* and plagiarised in bad woodcuts aimed at the illiterate. 'If a French or Dutch army had landed, my friends, we would know of it!'

'He lies! The French are here! Look now, toward Moorgate!'

Angry shouts of defiance mingled with the sounds of men running, as several of the brave fellows of a few minutes earlier fled at the sight of what they assumed to be King Louis' musketeers, filing out into Moorfields through the Tudor gatehouse, intent upon rape, plunder and murder.

The terror lasted only for a moment; the moment it took for the many lanterns and blazing torches illuminating the fields to reveal the familiar red uniforms of troops from the London Trained Bands and the royal Life Guards.

* * *

It took hours to quell the riot completely. There were new rumours and new shouts all through the night. There were the diehards who were convinced that the Trained Bands were actually French dragoons in disguise, wearing English uniforms to lull their victims. There were the fanatics who proclaimed that it did not matter if these really were English troops: they were the instruments of the Duke of York and thus of Popery and arbitrary government, sent to enslave or murder God-fearing people. Fights broke out at the slightest provocation, the Sceptres and I intervening to break up at least a half dozen of them. Slowly, though, order returned, and in whole swathes of the fields, tired, desperate people lay down and tried to find some sleep. Miraculously, few, if any, seemed to have died, although there were countless cases of broken limbs and other injuries.

With daylight, hungover men looked sheepishly at each other. Shamefaced youths, who had been all for fighting the French a few hours before, slunk back to their mothers. Francis disappeared into the crowd, intent on providing reassurance to those who still feared. The Sceptres and I went back into the City, through the Moorgate, and devoured a breakfast of bread, ale and mutton at a tavern close by Armourers' Hall, which had just avoided the flames and the fate of so many other livery halls. I had just ordered the men to return to the ship at Woolwich when I heard cheering at the end of the lane, went to investigate, and saw a familiar figure upon horseback, flanked by red-coated guards.

Carvell and I followed the King back into Moorfields. Thus I was close behind him when he halted in the middle of that great space, a vast but quiet and respectful crowd forming all around him. So I heard the speech that Charles the Second addressed to his people.

'My friends,' he began. 'Good subjects all. First, so that there should be no repetition of what happened here last night, I assure you that the enemy has not landed. Prince Rupert keeps command of the sea, and not one French or Dutch soldier stands upon English soil.' The King scanned the thousands of dirty, frightened people before him – although how many actually heard him was quite another matter. 'My heart bleeds for the loss you have suffered – the loss we have all suffered. For make no mistake, I have suffered too. London has been dear to England's kings since the days of the Confessor. It is the jewel in our crown. So if God has seen fit to destroy London, then it is a judgement upon England, and upon England's King.' I noticed a few smirks; even in the solemnity of the occasion, not a few – myself included – were thinking of Charles Stuart's notorious whoring. 'But we will rebuild it. I give you my word upon that – the word of the King. Legal obstacles will be swept aside. You will have new houses, better houses, better and wider streets. There will be a new Guildhall and a new Royal Exchange, greater and better than those the fire has consumed. We will build the churches anew. Above all, we will rebuild Saint Paul's into a fitting monument to God's glory.' There were cheers now, and applause. 'So, yes, you will have to sleep under the stars for days, even weeks. But long before winter comes, you will be safe again – safe in the new, rising London, of which we will all be proud. So for now, be of good comfort, dear people, and know that you have the love of your King.'

A great cheer went up, hats were flung into the air, and 'God save the King!' re-echoed around Moorfields.

Charles the Second had never been more loved, would never be so loved again. Every man, woman and child listening to him that day had heard the stories of how he and the Duke of York had heaved water buckets or wielded spades alongside their subjects, oblivious to the threat of regicide. They had battled to save London, despite what London had done to their father. I was one of the few people in

Moorfields who knew that all Charles Stuart's kind words about his capital city were cant and hypocrisy, for like all the Stuarts, he detested the place. But this King was politician enough to know that you tell people what they want to hear, and he was a master of that.

Of course, the outpouring of unvarnished affection towards Charles Stuart did not last. In truth, it barely lasted until the winter. But there, amid the tents and timber shelters erected all across Moorfields, I witnessed it, and remember it still.

* * *

The King dismounted to speak with individual members of the crowd, who kissed his hand as though he were the Second Coming. I pushed my way through, Julian Carvell following close behind me, and bowed when I was before the King.

'Damn it, Matt Quinton,' said Charles Stuart, 'are there six of you now? You've been everywhere, man. You and my brother, too. Thank God England had men prepared to exert themselves so! More than some others, that's certain. Come, though, Matt, I'll tell you a witty story, lately told me by Sir William Penn. Now, tell me, what kind of thing did men bury for safety during the fire, eh?'

'I heard of many a goldsmith burying his horde in cellars, Majesty.'

'Gold, naturally. Penn buried his wine – also good English common sense, that. But our friend Mister Pepys buried his *Parmesan cheese!*'

The King laughed, and I joined in dutifully, as did the Life Guards within earshot. Unlike them, though, I knew Sam Pepys, and knew it was exactly the kind of thing he would do.

'So who's this fellow, Matt?' said the King, scrutinising Carvell.

'This, Your Majesty, is the bold coxswain from the *Royal Sceptre* who taught me the stratagem for blowing up buildings.'

Carvell bowed deeply, and the King examined him still more closely.

'To think, Sir Matthew, that *I* am known as the Black Boy. Well, here's a pass. A most excellent pass. Up, man, and take the hand of your King!'

Carvell rose, reached out uncertainly, and kissed, then shook, the proferred royal hand.

'M-majesty!' he stammered. I had never before seen the garrulous, jolly fellow so tongue-tied.

'Your name, good fellow?'

'Carvell, Majesty. Late of your royal colony of Virginia.'

'Virginia, eh? That explains it. You must tell me of Virginia, Master Carvell, for I have a mind to keep you close at hand. Such eminent service as you have rendered deserves reward, and I have the very thing in mind. The shipkeeper of the *Royal Escape* is lately dead. Sir Matthew, would you say this fellow is qualified for the post?'

'Amply so, Your Majesty.'

'Excellent. And you, Coxswain Carvell. You have facilitated my second royal escape, by God, so what say you to taking charge of the first?'

It would have been nearly possible to cram an entire sheep into Carvell's gaping mouth.

'Your Majesty's bounty is… is…'

'Splendid. A black boy to mind the ship that saved the Black Boy – what could be better? Then we are agreed. I'll get my brother to command Mister Pepys to draw up a warrant. That's assuming he's finished exhuming his cheese, of course.'

The King laughed, mounted, and rode off, leaving the captain of the *Royal Sceptre* and the new shipkeeper of the *Royal Escape* alone. But Julian Carvell seemed to be on another planet, as though a cannon-of-seven had gone off in his ear. In one sense, the *Royal Escape* was the meanest vessel in the inventory of the King's Navy: a simple Brighton fishing smack, no more. But in another, it was by far the most important ship in England. For this was the craft that had secretly smuggled Charles Stuart to safety in France following his defeat at the Battle of

Worcester at the hands of Oliver Cromwell and his army. For weeks, the King had made his way across England in disguise, constantly in fear of being recognised and captured, hiding from Roundhead patrols – most memorably, in the branches of an oak tree at Boscobel House, and then disguised implausibly as perhaps the only six-foot-tall woman in England. But finally, he got to the coast, and the captain of the smack was persuaded to take him across the Channel, despite knowing full well who he was. Thus the humble vessel saved the life of the King, and when he was restored to his throne, he bought it, rechristened it *Royal Escape*, and moored it opposite the Palace of Whitehall, as a permanent reminder of his good fortune; and, indeed, as a warning, to ensure he never went on such travels again.

'Jesus' sake, Sir Matthew,' said Carvell, at last, 'what do I do?'

'What you do, Mister Carvell, is to gather some of your fellow Sceptres, find an alehouse, get them to toast your good fortune, and get constable-baiting drunk. And if you wish to consider that an order, you may do so.'

* * *

I made my way westward, then south down Shoe Lane, through the smouldering ruins of Farringdon Without, then out onto Fleet Street. Everywhere, people were swarming over the ruins: householders trying to locate the charred remains of their homes, shopkeepers and artisans salvaging what they could from the wreckage of their businesses. Blackened brick chimneys poked above piles of rubble, the only standing testimony to the houses they had once warmed. Children played particularly lengthy games of hide-and-seek, there being innumerable places in which to hide nearly indefinitely. To the east, everything was devastation, across the Fleet River and up to the blackened, half-fallen walls of Paul's Church.

I turned westward again and saw how, quite suddenly, the devastation stopped. It was as though an invisible wall had been erected, beyond which the fire could not pass. There, to the south of Fleet Street, stood the Temple and its glorious round-naved church. To the north, Saint Dunstan in the West survived, seeming a kind of gatehouse to the untouched buildings beyond it.

One of the first of which was Ravensden House.

My brother's wish for the great fire to consume it had not been granted. The house still stood, entirely intact; or at least, as intact as its manifold cracks and defects permitted it to be. I found Musk inspecting it for damage.

'How it remains standing is a mystery that passeth all understanding,' he said. 'In five hundred years' time, antiquaries will be crawling all over it and puzzling over how it still survives, when the rest of London's been reclaimed by forests and meadows centuries before.'

'Are you turned seer now, Musk? The new Mother Shipton for our times?'

He gave me a look that indicated the question was beneath contempt.

'Expect you'll want to know where Her Ladyship is. Still at Whitehall, is where she is, supervising the loading of everything that's now got to be brought back here. That's if she's not taking tea with Mistress Stewart or Lady Ossory.'

'And her…'

'Her health excellent, child kicking.'

'And Captain Ollivier?'

'With the Duke of York. Now the fire's over, His Royal Highness's thoughts have turned back to the sea, it seems, and the prospect of battle with the French. But he'll never get anything out of the captain. The Duke's too tight with his wine, thinks half a glass is enough for an entire meal. If it was me, I'd pour an entire hogshead down Captain Ollivier, and would soon have every one of King Louis' secrets out of him.'

I left Musk to his inspection and his complaining, and went to my brother. Charles had been installed in a bed newly erected in the library, on the ground floor at the back of the house, thus obviating any need to get him back upstairs. He was evidently much improved, sitting up against his pillows, studying various papers in cipher.

'Matt,' he said, embracing me as warmly as he ever did. His voice was stronger, too. 'Well, my young brother – the saviour of the realm from a second regicide!'

'The King did much to save himself,' I said. 'And Goodman undoubtedly would have done the deed, were it not for Mistress Behn.'

'Thank God. I dread to think what would have transpired if he had succeeded. The infant Duke of Cambridge made King at three years old, and who for a regent? His mother, Clarendon's daughter? There would be rebellion in the blinking of an eye, and civil war would be come again.'

I nodded. The chief minister, the Earl of Clarendon, was universally detested, not least because his ugly daughter had ensnared the Duke of York into marriage through the simple stratagem of lifting her skirts and grabbing hold of his manhood.

'It's a miracle there was only the one attempt,' I said. 'The King and the Duke earned much credit with the people by being out on the streets, helping to pull down buildings and pump water. But it would have taken only one bitter old former New Model trooper with a pistol or a blade to hand.'

'The paradox of royalty,' said Charles. 'Be remote and aloof, as our royal brothers' late father was, and you are hated. Go out among the people, and, yes, you might be better loved – but you also place yourself in harm's way, and become a target for every malcontent and madman in the land.'

We talked for a while of the fate of London, the great buildings that were gone, the wealthy men said to be ruined, and those who had demonstrated craven cowardice during the fire (the name of Sir Thomas Bloodworth, Lord Mayor, being high in that particular reckoning). Then, as our conversation seemed to be drawing to an end, when he was clearly tiring and in need of rest, Charles abruptly changed the subject.

'Now that the matter of the Horsemen is concluded, I have thought fit to send Mistress Behn back to Antwerp. There, she is eminently useful to the King's cause. Here, though…'

It seemed as if he intended to say more, but thought better of it. I wondered: *does he know?* Even if he did not know of the sin I had committed with the lady in question, had he somehow heard of the interest shown in her by both the King and the Duke of York? The politics of the court were fraught enough without Aphra Behn becoming a new mistress for either Charles or James Stuart – or, God help us, both – and Lord Percival might very well have calculated that temptation ought to be distanced from both brothers, as well as from Sir Matthew Quinton.

As always, though, my brother's face was unreadable.

Nevertheless, my thoughts were in turmoil for the rest of the day, especially so when Cornelia returned from Whitehall. As we embraced, and she wept copiously – for she, too, knew of what had transpired in Great Saint Bartholomew's – a part of me wanted Aphra gone, and far away in Antwerp. But another part of me wanted her close. Very close.

Chapter Twenty-Four

I could have let her go without a word.

Perhaps I should have done. Indeed, even as I rode out over London Bridge, that was still what I was minded to do. True, I had an explicit order from the Lord High Admiral, directing me to return to the *Royal Sceptre* at Woolwich to expedite her fitting out for sea; but both the Duke of York and I knew that this was a fiction, for my ship would not be coming out of dry dock before the winter. Whether she would come out after that was a moot point, as there was already talk that the King had too little money to contemplate setting out a fleet the following year, especially with London, the great fount of money, in ruins. On the other hand, Woolwich removed me from any prospect of an encounter with the Duke of Albemarle, who had arrived in London to save it, only to find all the fires put out days before His Obesity returned to the capital. It removed, me, too, from any further obligation to Captain Ollivier, whose parole had been taken up by the Duke of York himself. And it also removed me from the risk of betraying myself to Cornelia, although I had to trust in God that Phineas Musk would not somehow give me away instead. But the Lady Astraea was aboard a ship at Gravesend, waiting for the wind, and Gravesend was not so very far from Woolwich.

At the south end of London Bridge, I halted and turned in my saddle. When I had last been at that precise spot, only some three weeks earlier – *three weeks*, for Jesu's sake – I had looked out at a London that was still intact and proud. Now, I could have been looking upon a scene painted by old Brueghel. Only a few blackened remnants of church towers, walls and brick chimneys stood above a vast heap of rubble, some of it smouldering. And overlooking it all, the shattered remains of old Paul's, its roof and large parts of the walls gone. Yet even from the south bank, I could see tiny figures of men clearing space amid the wreckage, starting to erect the timber frames of new buildings. There had been no official permission to do so; but that was the way of Londoners. Nothing was more certain than that a new London would rise from the ashes. Whether it would be the sort of London that the King and his advisers in such matters, the likes of Christopher Wren, wished to see, was quite another matter.

I rode on, down the familiar highway that led through Deptford and Greenwich toward Kent and the sea. I cut inland to avoid the sight of Woolwich yard and the masts of the *Royal Sceptre*; I would be there soon enough, fighting pointless battles with Identifiable Pett. Instead, I pressed on to Gravesend, where the usual mass of ships huddled beneath the protecting, comforting walls of the blockhouse, some waiting to proceed up river, others out into the open sea.

Aphra Behn's ship was a small flyboat, bound for Antwerp. The lady in question watched my approach as I was rowed out from the shore, and was waiting for me on deck when I got aboard.

'Sir Matthew Quinton,' she said. 'I had not expected you. Not expected you at all.'

Now that I was there, a few feet in front of her, overwhelmed once again by her charms, I realised I had not the slightest idea what I intended to say to her.

'I – I could not let you go without a word.'

She smiled.

'Ah, the famous Quinton sense of honour. I'd have thought you knew enough of the world to realise that there are times when it is better to let matters rest – to part, indeed, without a word. The firing of London and the saving of the lives of the royal brothers would have marked a fitting break between us.'

I knew that her words were true, and sensible, and right. But to hear them from her lips felt like a culverin ball hammering into my chest and blasting my heart clear of my body.

'I wanted to say – that is, I meant to say…'

She raised a finger to my lips. The touch of her flesh, even such a tiny part of her flesh, made me shiver.

'To you, perhaps, I am a temptress,' said Aphra. 'What the preachers would call a fallen woman, a brazen harlot, or words to that effect. Perhaps, though, since the King's return, we live in a time where the more enlightened might think of me as a woman of independence, striving to make her way in the world by whatever means she can. Or at least, I hope they would.' She looked away, but I could have sworn there was a hint of a tear in her eye. 'Ours was but a single, strange moment in time, in this strangest of years. The year of the Great Fire. The year of the Beast.' A hint of her smile returned. 'You should put me behind you, Matthew. Soon, you will have a child, and your world will change. And if you become Earl of Ravensden, it will change even more. But there is no world you can inhabit that has a place in it for the Lady Astraea.'

I could think of no reply; no reply that mattered, at any rate.

'You will be safe?' was all I could manage.

'Those whom I watch in Flanders, on behalf of your brother and Lord Arlington, are milksops compared with our friends the Horsemen. But don't concern yourself for me, Matthew. Concern yourself for the things that matter in your world – that truly matter. Who knows, though, perhaps one day I shall model a character upon you.' She was smiling broadly again. 'A worthy knight. A man of rare honour in a dishonourable world. Yes, I think a playwright could make something of that. With embellishments, of course, and dramatic licence, for that is what we do.' There was a curious edge to the smile now. 'A little more roguish, perhaps. More of a rover.'

I could see the shipmaster fidgeting. I knew that stance: the eternal impatience of the captain who knows that the conditions are very nearly right to take his ship to sea. The wind was set fair for Flanders, and the wind must not be denied.

* * *

We parted, and I returned ashore. A little later, from the roof of Gravesend blockhouse, beneath the fluttering colours of the Union Flag that flew above it, I watched as the ship carrying Aphra Behn unfurled sail, picked up momentum, and began to move down Long Reach. Soon, it disappeared behind the land and the other hulls and sails thronging that stretch of the Thames. And as I watched it, I struggled with all that welled up inside me.

When I next met Aphra, some years later, both of our circumstances were different; very different indeed. For one thing, I was a father. The birth was long and difficult, the child a thing of wonder, the mother doting, and the christening, held on a freezing winter's day in the miraculously preserved Temple Church, a splendid affair, proving that new life was returning to London. My brother, restored to as good a state of health as it was his wont to enjoy, was able to attend, as was my mother, the Dowager Countess, who managed to struggle down the icy roads from Bedfordshire. Tristram was there, resplendent in his doctoral robes, as was my sister Elizabeth and her husband Sir Venner Garvey, now a member of the Parliamentary committee enquiring into the causes of the Great Fire of London. A committee that was blissfully unaware of the existence and purpose of the Horsemen of the Apocalypse, which was exactly how my brother and I intended it to remain.

But all thoughts of conspiracies, and politics, and even of a return to sea, were put aside as Cornelia and I went to the font. There, we were joined by the principal godfather, grinning broadly. King Charles the Second loved children almost as much as he loved the act of begetting them.

And so Francis Gale baptised the sand-haired, keen-eyed, curious infant who from henceforward would go by the name of Madeleine Quinton.

Epilogue

'Make way, there! Make way for the Honourable Sir Matthew Quinton!'

I can still hear Phineas Musk's unmistakeable voice, can smell the mass of humanity pressing into the courtroom.

'Make way, I say!'

Phineas Musk enjoyed few things in life better than pummelling those who were too slow to get out of his way, and clearing a path for me into the courthouse provided him with much opportunity for pummelling. For the crowd attempting to squeeze into the court, hastily designated to replace the burned Old Bailey, was a large and fevered one. This, after all, was the chance to look upon the face of the man who had supposedly confessed to starting the Great Fire of London, and it seemed as though the whole of the cremated city had turned out for the occasion.

Musk obtained a stool for me – I did not enquire how, but suspected that it involved more pummelling – and I settled down to view the proceedings. Insofar as I could, at any rate; the throng meant that even someone as tall as I could not quite see everything. Of course, I had been in a courtroom before, but Bedford Assizes could not compare to this in spectacle, and the trials of those caught poaching on Ravensden land certainly could not compare for attendance, nor the atmosphere of gravity, anger, and vengeance. Nor could a circuit judge compare with the red-robed, bewigged magnificence of the Lord Chief Justice of England himself, Sir John Kelyng, who had earned the undying respect of my mother by virtue of his having sentenced the fanatic Bunyan at Bedford Assizes.

My bones turned to marble, my flesh to cold gunmetal, my blood to ice.

A fleeting gap had opened in front of me, and through it, I caught my first glimpse of the accused. Since Aphra's departure for Antwerp, I had been principally at Woolwich dockyard, returning only that morning, and was thus out of touch with London news. So the only thing I knew of the supposed arsonist was his name. Robert Hubert, a Frenchman, originally of Rouen, latterly of London. But names did not matter, there in the courtroom, as I shivered at the implications of what I saw in front of me.

For I had seen this man, this Robert Hubert, before.

He was the simpleton in the Swedish ship at Saint Katherine's, when Aphra and I had first boarded it in search of the Four Horsemen.

*　*　*

Slowly, very slowly, my heart quietened, and feeling returned to my limbs. Robert Hubert's presence aboard the *Milkmaid* could surely have been nothing but coincidence; how could it be otherwise? Indeed, this conviction was swiftly reinforced as the trial began, and the pathetic nature of the accused Frenchman became apparent.

'How do you plead?' demanded Kelyng, after the reading of the charge.

Silence.

A clerk mumbled something to the Lord Chief Justice: presumably, the information that Robert Hubert could speak almost no English. Kelyng rolled his eyes to the heavens, shook his head at the jury, growled an order to the clerk – seemingly, to find an interpreter, for a pale, stooping law student from one of the Temples was swiftly plucked out of the crowd and fulfilled this role for the rest of the trial – and then turned back to the accused.

'How do you plead?' repeated Kelyng, this time in execrable French. *'Coupable, ou non coupable?'*

'Coupable,' said Hubert, so quietly that most of those at the back of the court missed what he said.

There was a groan from those who had heard. A guilty plea meant no evidence, no explanation, and no entertainment. Kelyng saw the matter rather differently, and smiled. He nodded to the clerk of the court to make ready the black cap. No doubt his thoughts were on a quick sentence and an early dinner.

Suddenly, though, Hubert laughed, as if at some private joke.

'Coupable,' he said, *'non.'*

Loud murmuring ran around the courtroom, and perplexed jurors whispered frantically to each other.

'What in God's name does that mean?' snapped the Lord Chief Justice, in English. He resorted to French once again. 'Are you pleading guilty, or not guilty? I remind you that you have signed a confession.'

The Frenchman stared at him as though he were the man in the moon. His mouth opened and closed several times.

Then, loudly and happily, he said, *'Non coupable.'*

The crowd cheered.

* * *

Within an hour, the hostility that had been present in the court at the beginning of proceedings was all but abated. Within another, there was a palpable sense of pity. By then, Hubert had changed his plea two or three times; or rather, nobody was entirely certain whether he had or not, least of all his confused interpreter, the jury, and Lord Chief Justice Kelyng. The watchmaker seemed to be in another world, engaged in some peculiar dialogue with himself. He was certainly incapable of mounting his own defence, as any Englishman brought before a court would expect to do.

Lowman, the keeper of the Surrey county gaol, was called as a witness, and testified that some days before the trial he had taken Hubert to St Katherine's Dock, so that the watchmaker could show him where the Swedish ship that brought him to London had lain. He could find no such ship, said Lowman. Of course he could not: he was looking for a ship called the *Skipper*, which is what Hubert, in his written confession, had said it was called. The poor, confused Frenchman had somehow conflated the colloquial title of the ship's master with the name of the ship itself – or, if you prefer, he had all too easily thrown Lowman off the scent of the real ship, the *Milkmaid*.

I knew, as almost no one else in the courtroom did, that the ship in question was long gone. It had been released by direct order of the Privy Council, responding to a most pressing request from Lord Leijonbergh, the Swedish ambassador. He, in turn, was seemingly acting at the behest of Lord Hagerstierna, the richest man in Sweden; and Hagerstierna was a close friend of both Magnus de la Gardie, the High Chancellor, and that kingdom's enigmatic former ruler, Queen Christina, both of whom I had encountered during a desperate business only a few months before.* In the more than sixty years since the Great Fire and the trial of Robert Hubert, I have sometimes wondered whether that was all mere coincidence: whether it was nothing, or was everything. I never pursued it, but perhaps one day, another man will.

Anyhow, on that October day in 1666, Lowman continued his testimony. At the Frenchman's insistence, he said – for this had been during one of the interludes when Hubert was proudly proclaiming his guilt – he had taken Hubert from St Katherine's into the charred ruins of London, where the watchmaker made unerringly for the site

* *The Lion of Midnight*

of Farriner's bakery. How could he have known where it was, unless he had been there before? There were knowing nods all around the courtroom. But Musk and I exchanged a glance. Even a two-year-old child could have pointed out the spot where the Great Fire of London began: for it was the one place among all the ruins where, every day without fail, a large crowd gathered to stare pointlessly at the charred pile of wood and rubble that had once been Pudding Lane.

Finally, Hubert himself was called to give evidence, muttering *'coupable ou non coupable'* time and time again, as though he were some lesser version of Shakespeare's Dane.

'And how did you put the fireball within the bakery?' barked Kelyng.

The student translated, and Hubert became animated, waving his hands, then mimicking the act of pushing something upwards. The student leaned close to catch his mumblings, then turned to address the jury; the youth seemed to be revelling in the attention, no doubt reckoning that an impressive performance before the Lord Chief Justice of England might advance his future legal career.

'He says, My Lord, that he placed it on the end of a pole, and put it through an open window.'

'On the street side?'

The question was translated back to Hubert.

'Yes, My Lord, on the street side.'

Farriner, the baker, a large man who had evidently sampled too much of his own produce, was sitting close to the accused, following proceedings intently. As well he might, for upon the verdict hinged the question of whether both the current populace of London and the whole of posterity until kingdom come blamed Robert Hubert and Thomas Farriner for the Great Fire of London.

The baker got to his feet.

'My Lord, there was never any window on that side!'

'Be silent, Mister Farriner!' snapped Kelyng. 'You will have your chance to give evidence in due course.'

The baker sat down amid a considerable hubbub which, for some moments, Kelyng did not seek to restrain. Not a few brows were furrowed now, Musk's among them.

'What's he playing at?' he said. 'If he wants the Frog to hang, why not stay silent about the window? Or agree that there really was a window? Nothing to prove otherwise, after all. The evidence is a pile of ash, like the rest of London.'

I nodded. Thomas Farriner would surely want Robert Hubert to swing. Moreover, he, his son, and his daughter, were three of those who had brought the original indictment against the Frenchman. Suddenly, though, I saw that there could be only one plausible explanation for the baker's behaviour; and my opinion was reinforced by the attitude of his children, who were scowling and giving him black stares.

In truth, Thomas Farriner was a remarkably stupid man.

* * *

The afternoon wore on, with Hubert's testimony becoming ever more rambling and self-contradictory. There was more and more shuffling in the courtroom, and a steadily increasing level of whispering as the audience's attention wandered. My mind drifted away to thoughts of Cornelia, and Aphra, and my brother, and my ship. The fleet had come in to pay off, and the forlorn attempt to get the *Royal Sceptre* back to sea had been abandoned. Sir Robert Holmes was come up to London to deliver a report to the King on the fleet's condition, and I had promised to drink with him once the day's proceedings in court were concluded. In this particular instance, no one expected the course of justice to take very long. The next day, I was to dine at Ravensden House with Julian Delacourt, Lord Carrignavar, whose conscience had mastered him after all, so he was destined for the long road to County Kerry and a lifetime of worry.

From time to time, my attention returned to Robert Hubert. The poor fellow was a lunatic, as was evident to all. Quite why he should insist so vehemently that he had put a fireball into Farriner's bakery in Pudding Lane, and thus seek the martyrdom of the noose, was a mystery. But it did not matter. Robert Hubert would swing for the Great Fire of London, whether he had started it or not. And it was obvious to me, just as it was obvious to every man from the Lord Chief Justice of England downwards, that he had not started it.

Then he said something that I nearly missed. Something that teetered at the very edge of my mind, almost falling out of it entirely. But then he repeated it, and added one point of detail that caused me to sit bolt upright upon my stool.

At first Hubert had stated that he was part of a small army of twenty-four men, intent on destroying the city. Of course, there was one very obvious flaw with this testimony. As I looked around the courtroom, and saw the shaking heads and the furrowed brows, I knew that one did not have to be a captain in the King's Navy to wonder how, exactly, that could be so, if the would-be destroyer had been aboard a ship that had not been destined for London at all, and only sent there as a result of its fortuitous capture at sea. But then, as so often during the trial, Hubert changed his testimony, very nearly in mid-sentence, his interpreter struggling to keep up or to make sense of his words. Now there was a new number of conspirators, and the watchmaker proclaimed it time and time again. *Quatre*. Hubert seemed to be claiming that he was one of four men who designed to fire London. *Four men*. And he gave the name of the man, a fellow Frenchman, who had recruited him, and come to London with him in the same ship; so this must have been the second man, the older man, that we had encountered aboard the *Milkmaid*.

Stephen Piedloe.

It was a name I had heard before, only once, and which I had very nearly forgotten. But Aphra had mentioned it in passing, as a mere detail during the conversation on our coach journey to Chelsea College in August, when we were first setting out on our frantic search for Mene Tekel and the Precious Man. She was recalling her dealings with the Horsemen in Surinam and trying to describe their appearances to me. And then the name of Stephen Piedloe had come up.

Phineas Musk's face told me at once that it was a name he knew, too. He would have read it on the papers he'd checked during our first visit to the *Milkmaid*. The papers I had judged so insignificant that I'd never even asked him what they contained, and that Musk had judged so insignificant that he'd forgotten their contents almost immediately. The papers that contained the names of the two Frenchmen we had discovered.

No, poor, mad, soon-to-be-dead Robert Hubert could not possibly have been one of the Four Horsemen of the Apocalypse.

But the French Huguenot who had supposedly died before going to Surinam, the colleague of Schermer, De Wildt and Goodman – the one Horseman whom Aphra Behn had never seen, and thus could not have identified even if she encountered him face-to-face, say, on a ship moored off Saint Katherine's Dock – most certainly was.

Stephen Piedloe was the name of the fourth Horseman of the Apocalypse.

* * *

'You could not have done any other, you know,' said Charles Quinton, Earl of Ravensden, who was sufficiently recovered to go out with me in his coach to watch the execution of Robert Hubert at Tyburn.

It was the seventeenth day of October in the year of Our Lord, 1666; or, as some still had it, the year of the antichrist. A fortnight since the jury had brought in a swift and entirely expected verdict, and a black cloth had been placed atop Lord Chief Justice Kelyng's wig.

'I could have stopped the trial,' I said, albeit without conviction.

All the guilt and rage I felt that day in the courtroom, all the doubts and fears I had experienced since, came back to me in a great wave.

'On what grounds? One name? Kelyng would have slapped you down, and rightly so. You had no evidence, Matt. No proof. We do not know – will never know – whether you killed Schermer and de Wildt before or after they attempted to fire the City. We will never know whether Piedloe succeeded in their stead. For all we know, it could have been pure chance that a fire broke out in Pudding Lane on the very night that the Horsemen were preparing their attack. Or God's will, if you prefer. One way or the other, London was destined to burn that night. You couldn't have stopped destiny, Matt. No man can ever stop it. Not even Lord Percival.'

The coach was moving slowly through a vast crowd, thronging all sides of the scaffold, probably thousands strong. Musk was sitting by the coachman, both of them using their whips to clear a path. The scaffold was in sight now, surrounded by a ring of musketeers from the Trained Bands. Robert Hubert was already upon it.

'And it is that man's destiny to hang,' I said. 'That poor, simple fellow who barely knows what he says.'

'He made his own destiny. God knows why – perhaps it is just the weakness of his mind, as you say, or perhaps there is more to it. After all, brother, some men seek nothing more than martyrdom.'

'But martyrdom in what cause?'

Charles looked out at the scene, and was silent for some time. The noose was around Hubert's neck. We could not hear the priest's prayers, although we were close enough; there was a constant noise from the crowd, jeers, boos and angry shouts, and it grew louder by the second.

'Another thing we shall never know,' said my brother. 'Perhaps no cause other than this – for history to discount the notion that such a colossal horror as the Great Fire of London could possibly have been started by such a deluded simpleton, and thus conclude that it could only have been an accident.'

At that moment, Robert Hubert dropped. His legs danced, and

then were still. The body hung limp in the breeze. I can remember the noise that the crowd made, for in all the years of my life since that day, I have never heard anything remotely like it again. At once a cheer and a scream, it seemed as loud as the greatest broadside, and shook the very ground itself.

'And for history not to pursue Stephen Piedloe,' I said, as the noise subsided a little.

'Amen,' said Charles, although whether to my words, or to some prayer he had silently offered for the dead, I could not tell.

The mob was already flooding away from the scaffold, pressing so tightly around us that it was impossible for our coach to move. Hubert's body had been cut down, and was being bundled into a cart; it was common knowledge that the corpse was to go to the College of Surgeons, there to be dissected. The carter started his donkeys, a file of troopers from the Trained Bands fell in on each side, and the cart began to come down Tyburn Hill, directly towards us.

The cart was very nearly alongside our coach when it began. To this day, I am not certain whether it was an accident or not. Whether a meanly dressed bald man from among the crowd simply stumbled due to the press of people, and stretched out his hand to grab the site of the cart for support. Or whether he had intent in his mind from the very start. In either event, the troopers did nothing to stop him. The fellow pulled himself up, looked into the cart, then struck out and punched the corpse of Robert Hubert.

A woman shrieked. Not a shriek of horror, but one of delight. She flung herself forward, pulled herself into the cart, and began to tear off Hubert's shirt. A short man climbed up beside her, then another, then a boy of ten or so, who snatched the Frenchman's left hand and tried to rip off his thumb. The troopers did nothing. More and more climbed aboard; more and more hands snatched at the watchmaker's corpse.

Within seconds, fingers were tearing at Hubert's flesh, pulling it apart, ripping it from the bone. A woman scoured out an eyeball. A man produced a large knife and began to hack off the head. But as he did so, the Frenchman's ghastly, torn face turned toward me. To this very day, I can still see the expression that Robert Hubert must have had on his face when he died, and I will swear upon oath that it was a smile.

The Great Fire of London
The Curious Case of the Fire-Raising Watchmaker, the Elusive Sea Captain, and the Queen of Sweden's Tailor

A HISTORICAL INVESTIGATION

Until I started researching and writing *Death's Bright Angel*, my knowledge of the Great Fire of London came from a combination of general knowledge, facts learned at school, TV programmes, Pepys' diary, and a couple of books on the matter, read more than a decade ago. I suspect, if pushed, most people would admit similar. However, I'd also taught the subject quite often, usually to twelve year olds (Year 8, in British education parlance), frequently employing ancient BBC educational programmes with shockingly cheap special effects. It's a subject that goes down well with schoolchildren – lots of drama and destruction, vivid first-hand accounts, even some humour ('he buried a *cheese*?'), and best of all, nobody dies; well, hardly anybody. Unsurprisingly, the Great Fire is a mainstay of the National Curriculum in History for schools in England and Wales, and some ten children's books about it have been published since 1995 alone. Within the same period, three full-length, fully referenced adult studies of the Fire have also gone into print.

J. D. DAVIES

I duly read or re-read all three of these books, and several earlier ones, as research for *Death's Bright Angel*, and as I did so, felt a mounting disquiet. All described mid-seventeenth-century London, the actual course of the Fire, and its various aftermaths, competently enough – sometimes quite brilliantly. But when it came to the aspect in which I was most interested, the different theories circulating at the time to explain why the Fire began, and especially the confessions, trial, and execution, of the supposedly simple-minded French watchmaker Robert Hubert, alarm bells rang.

All recent books on the Fire explicitly derive large parts of their accounts – of the theories, of the Fire's outbreak in Farriner's bakery in Pudding Lane,* – from a single earlier secondary source, *The Great Fire of London* by Walter George Bell. This was originally published in 1923 and republished several times since, and the principal primary source upon it relied, William Cobbett's *Complete Collection of State Trials*, was published between 1809 and 1826, incorporating earlier material from editions dating back to 1719. All the modern books accept without question Bell's judgement that 'this fact *(the accidental outbreak in the bakery)* does not admit of doubt… the judgment that must result from a calm consideration of the evidence, *[is]* that the Fire in its origin was due to carelessness, and was not criminal'.

What of it? Surely all that Bell (a journalist and astronomer, incidentally, not a historian) did was follow the orthodoxy rapidly accepted by enlightened contemporaries like Samuel Pepys, the orthodoxy allegedly followed by the Lord Chief Justice who had actually sentenced Hubert

---

* Or perhaps not in Pudding Lane; just before *Death's Bright Angel* went to press, the historian Dorian Gerhold discovered new evidence proving that the fire did not actually break out there at all, but in the part of Farriner's yard that backed onto what is now Monument Street *(Country Life*, 10 February 2016). Whether that affects the credibility of the evidence of Robert Hubert and Thomas Farriner would probably need to be established by further research.

and which, when partisan fervour and religious bigotry eventually died down, became accepted by most of the general public, too? The Great Fire began by accident; as I indicated in the note at the beginning of this book, Robert Hubert's confession to having started it was written off almost immediately, as it has been ever since, as the rambling of a madman who did not even arrive in London until after the Fire began.

Even so, I wanted to see exactly how Bell reached the conclusions, upon which all recent books about the Fire depend. I also wanted to examine the source material about Robert Hubert in a more forensic way than has been attempted before, and to see if there were any sources that had been completely ignored in previous studies. This might seem a curiously intensive research strategy for a work of fiction, but I knew from the outset that the storyline for *Death's Bright Angel* would only have sufficient drama if it posited arson, or strong suspicions of arson, as the cause of the Great Fire. To make the book as convincing as possible, I knew I had to investigate that possibility as rigorously as I could.

In other words: once a historian, always a historian.

1666: A YEAR OF PROPHECY

In Chapter Eight of this book, Matthew Quinton is briefed by Aphra Behn and the Earl of Ravensden about the extraordinary number of rumours and threats circulating during the summer of 1666 – what might now be termed 'terrorist chatter'. I took a liberty by bringing the doyenne of women playwrights back to London, when she actually spent the whole of that year in Antwerp, but as the plot of this book posits, she was certainly in Surinam, then an English colony, in 1663-4, when she was already acting as an agent for Charles II's government, a role she was still playing in Spanish Flanders in 1666 under the code name of Astraea (the elusive Mr Behn having died sometime between those dates, after a very brief marriage).

I also invented the names and 'back stories' of the book's 'Four Horsemen of the Apocalypse', with the debatable exception of the final plot twist concerning Stephen Piedloe. Apart from those elements of dramatic licence, everything recounted to Matthew in that chapter was actual intelligence that came before the King's government during that year, and the Rathbone Plot took place exactly as described. Rumours about potential rebel leaders called 'Mene Tekel' and 'the Precious Man' were legion, while it was widely believed that something dramatic, even cataclysmic, would take place on or around 3 September, the anniversary of the death of Oliver Cromwell and of two of his greatest victories, the battles of Dunbar and Worcester. Above all, many preachers, pundits and bar-room recidivists galore held forth on the supposed significance of the year 1666 itself: the date containing the number of the Beast.

As with all predictions (to date) of the world's end, this was a potent blend of wishful thinking, paranoia and hysteria. But the fact that the Great Fire of London took place after so many predictions, so many prophecies (even, inevitably, one from Nostradamus), and so much prayer on the part of the disaffected, was simply too great a coincidence for many at the time, and for many years afterwards. Just as on 9/11 and other occasions, the official explanation was just too pat. There had to have been some greater conspiracy afoot. Unfortunately for those of this mindset, the Great Fire of London's Osama Bin Laden (or Dick Cheney, depending on your viewpoint) seemed to be a mentally ill twenty-six-year-old French watchmaker named Robert Hubert.

ROBERT HUBERT: THE UNUSUAL SUSPECT

In a nutshell, the commonly accepted story is this.

During and after the Fire, many Londoners maintained that not only was the blaze begun deliberately, but that *they had actually witnessed people starting fires* (or, as is often the way in such cases, they knew someone who claimed to have witnessed it). In the short term, such stories helped generate the wave of xenophobia leading to several attacks on and attempted lynchings of French and Dutch residents of London in particular. A Frenchman was nearly torn apart because he was found to be carrying several 'fireballs', which turned out to be tennis balls. A poor widow was attacked on suspicion of having fireballs in her apron, and closer inspection revealed them to be chickens. This is the real historical (and hysterical) context underpinning the fictional attack on Cornelia Quinton and Captain Ollivier in this book.

Many of these tales of arson were eventually recounted to the Parliamentary investigation into the disaster, and are considered in more detail below, but one in particular developed an unstoppable momentum. This was the odd saga of one Robert Hubert, a twenty-six-year-old French watchmaker, who left the City after the Fire (as did many foreigners, fleeing both the flames and the wrath of the Londoners). He was apparently heading to one of the east coast ports when he was apprehended in the Romford area and taken before Carey Harvie, a Justice of the Peace, at Havering-atte-Bower.

The tale Hubert told Harvie was extraordinary. He claimed to have been one of twenty-four men, led by a fellow Frenchman named Stephen Piedloe, who had set out to destroy London. (Subsequently, Hubert would claim they originally intended to do so in 1665, but abandoned that plan due to the plague.) Hubert even confessed to Harvie that he had thrown a fireball into a building – although he said this was near the palace of Whitehall, and that he only did so after the fire in the City itself was already raging.

Hubert was sent up to London, to the White Lion Gaol in Southwark. He appeared at the substitute Old Bailey in October, and now told a different story. Now there were just four arsonists, including himself and Piedloe. He, Hubert, had been recruited in Paris by someone 'that he did not know, having never seen him before'. Hubert and Piedloe went to Stockholm, for reasons unknown, but took passage in a ship which brought them to London at the end of August. During the night of 1-2 September, Piedloe took him ashore, ending up before the bakery in Pudding Lane, where he told Hubert to put a fireball through a window. Hubert attached a ball to a long pole, lit it, and put it into the building, waiting to be certain that it was ablaze before making off. He claimed to be a Catholic, and to have carried out the attack for money. He had only received one gold coin from Piedloe, with a promise of five more when they got back to France. Despite all the contradictions in his evidence, Hubert clinched the case against himself by insisting on being taken by his gaoler, John Lowman, to identify the site of the bakery amidst the charred rubble of Pudding Lane, which he duly did, despite Lowman's best efforts to confuse him and get him to retract.

Some contemporaries clearly found it all unlikely, not least because the Farriners – who had good cause to encourage belief in Hubert's guilt – stated that there had never been a window where Hubert claimed to have inserted the fireball. Hubert's evidence was full of contradictions, and he pleaded not guilty at the beginning of his trial, thus effectively retracting his confession before Harvie, before reaffirming the confession once again, and then retracting it again on the scaffold. Even the notoriously draconian Lord Chief Justice Kelyng, who presided over the trial, said of Hubert, 'all his discourse was so disjointed that he did not believe him guilty'. The Lord Chancellor, the Earl of Clarendon, claimed that 'nobody present credited anything [Hubert] said', concluding that he must have been 'a poor distracted wretch, weary of his life, and chose to part with it this way'. Sir Edward Harley, one of the MPs who examined Hubert, reported that 'he said some extravagant things that savoured of a disordered mind'. But, faced with a confession that the accused simply refused to retract, despite all the doubts over its veracity, the jury had no alternative but to convict. Robert Hubert was hanged at

Tyburn on 17 October 1666;* his body, intended for dissection by the Barber Surgeons Company, was reputedly torn apart by a furious mob ('reputedly' being inadequate evidence for a historian, but ideal for a novelist seeking an ending for his book). Fifteen years later, the Swedish captain of the *Milkmaid*, the ship that supposedly carried Hubert to London, provided written evidence that he could not have started the Great Fire. According to the captain, Hubert did not go ashore until Tuesday, 4 September, two days after the blaze broke out in Pudding Lane. London had hanged an innocent man, albeit one who'd been determined to convince everybody he was guilty.

ROBERT HUBERT: EVERYBODY EXPECTS THE SPANISH INQUISITION

For many, Hubert's guilt was unquestionable. The Great Fire was

---

* All published sources about the Fire which provide a date for the execution, from *Wikipedia* to *The Oxford Dictionary of National Biography* via all modern books on the subject, claim that it took place on 27 October. Yet a report of the event can be found in a newsletter dated 20 October, addressed to Sir Edward Mansel of Margam Abbey, which has always been easily accessible in the *Calendar of State Papers*; the other events described in that newsletter also took place just before the 20th. This discrepancy can be explained by all writers having blindly followed British Library Additional Manuscript 27,962R, the despatches of the Florentine ambassador Giovanni Salvetti, seemingly the only source to give a precise date for Hubert's execution – which gives it as Wednesday 27 October, following his conviction on Monday 25. However, a simple countback from there would quickly reveal that, by this reckoning, 2September, the day on which the Great Fire began, was a Thursday, rather than the Sunday on which it actually broke out. In other words, the usual dating for the fire and all subsequent events uses the 'Old Style' Julian calendar, but Salvetti, whose dating was presumably copied by one writer and then recycled unthinkingly in all other accounts, used the 'New Style' Gregorian calendar current in Florence and the rest of Europe – and this was ten days ahead.

a tragedy so colossal, taking place against a backdrop of so many signs and portents, that it could only have been started deliberately. Hubert was French, a citizen of an enemy country; the French were mostly Catholics; therefore Hubert was a Catholic, as he himself testified (although virtually everyone who knew him judged him to be a Protestant). By the perverse form of circular logic employed by seventeenth-century English Protestants, Catholics were assumed to be arsonists, and vice-versa. 'Papists', especially foreign Papists, were 'the other' of the age, the archetypal bogeyman, cast in the same role that Jews, witches, Communists and Muslims have played in other eras. In seventeenth-century England, though, this fearful mindset seemed to be supported by the lessons of history – the burnings of Protestant martyrs by 'Bloody Mary', the Gunpowder Plot, the stories of the treatment of English sailors at the hands of the Spanish Inquisition, and so forth. The Jesuits were even believed to run entire colleges where they trained fire-raisers. In the seventeenth century, Catholicism was synonymous with fire: QED.

Cobbett, Bell, and the authors who have relied on their accounts, all reject such simplistic thinking, and take the more rational – and more comfortable – line that Hubert was a simpleton, who, for whatever reason, confessed to a blaze that started accidentally. At the same time, these authors have sometimes turned equally unreliable hearsay and second-hand gossip into gospel. For example, the suggestion, repeated uncritically in some modern accounts, that Hubert was disabled, and thus physically incapable of lifting a fireball on a long pole, seems to have first appeared in issue 370 of *The Observator,* published in 1683, a source I'll examine in detail later. According to its author,

> I am told, that Hubert had a dead palsy on one side, one arm useless, and much ado to trail one leg after him; was not this a fit man to manage a long pole, clap a fireball to the end of it, and this fireball to be put into a window, where there was no window

at all?...Here's Hubert, a lame, creeping miserable wretch, a Protestant brought over in a ship, that was not designed to come hither, a known madman singled out for a conspiracy. Here's Hubert setting the town a fire with a long pole, that must reach from St Katharine's [Dock] to Pudding Lane; and in short, he's as mad as Hubert, that does believe it, and a Jesuit that does not.

Even though the opening remark ('I am told') should have rung some alarm bells, this assertion was repeated in pamphlets throughout the eighteenth century, and eventually became accepted orthodoxy. In fact, the only basis for all this seems to be John Lowman's statement that he placed Hubert on a horse 'by reason of his lameness'. It was never suggested that this would have prevented him lifting a long pole to a window, and Lowman, who was seemingly determined to undermine Hubert's confession if he could, would surely have mentioned such a severe disability.

There is a similar silence in other contemporary sources. The best chronicler of the age, Samuel Pepys, who invariably recorded such things in minute detail, relates a conversation he had on 24 February 1667 with Sir Robert Vyner, the King's goldsmith, who had been the Sheriff of London at the time of the Fire. Vyner referred explicitly to the issue of the fireball being stuck through the window. He did not argue that Hubert could not have done this due to an infirmity, merely that the Farriners had said no such window existed. Instead, Vyner stated that he found the Frenchman 'though a mopish besotted fellow, [he] did not speak like a madman'.

Vyner's interestingly nuanced assessment was supplanted in later years by the orthodoxy that Hubert was simple-minded, and would confess to anything: what would now be called a serial confessor. For example, *Observator* 370, as well as trumpeting (and perhaps greatly exaggerating) Hubert's supposed 'disability', also claimed that the watchmaker had previously confessed to a murder and was to be hanged for it, but the day before he was meant to go to the gallows, the real murderer was caught and Hubert set free. There appears to be no corroboration at all for this statement.

A similar story can be seen across the board in the literature about the Great Fire: secondhand 'evidence', or pure hearsay, has become accepted fact. Many authoritative-looking references citing pages in Cobbett's *State Trials* (could any book wish for a more intimidatingly impressive title?) are actually citing the footnotes on those pages, which are not drawn from accounts of 'state trials' at all. Instead, those notes comprise lengthy quotations from other vaguely contemporary, but sometimes deeply flawed, partisan accounts pedalling rumours that circulated years after the Fire. Such sources include the Earl of Clarendon's *Life*, essentially just second-hand recollections of some trial evidence, written in exile, from memory rather than documentary sources, six years after the Fire. *The History of My Own Time*, written by Bishop Gilbert Burnet, largely in the early eighteenth century, was a partial, error-strewn and unreliable narrative, with most statements about the Great Fire being explicitly secondhand and prone to namedropping ('[Archbishop] Tillotson told me...', 'was told me by...the Countess of Clarendon', and so forth). Several other of these misleadingly quoted works were written even later: Laurence Echard's *History of England* (1718), Paul Rapin de Thoyras' *Histoire d'Angleterre* (1723-5), John Oldmixon's *Critical History of England* (1724-6), and James Ralph's *History of England* (1744-6). Fortunately, it is possible to get past this edifice of myth-building, and to study some of the original sources relating to Robert Hubert, rather than much later printed versions. These sources paint a very different picture.

ROBERT HUBERT: 'JUST THE FACTS, MA'AM'

The original of Hubert's first deposition, taken before Carey Harvie or Hervey, Justice of the Peace, at Havering-atte-Bower on 11 September 1666, survives in the Mildmay manuscripts at Somerset Record

Office, Taunton, but this document seems not to have been studied – and has certainly not been quoted – by any previous writer on the Great Fire of London. The deposition contains a number of deletions and amendments, casting new light on the story.

According to it, Hubert left France about the middle of the previous Lent ('5 or 6 months since' was crossed through; the middle of Lent would have been about the end of the third week in March) with a French gentlemen named 'Piedelow', with whom he travelled to Sweden. They spent three or four months there before going to London, where 'Piedelow' gave him a fire ball, keeping two others for himself, 'wishing him *when the city was on fire* [my italics] to cast the same ball into an house *[sic]* in Whitehall'. But 'in Whitehall', repeated slightly later in the document too, was an afterthought or correction; the original location written down, but then crossed through, was 'in London'. Piedelow gave Hubert a shilling in advance, promising him 'a greater reward when they came into France'. Hubert carried the fire ball 'some time about him in his pocket' before throwing it into a house; 'in the window' was added.

After the City was ablaze, Hubert claimed he went aboard a Swedish ship moored near St Katherine's Dock, by the Hartshorn brewhouse, 'where Piedelow was, *and saith that he should be well rewarded when he came into France* [the passage in italics was inserted subsequently]'. (It is interesting that Hubert was so precise about the location of the ship and so vague, in this deposition at least, about the location of the house he claimed to have set on fire.)

The next sentence is particularly important, and is printed here as it appears in the manuscript deposition: 'the ~~master's~~ name of that ship was ~~Skipper~~ Schipper, ~~and that was also~~ the name of the ~~ship~~ master of the ship was ~~Skipper~~ Schipper'. Clearly both Hubert and the clerk recording the deposition were confused, which probably explains the unlikely repetition. According to Hubert, though, the mysterious ship master gave him leave to go ashore and confer with Piedelow, 'if he could find him and go about his business'. This phrase was inserted into the text and then effectively repeated a second time, but with one crucial difference crossed through, and thus absent from the printed versions. Hubert seems to have said originally that 'the master *and Piedelow*' told him to go about his business.

Hubert was sent to the White Lion Gaol in Southwark, and on 16 September, indicted before the Middlesex Assizes, charged as follows:

True Bill that, at St. Martin's (-in-the-Fields), county Middlesex on the said day, Robert Hubert late of the said parish, labourer, set fire to a certain fire-ball compounded of gunpowder brimstone and other combustible matter, and with it fired and destroyed the dwelling-house of a certain man to the jurors unknown. Robert Hubert put himself 'Not Guilty' to this indictment, process on which ceased, because the said Robert was hung in London on another indictment.

This corresponds to the evidence in the Havering-atte-Bower deposition, namely that Hubert attacked a house 'in Whitehall'; and it provides the intriguing lead that Hubert was a 'local', a resident (at least occasionally) of the parish of Saint Martin-in-the-Fields. All of this, though, must have been overtaken by events, because Hubert simply went back to prison. Meanwhile, two separate official investigations into the causes of the fire got under way. The first was ordered by the King, under the auspices of the Privy Council, and was chaired by the Lord Chief Justice, Sir John Kelyng. On 25 September, too, the House of Commons appointed its own committee of no fewer than seventy members, chaired by the young and fiercely independent-minded Sir Robert Brooke, MP for Aldeburgh, to enquire into the causes of the disaster, and this began sitting the next day. It heard many supposed 'eyewitness' accounts of Catholic and/or Dutch and/or French incendiarism, although the committee had not formally reported by the time Parliament was prorogued on 8 February 1667, and it was never reconvened.

Thus Robert Hubert's was simply one of many depositions given to the committee. It was set down as follows (spellings, etc, modernised):

> Robert Hubert of Rouen in Normandy, who acknowledged
> that he was one of those that Fired the House of Mr. Farriner a
> Baker in Pudding-Lane, from whence the Fire had its beginning,
> confessed, that he came out of France with one Stephen
> Piedloe about four months before the Fire, and went into Sweden
> with him, where he also stayed with him as his Companion
> four months, and then they came together into England in
> a Swedish Ship called the *Skipper*, where he stayed on board with
> the said Piedloe till that Saturday night, in which the Fire broke
> out. When Piedloe taking him out of the Ship, carried him into
> Pudding Lane, and he [Hubert] being earnest to know whither
> he [Piedloe] would carry him? he would not satisfy him till he
> had brought him to the place, and then he told him, that he had
> brought three [fire] Balls, and gave him one of them to throw into
> the house. And he would have been further satisfied in the design,
> as he said, before he would execute it: But Piedloe was so impatient
> that he would not hear him, and then he did the Fact, which was,
> That he put a fireball at the end of a long Pole, and lighting it
> with a piece of Match, he put it in at a Window, and stayed till he
> saw the House in a flame. He confessed that there were three and
> twenty accomplices, whereof Piedloe was the Chief.

There is no suggestion that the committee originally placed any more
weight on Hubert's testimony than on any other evidence it heard,
much of which was fanciful, much pure hearsay. There was even an
attempt to attribute dire significance to something an Irishman had
supposedly said in a pub, a species of evidence not normally considered
legally watertight. As one of the MPs serving on the committee noted,
'all the allegations are very frivolous and people are generally satisfied
that the fire was accidental'.

Perhaps inevitably, accusations had been levelled against Monsieur Belland of Marylebone, the King's French firework-maker, who was supposedly hunted down by a mob and found hiding in Whitehall Palace. William Champneys, hatband maker of Horselydown, came across a constable in Shoe Lane who had arrested a Frenchman for throwing fireballs, and asked Champneys to assist him; the Frenchman was supposedly turned over to the Life Guards. Yet another Frenchman was seized in Southwark, supposedly carrying fireballs on his person, was turned over to the Guards, and again disappeared without trace; and a man allegedly caught in the act of firing a house in West Smithfield was seized at gunpoint by the Guards from the clutches of the mob. Still another fire-raising Frenchman was arrested by a constable who then propitiously encountered the Duke of York, who took the man off into his own custody, saying 'I will secure him.' Again,

On Monday the third of September, there was a Frenchman taken firing a House; and upon searching of him, fireballs were found about him. At which time four of the Life Guard rescued the Frenchman, and took him away from the People, *after their usual manner in the whole time of the Fire.* [emphasis in original source]

Nothing more was heard of these stories, several of which seem like attempts to suggest that the King's Guards, the King's brother, and by implication the King himself, were in league with Papist and foreign arsonists. This agenda was favoured by many inhabitants of London, and not a few members of the parliamentary committee of enquiry.

The brief 'headings' Sir Robert Brooke reported to Parliament on 22 January 1667, other evidence supposedly submitted to his committee, and the evidence given at Hubert's trial, were combined into a pamphlet entitled *A True and Faithful Account of the Several Informations,* published in 1667. This found its way into later collections of 'primary' sources, including Cobbett's *State Trials,* thus becoming the basis for much of Bell's account, and more recent books about the Great Fire. Sources that did not end up in the *True and Faithful Account*, on the other hand, or in the equally accessible *Calendar of State Papers* – such as the original Havering-atte-Bower deposition and the record of Hubert's appearance before the Middlesex sessions – have been ignored. In one sense, they make Hubert's story even more confused and self-contradictory than it already appears to be. They also pose new and problematic questions.

ROBERT HUBERT: PATSY *PAR EXCELLENCE*

Hubert's appearance before the parliamentary committee was generally recognised to be pathetic: he was described shortly afterwards as 'an inconsiderable fellow', and it was said that 'little credit has hitherto been given to his discourse'. Nevertheless, the alternative royal-sponsored enquiry into the fire found the case against him serious enough to press charges. Hubert was indicted on 8 October, and went for trial before the London City assizes. It is worth noting that three of the signatories to the letter of indictment were Thomas Farriner, the owner of the bakery in Pudding Lane, his son, and his daughter, for whom the Frenchman's confession must have been a godsend. Without it, the entire population of London would have blamed the Farriners for the Great Fire.

However, the assumption that Farriner, or one of his family or employees, made a careless mistake on the night of 1-2 September 1666, and sought to offload the blame onto Hubert, is too easy. There were suggestions that some fuel had been placed next to, or even in, one of the bread ovens, to allow its more speedy lighting the next morning. Farriner, who had the contract for supplying the Navy with ship's biscuit (which seems to be the sole reason for so many sources describing him as 'the King's baker') could have been under pressure to fulfil a bulk order for a fleet six weeks away from port. At the same time, though, he would have been more aware than most of the dangers of fire, and must have followed exactly the same routine to guard against it every single night of the thirty-seven years since he'd begun his apprenticeship.

Moreover, as Matthew Quinton points out in Chapter Sixteen, if you wished to start a fire that was likely to cause significant damage in London during the dry summer of 1666, *regardless of the direction of the wind*, you would almost certainly start it somewhere near Pudding Lane, given the immediate proximity of countless warehouses, wharves, and workshops, filled with highly flammable material. And you would certainly start it on a Sunday, when fewer people would have been up and about to fight any fire.

Hubert's confession inevitably focused attention entirely upon him, but this has led to a dismissal of all other accounts of the Fire's origins. Quite apart from all the stories recorded by the Brooke committee, there was the testimony of Edward Taylor, a ten year old boy, who testified before Lord Lovelace on 9 September that he, his father and his Dutch uncle, John Taylor, had set off fireballs in Farriner's bakery and elsewhere in London.* There is also a previously unknown – or, at least, uncited – letter about the Great Fire in the National Library of Wales, written on 6 September, from an anonymous correspondent in London to one of the Wynn family of Gwydir, on the Caernarfonshire-Denbighshire border, suggesting that at least some contemporaries believed in a middle ground between the 'conspiracy' and 'cock-up' theories. This letter suggested that the fire did break out accidentally in Farriner's bakery, but was then spread by the 'malstring industry' of the

---

* If 'Uncle John' was Dutch, why wasn't young Edward? John Taylor is hardly a Dutch name. Assuming that such a person existed, and wasn't the product of the overactive imagination of a guilt-ridden ten-year-old (or, as Bell described him, 'a little liar' – perhaps one who might have had a now obscure grudge against his nearest and dearest), it raises the possibility that the uncle might have been one of the many English republican exiles living in the Netherlands; many more would be involved in the Dutch attack on the British fleet at Chatham in the following year.

French and Dutch using fireballs, of which the writer claimed to have seen one or two. A similar tale appears in a letter from John Tremayne, a nineteen-year-old student at the Inner Temple, to his father Colonel Lewis Tremayne of Heligan in Cornwall. Although the surviving version was written on 22 September, it repeats the information given in a letter John had sent on the eighth, but which had apparently miscarried. John Tremayne provides a dramatic eyewitness account of proceedings:

> we were all in arms in the beginning, it being certainly said that it was a plot, but I rather think it God's judgment for our sins and devil ways; though I saw several French & Dutch taken with fire balls setting houses on fire, and some of them in woman's clothes, yea there were some English taken likewise. One I saw taken in the Temple garden with fire balls, but would not confess what he kept them for; God be praised, the villains never gathered to any head, though several outcries were made to that purpose, and one in the night which forced us to leave all in the fields [and] take arms, but it was presently over. They fired also several places [such] as Southwark, Westminster behind the Abbey, St Martins in the Fields, etc. There were several taken and killed outright: one woman that had fire balls was drawn in pieces per the multitude, and any that had but the look of a Frenchman was taken and carried to prison, or cut and slashed per the people, they were so violently bent against the French.

These two previously unpublished sources corroborate Robert Hubert's original deposition (as well as, potentially, some of the other tales of arson attacks too), which stated that the French watchmaker threw a fireball into a house somewhere in London *after the fire had already begun*. Both letters were written privately, before Hubert made his deposition, so none of these sources could have drawn on any of the others.

In one sense, though, Hubert made a perfect scapegoat, and not just for the Farriners. If the Great Fire was an accident, tenants would have to rebuild their burned properties at their own expense. If it was arson, carried out by a subject of a nation with which England was at war, the tenants would not be liable. From the point of view of most Londoners, then, the self-confessed guilt of Robert Hubert could not have been more fortuitous.

It was this decision over legal responsibility that encouraged tenants to rebuild their properties rapidly, on the same footings, and within much the same street pattern, thereby stifling at birth the ambitious plans developed by Sir Christopher Wren and others for a new, more rationally laid-out London, with wider streets and grand vistas. If someone was setting out to arrange such a thing, then, a Great Fire of London that could be pinned on a 'lone gunman' – or rather, a lone Frenchman – was truly the 'insurance scam' from Heaven. There may be sinister significance to the way Hubert's testimony shifted from him attempting to fire a house 'near Whitehall' (in other words, outside the City of London), back to what he seems originally to have said at Havering-atte-Bower before his deposition was modified, namely that the house was 'in London' (that is, strictly speaking, within the City). His insistence on identifying the Pudding Lane bakery as his target, meanwhile, seemingly clinched the matter.

In 1666 and thereafter, it suited the royal and civic authorities to demonstrate that Hubert was a Protestant madman who, if he attacked anything at all, attacked a building outside the City.[*]

---

[*] Was Hubert, perhaps, the anonymous individual mentioned by Newton Killingworth, a witness who reported to the committee of Parliament that 'he apprehended a person during the fire, about whom he found much combustible matter, and certain black things, of a long figure, which he could not endure to hold in his hand, by reason of their extreme heat. This Person was so surprised at first, that he would not answer to any question; But being on his way to Whitehall, he acted the part of a madman, and so continued while he was with him'?

Conversely, it suited London property holders, and the fevered mood of public opinion, to demonstrate that he was a Catholic terrorist who threw a fireball into Farriner's bakery, *within* the City. Whether the impressionable Hubert was ever 'leaned on' to ensure his testimony conformed to the latter story will never be known. What we do know is that the crime he was charged with, and apparently confessed to, changed between 16 September and 8 October 1666, from throwing a fireball into an unspecified house in the parish of Saint Martin-in-the-Fields (consistent with his original Havering-atte-Bower deposition), a charge to which he pleaded not guilty, into throwing one into Farriner's bakery in Pudding Lane, to which he pleaded guilty. Quite how and why this came about remains a moot point.

Robert Hubert is always assumed to have been a watchmaker, despite the Middlesex Sessions indictment describing him as a 'labourer'. But no one, to date, has analysed this assumption, or the generally held belief that Hubert's father was a famous watchmaker of Rouen. In fact, significant information about the Hubert dynasty is accessible. In 2014, the clock museum at Saint Nicholas d'Aliermont, near Dieppe, mounted a substantial exhibition of the work of Normandy watch-and clockmakers of the seventeenth century, the catalogue of which, available online, includes much information about the Huberts.

The founding father was Noel Hubert, who died in 1654; he seems to have had eight sons, several of whom became noted watchmakers in their own right, as did several of their sons in turn. Robert Hubert 'the arsonist' has not been directly connected to this family tree, but this signifies nothing. For one thing, there were several other Huberts in Rouen, working in related crafts, and almost certainly brothers, cousins or nephews of Noel Hubert. In 1660, for example, Timothy and Salomon Hubert were master locksmiths in the city, and are known to have been related to Noel. Moreover, the known grandsons of Noel Hubert were all born between 1634 and 1654, which would place Robert's likely birthdate of 1640 squarely in the right timeframe for that generation of the family. The increasingly vicious persecution of French Huguenots after 1660, mentioned in this book in the context of Captain Ollivier, ultimately led many members of the Hubert family to seek their fortunes elsewhere. By the 1680s, 1690s and 1700s, family members could be found in Geneva (an important connection, to which I'll return), Amsterdam, and, indeed, London, where David Hubert, a great-grandson of Noel, was a prominent member of the Watchmakers Company by 1714.

One further, critical, piece of evidence should be emphasised: Robert Hubert was almost certainly not a Roman Catholic, although his various contradictory statements muddied the waters. Further confusion was introduced by a visit supposedly made to him in prison by Father Harvey, confessor to the much-mistrusted, Portuguese and devoutly Catholic Queen. Some accounts have Harvey converting Hubert to Rome; others have Hubert refusing to renounce his Protestant faith. Still others, always second-hand, maintain that on the scaffold Hubert recanted both his confession and his apocryphal conversion, thus dying a Protestant.

Despite being a publication that needs to be taken with a pinch of salt, *Observator* 370 stated categorically that Hubert was a Huguenot, and that the French Protestant Church in Stockholm could testify to the truth of that. I contacted that church's modern day incarnation, the *Franska Reform Kyrkan,* but it does not hold records from before the mid-eighteenth century. Nevertheless, the weight of evidence tends to confirm that Hubert was, indeed, Protestant, from a staunchly Protestant family. The 2014 exhibition catalogue from the museum in Saint Nicholas d'Aliermont indicates that the Hubert family was Catholic until the first quarter of the seventeenth century, but all members, without exception, then became Protestant, and in later decades, their response to the persecution of the Huguenots was absolutely typical of the French Protestant experience. It is highly unlikely, although not impossible, for Robert Hubert to have been a Catholic. Later in this account, too, previously unknown evidence will be presented about Hubert's possible Huguenot connections in Stockholm.

The political and legal squabbles over what Robert Hubert was – Protestant madman, or Papist conspirator? – also shaped the emergence, fifteen years afterwards, of the next substantial evidence about the outbreak of the Fire, Hubert's potential role in it, and the shadowy Stephen 'Peidelow', or Piedloe.

THE MYSTERIOUS STEPHEN PIEDLOE

Amid all the contradictions and confusions in Hubert's various statements, one element is consistent and unshakeable: his insistence on the existence, and central role in the outbreak of the Great Fire, of Stephen Piedloe. Moreover, unlike most other elements of Hubert's story, there appears to be corroboration for at least part of this. A man named Graves, a French merchant of St Mary Axe, testified that he had known Hubert since he was four years old, and had visited the watchmaker in prison (where Hubert had supposedly confessed his guilt to him). Graves said he knew Piedloe, too, and described him as 'a very debauched person, and apt to any wicked design'.

This, in turn, invites us to ponder Monsieur Graves. There is no trace of any individual by that name in the area around St Mary Axe, or in the City as a whole, in the 1666 Hearth Tax for London, but that is not necessarily suspicious. A Josephe Graves had been a vintner in St Helen's Bishopsgate, immediately adjacent to St Mary Axe, during the 1640s, so could well have been the same man, especially as this would probably make him about the same age as Hubert's father, whom he also claimed to know. Moreover, Hubert's original deposition at Havering-atte-Bower stated that Piedloe 'had a chamber in London', a sentence subsequently crossed out and thus absent from all published accounts of the Fire. If that was so, then as members of the French expatriate community, Graves, Hubert and Piedloe could have known each other, perhaps even worshipped together at the Huguenot Church in Threadneedle Street. In any event, it seems probable that Hubert and Piedloe knew the geography of London well.

We cannot be certain about the origins of the name 'Piedloe', which is also spelled 'Peidelow' in some contemporary sources and 'Peidlo' in slightly later printings. However, Piedleu or Piedeleu is an old French surname, common in Normandy and Brittany, and conspiracy theorists may delight in the fact that it means 'wolf's foot'. A William and Simon Piedeleu seem to have been merchants of Amiens, trading with the city of London as early as 1367. Various Piedeleus were prominent in civil life in Rouen during the sixteenth and seventeenth centuries; one held the noble title of Sieur d'Aunay, and to provide yet more grist to the mill for conspiracy theorists, several were prominent Freemasons. Marie Piedeleu was one of the first women in Rouen to obtain a divorce, after the French Revolution legalised the practice; and Piedeleus can still be found in Rouen (and even at Oxford University) today. So, again, it is possible that a Stephen 'Piedloe' could have known Robert Hubert, and probably his father too, through the Rouen connection, and could have moved in circles that made him known to the prominent London-based French merchant, Monsieur Graves.

THE EQUALLY MYSTERIOUS CAPTAIN PETERSON

Hubert's evidence is so confused, and contemporaries' confirmation of his simple-mindedness so substantial, that it is difficult to accept him as the instigator of the Great Fire. Hubert was in any case posthumously provided with an alibi by the captain of the ship who brought him to London, Lawrence Peterson, who wrote a letter on 17 December 1681 stating that Hubert could not have started the fire, as he was aboard his ship when it began.

There are several problems with Peterson's evidence, quite apart from the obvious question of why it took him fifteen years to come forward. First, who was Laurence Peterson? Hubert never actually named him; in his original deposition, the name of the captain of the ship he went aboard was 'Skipper', or Schipper. Not one witness who came forward in 1666 named this man in connection with Robert Hubert. But there certainly was a Captain Laurence Peterson, in the right place at the right time, as evidence produced hereafter will confirm, so we can take it for granted that he wrote the letter attributed to him.

Peterson's letter of 17 December 1681 stated that Hubert had been aboard his ship, near St Katherine's, when the fire broke out, having not gone ashore at all previously. The Frenchman 'did seem to rejoice and say, Fery well, fery well, which with the word Yes, yes, was all the English he could speak', at which Peterson took offence and clapped him in the hold. According to the Swede, Hubert managed to escape through a scuttle and got ashore at 'Mr Corsell's' quay, where the captain saw him being seized by the mob. This was the wharf adjoining Hartshorn's brewhouse, the building mentioned in Hubert's Havering-atte-Bower disposition. (Abraham Corsellis, who owned the business, was a wealthy brewer of Flemish origins, whose family became so respectable in English society that his grandson went to Eton and became an MP.)

The flaw in Peterson's evidence here is that Hubert was not arrested in London on 4 September, but in Essex seven days later. It is possible, of course, that Peterson either lied about, or 'misremembered', the timing of Hubert's going ashore and how, when and where he ended up captured. But he made no reference to Stephen Piedloe having been aboard his ship: a curious omission, given the precision of other recollections from fifteen years earlier. The remainder of Peterson's evidence, too, stretches credibility. Peterson stated that he never heard of Hubert again until he went to his father in Rouen to claim back the three pounds ten shillings he was owed for the son's passage in the ship. At this, the father said his son had been hanged for starting the Great Fire of London; 'which much amazed this informant, he well knowing the contrary to be true'.

Why did Laurence Peterson wait fifteen years before providing a statement setting out his recollections of Robert Hubert and the Great Fire of London? The political context of the period might explain things. On 10 January 1681, the House of Commons resolved 'that it is the opinion of this House, that the City of *London* was burnt in the Year One thousand Six hundred Sixty-and-six, by the Papists; designing thereby to introduce arbitrary Power and Popery into this Kingdom'. This was one of a series of resolutions passed by a House consumed by fears of the (entirely fabricated) 'Popish Plot', and which was determined to exclude the Catholic Duke of York from the succession through the efforts of the new, ferociously anti-Catholic 'Whig party'. Charles II's response was to prorogue, and shortly afterwards to dissolve, this Parliament. Another met at Oxford in March, but this, too, was swiftly dissolved, and a loyalist backlash began, with another new party, the pro-crown and anti-exclusion Tories, at its heart. It was in this frenzied atmosphere that the virulently anti-Catholic passage, quoted by Matthew Quinton in the prologue, was added to Wren's Monument. For some time, there was real prospect of a new civil war: on 2 September, the fifteenth anniversary of the outbreak of the Great Fire, 20,000 Protestant apprentices of London presented an address to the Lord Mayor to mark 'the burning of that famous city by Papists'.

Captain Peterson's 'testimony', dated 17 December 1681, might have been orchestrated from within the court, or by someone loyal to the Stuart brothers, as a way of countering the still widespread idea that the Catholics began the Great Fire. Peterson's statement seems to have been first published in issue 370 (5 July 1683) of Sir Roger L'Estrange's newspaper, *The Observator*, a staunchly royalist propaganda vehicle (although this makes us wonder why the letter was apparently not disseminated for over eighteen months). As well as publishing the letter, L'Estrange attempted to explain the obvious discrepancy in Peterson's dates by claiming that after being seized by the mob on 4 September, Hubert was taken before a Justice of the Peace in Mile End Green who found no cause for suspicion and released him. He was later arrested again at Romford, where the local mob demanded to know '"What? Are you one of the rogues that fired the City?" "Oui, oui," says he.' Quite apart from the *Allo Allo* like nature of the dialogue (which begs the questions of L'Estrange's source for it, and why Hubert should say 'oui, oui' when, again according to L'Estrange, '"yes, yes" was all the English he could speak'), this still leaves seven days unaccounted for in Hubert's movements. In the late seventeenth century, or even in the worst gridlock of the early twenty-first, it could not take seven days to get from Mile End to Romford.

It is also worth pointing out that Peterson's statement was not, in fact, sworn on oath, as some have claimed. The Swede's closing remark stated that he was 'ready to make oath' of what he had written, if necessary. In reality, there was not the remotest possibility of him being required to swear to that effect. Contrary to what some modern accounts state, there was no active enquiry into the Fire in December 1681, there was no Parliament, and Peterson was almost certainly not in England. He signed his letter as 'master of Drottningholm', and evidence generously supplied to me by the Swedish Maritime Museum shows that a Lorenz Peterson was, indeed, captain of a ship of that name in 1681, and remained so until she was wrecked in 1684.*

In these circumstances, and given that Peterson's account of Hubert's departure from his ship was dubious, we might ask whether the Swedish captain ever actually wrote such a document at all – especially

---

* My thanks to Malin Joakimson of *Statens Maritima Museer*. The *Drottningholm* was a 'kompaniskepp', i.e. it was owned by one of Sweden's major monopoly companies.

because, if the original but deleted words in Hubert's Havering-atte-Bower deposition contain a shred of truth, then the captain and the mysterious Monsieur Piedloe might have been working together. But even if Peterson did write it, this still begs two critical questions: the one already stated, namely why did he write it when he did, and why did he not mention Stephen Piedloe?

Roger L'Estrange seems to have anticipated exactly such charges being laid against Peterson's testimony, as he took great pains to establish the veracity of his source:

The Master *(Peterson)* was here again some two or three year after; and makes this voyage commonly once a year; he was here this very last spring. He has several times told this correspondent, how much it has troubled him, that he did not give Hubert a visit, when he was in prison; which would infallibly have sav'd his life. Now as to the information of this Peterson, I can prove it by several persons; and I dare appeal to my Honourable friend the Lord Leyemberg *(Leijonbergh)*, the Swedish minister, for the credit of what I have delivered.

(In the subsequent issue, *Observator* 371, L'Estrange added the names of the Houblon brothers, prominent London merchants of French extraction, as further witnesses to the truth. The younger brother, John, later became the first Governor of the Bank of England.)

Then there's a further question. If, as L'Estrange claims, Peterson knew Hubert was in prison, charged with starting the Great Fire, why was the skipper apparently so shocked when he went to Rouen and heard that Hubert had been hanged for exactly that offence (or so keen to stress that he hadn't heard of Hubert after he'd left his ship)? I'll return to the questions of Captain Peterson, and the timing of his letter, shortly. Before that, though, let's examine why his letter should have appeared in print in the summer of 1683, not before, and in *The Observator*, not any other publication.

SIR ROGER L'ESTRANGE, THE BIRTH OF RED TOP JOURNALISM, AND THE INVENTION OF HISTORY

Sir Roger L'Estrange (1616-1704) was one of the founding fathers of modern journalism. However, he detested the notion of a free press, and would have found the notion of media neutrality incomprehensible. His latest biographer describes him as 'violent in his battles and often brutal in enforcing his will on his enemies', so perhaps modern press barons owe him a debt, too. In April 1681, shortly after the Oxford Parliament was dissolved, he began to publish *The Observator*, 'the most powerful organ of Tory propaganda', and it was in its pages that he launched an attack on the Whig domination of the City of London which had resulted in the anti-Catholic inscription being placed on the Monument. In doing so, L'Estrange revisited the evidence surrounding Hubert's conviction in 1666, and in this context, Captain Peterson's letter of December 1681 emerged.

Without exception, all material L'Estrange published on the subject went into print for one purpose alone: to promote the Tory and court argument, that Hubert had not been a Catholic and could not have started the Great Fire. The subtitle of *Observator* number 370 (5 July 1683) was '*The whole story of Hubert's setting fire to the city (and consequently that of Sir Patience Ward's inscription upon the Monument) proved to be a mere sham*'. (Ward was the Whig Lord Mayor of London who had ordered the inscription.) This was part of a series of issues in which L'Estrange, who had a long track record as an apologist for English Roman Catholics, attacked the entire narrative of 'Popish plots', and was published at a time when the Royalist/Tory reaction against that narrative, and the Whigs who promoted it, was in full swing. The 'Rye House Plot', an alleged Whig plot to assassinate Charles II, had been discovered only three weeks earlier, and *Observator* 370 and the following number, which continued L'Estrange's 'analysis' of Hubert's guilt, came out at exactly the moment Whig leaders, such as

William, Lord Russell, and Captain Thomas Walcott, a veteran of the republic's army, were being arrested and/or put on trial for their parts in the Rye House conspiracy. Therefore, the discrediting of everything Whig, including that party's belief that Hubert was (a) a Catholic, and had (b) started the Great Fire, was in full swing in July 1683, a time when paranoia about plots – albeit of an *anti*-Catholic variety – was rampant once again.

In this respect, it suited L'Estrange and the Royalist/Tory 'party line' to rubbish the role, or even the very existence, of Stephen Piedloe, who was, naturally, as Andrew Marvell and others noted, a much more plausible conspirator and arsonist than Hubert. 'There was no Piedelou in the ship *[that brought Hubert to London]*; and consequently all the Flam of Piedelou falls to the ground,' L'Estrange wrote, citing Peterson's evidence, but in the process brazenly disregarding something obvious. Even if there was no evidence of Piedloe having been on the ship – and Hubert stated categorically that he had been – there was ample evidence (notably the inconvenient testimony of Monsieur Graves) for the existence of such a person. Moreover, if Captain Peterson wrote his letter of December 1681 in response to a request to do so from someone in England, probably someone in an official position – and why else would he have written it? – why did he not write one sentence confirming that Stephen Piedloe had never been on his ship? There are many answers to that question, from the simplest (he forgot), to those which lead us inexorably to the 'dark side', such as the possibility that Piedloe and Peterson were working together, as Hubert implied, or that Peterson, the unknown person who had invited him to write his letter, and Roger L'Estrange, all had a vested interest in writing Piedloe out of the story.

Ultimately, Roger L'Estrange wasn't interested in Stephen Piedloe at all, and certainly not in providing any evidence that he started the Great Fire. L'Estrange just wanted to convince the public that Robert Hubert, the man universally believed by Whigs to have started the Fire, could not have done so, thereby undermining the credibility of the Whig party and its belief in a long-standing succession of 'Popish plots'.

L'Estrange was also driven by a personal agenda of wanting to exonerate Roman Catholics, and to demonstrate that they were loyal citizens. To prove this case, L'Estrange systematically went through the statements that Hubert made in 1666, and some of the stories about him that had surfaced subsequently. This led him to produce, in many cases for the first time, several new pieces of 'evidence' about Hubert and the Fire, but unsurprisingly, it is not easy to tell fact from rumour and downright fabrication. Many authors have rightly dismissed all those wild stories that surfaced before the Brooke Committee, the countless tales of Frenchmen with fireballs, and so forth. At the same time, strangely, these same authors have accepted uncritically pretty well everything an out-and-out partisan propagandist published seventeen years after the event.

L'Estrange employed the classic *modus operandi* of supporting his 'facts' by citing the number and unimpeachable integrity of the witnesses who could support him, without actually mentioning their names. An example is the story of Hubert's supposed previous confession to murder, recounted earlier. L'Estrange provided no date for this, no location for the story, no names of any of the other parties involved. His sole claim to authenticity stated 'this subject… is warranted to me, by a very good hand'.

But some of L'Estrange's assertions have a ring of plausibility. For example, the *Observator* explains how Hubert managed to identify the charred remains of the bakery in Pudding Lane when Lowman took him there by pointing out that a crowd of curious onlookers had formed a circle around the ruin, making its significance blindingly obvious to Hubert. It would hardly have been difficult to identify the location attracting their interest, nor, in that part of London, to guess why they were there. (Matthew Quinton uses a variant of this explanation during the Epilogue.)

In a subsequent issue of the *Observator*, L'Estrange also claimed to have made enquiries at Rouen to confirm both Hubert's religion and mental health. But the watchmaker's father was dead, and his two brothers were living in Constantinople and Geneva, so it was taking longer than he hoped to obtain the information. This 'evidence' is plausible, especially as two watchmakers named Hubert, the brothers Étienne, born in 1648, and Paul, born in 1654 (so the right age to be younger brothers of Robert Hubert) were working in Geneva in the 1680s, and their father, another Robert (the third son of Noel Hubert), had died in 1680. But if L'Estrange did eventually receive further information about Robert Hubert, he never published it.

Quite simply, the imperative to do so stopped mattering, especially as L'Estrange was not interested in publishing facts for the record, but in scoring political points as viciously and as rapidly as possible. By the end of 1683, the Whigs were clearly defeated, the so-called 'Tory reaction' was in full swing, and in 1685, the accession of the Catholic King James II led to the erasing of the anti-Catholic inscription on the Monument. As far as *The Observator* was concerned, Robert Hubert had served his polemical purpose in 1683, and was now ancient history. To paraphrase the Earl of Oxford's epitaph for Queen Anne, he was as dead as Julius Caesar.

THE NAVAL HISTORY OF THE GREAT FIRE OF LONDON

According to the accounts published in *The Observator*, the ship in which Hubert was taking passage was actually sailing from Sweden to Rouen, where Hubert was meant to be reunited with his father. But it was intercepted at sea by Prince Rupert's fleet and sent into the port of London. This, one of the many flaws in Robert Hubert's testimony and conviction, was moderately inconvenient for anyone wishing to prove the Fire was caused by a deeply-laid, long-gestating conspiracy. In itself, the interception story is plausible enough – although Hubert's original deposition, at Havering-atte-Bower, makes no mention of being arrested by the Royal Navy, and seems to imply that his intention (and, by implication, his ship's) was always to go to London.

Following the Terschelling raid and Matthew's fictional departure from it, the fleet continued to operate in the North Sea, with scouting warships regularly seizing suspected prizes and sending them to London; Prince Rupert's nimble yacht the *Fanfan* was particularly successful in this respect. (Unfortunately, no log book survives for her; but that is true of every British warship at sea in 1666.) By the end of August, though, its principal objective was to prevent the conjunction of De Ruyter's Dutch fleet and Beaufort's French squadron. The British and Dutch fleets were in sight of each other on 31 August, but the incompetence of the British pilots and bad weather prevented more than a brief, small-scale action. The fleet put into Spithead to repair, and so was there when the Great Fire took place; the Duke of Albemarle was summoned back to London to help deal with the crisis, and never went to sea again.* In mid-September, Rupert sailed again against the French fleet, which had come as far as Dieppe. During the subsequent operations, the French Second Rate *Rubis* was captured, an incident that I used as the basis for the capture of the *Jeanne d'Arc* by Matthew Quinton's *Royal Sceptre* at the beginning of this book. (In reality, the capture of the *Rubis* had an air of farce about it: her captain mistook the

---

* Rather more immediate naval support for the firefighting effort was provided by parties of seamen and dockyard workers, who were sent to London on 4 September, the basis for my plot device of having some of the crew of the *Royal Sceptre* ordered into the City; and although Julian Carvell is, of course, fictitious, it was certainly seamen who provided both the idea and the method for blowing up houses in the path of the conflagration, thus creating far more effective firebreaks.

ensigns of the British White Squadron for French flags, and thus blundered into the middle of Prince Rupert's fleet.)

Throughout the Anglo-Dutch wars, it was common for neutral merchantmen to be seized and sent into English ports for examination. There were hundreds of cases of Dutch (and, from 1666, French) ships disguising themselves as neutrals, or of genuine neutrals carrying Dutch or French goods, and many Swedish vessels, along with ships of Lübeck, Hamburg, Spanish Flanders, and so forth, were arrested in British waters as a result. But if the Swedish ship had been sent up to London in this way, there ought to be a record in the voluminous archives of Charles II's government, especially if the ship was bound for Rouen, in a kingdom with which England was at war, and thus might easily have been carrying, or been suspected of carrying, contraband goods.

Hubert's testimony, both before the Havering-atte-Bower magistrate and at the Old Bailey, named one ship only, which he called the *Skipper*, claiming that its captain was also called Skipper. This is plainly nonsense, but could well have been the confused mishearing of a merchant captain's usual title by a young man with learning difficulties, who was unused to the sea and who spoke very little English (and presumably no Swedish at all). But in his original deposition, Hubert never claimed that this was the ship which brought him to England. That ship was not named, and the *Skipper* was stated explicitly to be the ship that he went to only *after* the Fire had broken out. There is no mention of this ship or its eponymous captain in the testimony of John Lowman, keeper of the Surrey county gaol where Hubert was held, and who took the Frenchman to St Katherine's dock on 2 October to point out where the Swedish ship had lain. Hubert indicated a berth off Abraham Corsellis' Hartshorn brewhouse (thus providing the single piece of corroborating detail about the ship that appeared in the printed record in 1666, and which also appears, perhaps suspiciously, in the

'Peterson letter' of 1681), but Lowman 'could neither find nor hear of any such vessel'.

This is, perhaps, unsurprising, if Hubert had got the name of the ship so badly wrong. However, L'Estrange's suggestion that the ship in question was actually called the *Milkmaid* can be corroborated from unimpeachable sources.* On 19 September 1666, the Privy Council met at Whitehall, a meeting attended by King Charles II, his brother the Duke of York, the Archbishop of Canterbury, and many of the other great figures of the day. Its second item of business was to hear a complaint from the Swedish ambassador, Lord Leijonbergh, about the illegal seizure of two Swedish ships, one of which was the *Milkmaid*, captained by a 'Lorenze Peterson'. These had been seized at sea and sent up to London, contrary to the terms of the prevailing Anglo-Swedish treaty, and attempts had been made to 'persuade' the masters to sell their cargoes (iron, copper wire, copper kettles, and so forth) on the local market, rather than at their destinations. The ships were meant to be taking salt back to Sweden, 'where there is great want thereof', but 'by their long detention their provisions are spent, the most part of their men run away and employed by the colliers'.

The Council referred the matter to the Lords Commissioners of Prizes, who were to examine the evidence and release the ships if the ambassador's story proved correct. In fact, the Prize Commission was already on the case; a week before, on 12 September, it had referred the case of the *Milkmaid* to the judge of the Admiralty Court, Sir Leoline Jenkins. Curiously, though, the matter then goes silent. The Prize Commission minutes assiduously record the names and details of all ships discharged, having been proved not lawful prizes; but of the *Milkmaid*, there is no further word. This is very much a provisional

---

* I am grateful to Professor Steve Murdoch of the University of St Andrews, and to his PhD student Adam Georgie, for carrying out research into these matters on my behalf in both the Swedish and British archives.

judgement on my part, though. The High Court of Admiralty papers are voluminous, unwieldy, and very poorly catalogued and indexed (if at all), so it is possible that other references to Captain Peterson and his ship are lurking in some obscure folio within some forgotten box of dusty papers. Furthermore, the surviving port books for London for that year, incomplete in any case, are currently inaccessible due to mould damage.

But the *Milkmaid*'s trail can be picked up in the Swedish archives. Her owner was Claude Hägerstierna, a nobleman with extensive business interests. And as with everything else in the story of Robert Hubert and the Great Fire, the story is complicated. Claude's original name was Roquette: he was a staunchly Huguenot Frenchman from Languedoc, who settled in Sweden, made a fortune, became a supplier to the royal court, and was ennobled in 1654, taking a Swedish name. His interests included iron, salt, and luxury goods for the court of Queen Christina, such as silk fabric, hats and gloves. Indeed, several accounts describe him as the Queen's 'tailor', although he was much more important than that. Significantly, his principal trading connections included export trades to both Rouen and London. He made substantial loans to the Swedish crown, and, in a curious echo of my fictitious 'Horsemen of the Apocalypse', he also funded the work of General Erik Dahlbergh, Sweden's leading military engineer, who would certainly have known how to blow up a wall or two.

Hägerstierna was so well connected that, when Christina began to plan her abdication, she secretly sent her fabulous art collection ahead of her aboard one of his ships. He was also a close friend of Magnus de la Gardie, Lord High Chancellor, arguably the most powerful man in Sweden from about 1660 to 1680 (and, coincidentally, a character featuring in the fourth Quinton novel, *The Lion of Midnight*, as Matthew reminds us in the Epilogue). Hägerstierna owned several estates, including a substantial house in Stockholm's fashionable Österlånggatan. However, his Calvinist religion conflicted with the

Swedish kingdom's official Lutheranism; consequently, services for like-minded French Huguenots in Stockholm had to be held secretly, sometimes in Hägerstierna's house.

On his behalf, the *Milkmaid* appears to have undertaken two voyages in 1666, carrying iron and copper (thus tallying with the evidence in the English Privy Council records). Several loads dated between 27 March and 7 April 1666 are recorded in the Stockholm *vågböcker* at the Swedish National Archives, then none until 23 June, followed by several more until a final one on 10 July. Although the evidence cannot be conclusive (this source records when cargoes were bought, not when they were shipped), it suggests that the *Milkmaid* might have made a round trip, destination unknown, between early April and mid-June, then perhaps sailed again in mid-July – the voyage which ended in her interception by Prince Rupert's fleet. If these suggested timings are correct, and given the usual length of a voyage from Stockholm, out through the Sound, and down the North Sea, it seems probable that the *Milkmaid* arrived in London perhaps as early as late July, certainly by about the middle of August at the latest, which again would fit with the reference to a 'long detention' in the Privy Council records.

DENOUEMENT

The new evidence about the voyage of the *Milkmaid* casts considerable doubt on the version of the story told by Captain Peterson in 1681. If the ship really did arrive in London well before the end of August, when it is usually assumed that she docked there, then it is surely inconceivable that both Hubert and Piedloe remained aboard for such a long time, especially when both seem to have had residences within the city, and when there was seemingly no reason not to go ashore. True, England was at war with France, just as it was with the Netherlands. Even so, there were thousands of Frenchmen and Dutchmen in

London, and in Britain as a whole, going about their business freely; the idea of interning citizens of enemy countries during wartime did not really take hold until Napoleon rounded up all British subjects in France in 1803, and then held them until his first abdication in 1814. As Matthew Quinton states, one of Charles II's principal ministers, Lord Arlington, really was married to a Dutchwoman, as was one of his principal courtiers, the Earl of Ossory; and at the height of the war, during the year 1666, Dublin and Limerick really did have Dutch mayors. In that sense, my fictitious '*Meinheer* Vandervoort', and the story that he spins, is perfectly plausible.

On 2 October 1666, the Southwark gaoler John Lowman found no Swedish ship lying off St Katherine's dock during the time just before and during the Great Fire of London. Of course, he was looking for a ship called the *Skipper*; but even so, one assumes he would have checked all Swedish ships in the vicinity in order to prove or disprove Hubert's story. Of course, as the Privy Council heard the case of the *Milkmaid* on 19 September, it is just possible that she had been released, and had sailed, before 2 October; but this would imply uncharacteristic speed and efficiency on the part of the Restoration government. Moreover, Hubert's depositions make no mention of the ship in which he came to London being seized at sea, as the *Milkmaid* certainly was.

If all this is so, then it is possible Captain Peterson lied in 1681; and it also has to be possible that the skipper of a ship which was definitely in London at the time of the Great Fire, *but which had not been meant to go there,* was prevailed upon to provide a statement seeming to disprove Hubert's guilt, at a time when doing so was very much an agenda King Charles II's government wanted to pursue.

It also seems implausible that a random Swedish ship master would have met the likes of Roger L'Estrange, let alone opened his heart to him upon several occasions. It seems similarly unlikely that that ship master should have permitted an innocent man to be hanged in 1666; and that the veracity of the story should depend, not only upon the word of several anonymous 'persons', but also of the Swedish ambassador (a person surely unlikely to contradict the principal propagandist of the court he was accredited to), and the Houblon brothers, moderate Whigs keeping their heads down in the frenzied atmosphere of 1681-3, whose prosperity depended on not rocking too many boats.

'Correlation does not imply causation', as the saying goes, but the story of the Great Fire contains so many intriguing correlations that one cannot help but point them out. Let's return to why Captain Lorenz Peterson said nothing about the Great Fire of London until 1681. There's no evidence that he was still connected to Claude Hägerstierna by then, but the latter seems to have died in August of that year, just four months before Peterson wrote his testimony about Robert Hubert's voyage aboard the *Milkmaid*.* At his death, Hägerstierna was allegedly Sweden's richest man. So was there some reason why Peterson could not speak out before his death? If Robert Hubert really was a Protestant, had he, too, been a part of Hägerstierna's circle while he was in Stockholm? If so, was he, too, a part of the secretive Calvinist gatherings that constituted the so-called 'French church in Stockholm', which could supposedly vouch for the watchmaker's religion (according to L'Estrange)? And if there is a truth in any of this, might it mean that Hägerstierna wanted a firm lid kept on any connection between himself and the Great Fire of London,

---

* I make this point in the knowledge that I, too, might be falling into the trap of peddling dodgy dates. A number of online sources, including Swedish genealogical forums, etc, give Hägerstierna's date of death as 1682. But the *Svenskt Biografiskt Lexikon*, the Swedish version of the *Dictionary of National Biography*, gives it as 1681, and his memorial in the *Västra Ryds kyrka*, Uppsala, where he was buried, gives it as 8 August 1681. With the exception of the first of them, though, the rhetorical questions that I pose in the remainder of this paragraph are not affected by the date of death.

no matter how tenuous, in case 'guilt by association' damaged his business interests?

Robert Hubert and Stephen Piedloe do seem to have come to London by ship – it was one of the few elements of his evidence to which Hubert adhered with absolute consistency – but thanks to all the new discoveries in primary sources, the 'alibi' supposedly provided for Hubert by Peterson, fifteen years after the event, no longer bears serious scrutiny. And, of course, there was never any alibi at all for Stephen Piedloe, the shadowy figure who got clean away: the man whom Robert Hubert consistently identified as the fire-starter of London, and whom Sir Roger L'Estrange was perhaps rather too keen to write out of the story.

* * *

Thomas Jackson, a nineteenth-century clergyman, once lampooned the nitpicking Biblical criticism of his day by using its methodology to prove that the Great Fire of London never actually happened at all. Unfortunately, the idiocies Jackson satirised are still with us, underpinning pretty much every conspiracy theory to be found in internet chatrooms and on social media. I don't propose to add to them here, except in one sense alone.

The Great Fire of London happened. It is overwhelmingly probable that it was an accident, caused by the carelessness of Thomas Farriner or one of his assistants. But this orthodoxy has become established because virtually all writers on the Great Fire of London, from the seventeenth century to present day, have automatically (albeit often subconsciously) discounted alternative explanations, then cherry-picked the evidence from a number of second-hand and secondary sources, of debatable provenance. Above all, there has been an uncritical acceptance of the 'evidence' produced by Sir Roger L'Estrange in 1683 – evidence published for overt political ends, in a context of feverish partisan politics.

Cutting through all this, common sense, along with the verdict of level-headed contemporaries commenting on the matter *during 1666 itself*, still leads to the conclusion that the fire began accidentally.

But to this common sense orthodoxy, I'd suggest three crucial, perhaps controversial, caveats.

1. The belief that the Fire began accidentally has always been regarded as the 'rational' explanation, even since the days in early September 1666 when it was actually still raging. Unfortunately, this has meant that the 'irrational' alternative explanations – the accusations against the French, Dutch and Catholics, and Hubert's bizarre behaviour – have not been analysed at all, or at best only in a superficial manner. Compare the treatment by historians of the Gunpowder Plot of 1605, arguably the closest historical parallel. Because the Plot undoubtedly *was* instigated by domestic terrorists, the motives, connections, methods, and prospects of success of those involved have been analysed exhaustively. But the perception of the Great Fire as an accident has become a self-fulfilling prophecy, with little attempt ever having been made seriously to examine alternative explanations, or to properly weigh other, perhaps rather inconvenient evidence that might support them.

Until now there has never been even a cursory attempt to research the backgrounds and connections of Robert Hubert, Stephen Piedloe, and Lawrence Peterson, or to test the known or supposed facts relating to those individuals. Moreover, since at least the time when the anti-Catholic inscription was removed from the Monument in the 1830s – or, perhaps, since the Dutch successfully invaded England in 1688 – even hinting at the possibility that English Roman Catholics, and/or the French, and/or the Dutch, might have been involved in the Great Fire of London, has been 'politically incorrect'.

2. Taking this argument a stage further: even if the Fire did begin accidentally, this does not preclude the possibility that it was then

exacerbated and accelerated by acts of arson, possibly by individuals disaffected toward the regime, possibly by a tiny minority of French or Dutch subjects living in London. It would be entirely conceivable that the latter could have wanted revenge for 'Holmes' Bonfire'; one letter written from London almost immediately after the Fire claimed that it was started 'in revenge of what our forces had lately done at Brandaris upon the island Schelling', while the Venetian ambassador, reporting the various rumours about the fire's cause, noted that one of them was 'due to many [Dutch] merchants rendered desperate by the burning of the ships at *[the Vlie]*, which rendered them bankrupt, and so they wished to get consolation for their own misfortune by a universal ruin'.

In that sense, posterity might have taken Robert Hubert more seriously had he been Dutch, for in September 1666, Dutchmen undoubtedly had motives in spades for wanting London to burn. As it is, the supposed eyewitness accounts of deliberate acts of arson, be they allegedly committed by Dutchmen, Frenchmen, or English Catholics, have invariably been dismissed as fantasy or mass hysteria. Yet the sheer amount of such evidence, along with its partial corroboration by previously unknown, and rather more dispassionate, sources like the letters to the Wynns of Gwydir of 6 September 1666, and of John Tremayne to his father (and, indeed, Robert Hubert's original Havering-atte-Bower deposition), suggest this possibility has been dismissed too readily.

3. Finally, if we accept that the timing of, and political context surrounding, Captain Peterson's statement in 1681 (and its subsequent publication in 1683), puts its truth in doubt, then Robert Hubert's supposed alibi must also be doubted. And if that alibi falls, then it is impossible to eliminate the possibilities that either the watchmaker of Rouen threw a fireball into a house in Whitehall when the fire in the City was already raging, as he originally claimed; or that Robert

Hubert – or his companion Stephen Piedloe – really did set off a fireball in Farriner's bakery in the early hours of 2 September 1666, thereby triggering the Great Fire of London.

Acknowledgements

This has been a more complex book to write than some of its predecessors in the series; consequently, I owe more debts than usual, to a broader body of people and sources.

My account of 'Sir Robert Holmes, his bonfire' is based closely on the historical record. My principal sources were Holmes' own account of the attack, printed in *The Rupert and Monck Letterbook* (Navy Records Society), Frank Fox's succinct summary in his magisterial *The Four Days Battle* (Seaforth Publishing), and the comprehensive study in Dutch by Anne Doedens and Jan Houten, *1666: de ramp van Vlieland en Terschelling*, which links to the website commemorating the 350th anniversary of the 'English Fury', http://1666.nu. Alan Marshall's excellent account of Aphra Behn's intelligence activities fortuitously came out just in time for me to consult it for this book ('"Memorialls for Mrs Affora": Aphra Behn and the Restoration Intelligence World', in *Women's Writing*, vol. 22, 2015). Leigh-on-Sea library provided invaluable material on the history of the town. For the historical essay, most of the principal sources that I consulted are identified and thanked at the appropriate points in the text. However, particular thanks must go to the staffs of the London Metropolitan Archives, the Society of Genealogists, Somerset Record Office and the National Library of Wales, Aberystwyth. For Roger L'Estrange's career and political attitudes, I referred to a 2011 doctoral thesis by Darrick N. Taylor (University of Kansas), and Mark Goldie's essay on *The Observator* in *Roger L'Estrange and the Making of Restoration Culture* (2008).

By far the best source for the Great Fire, though, was the City of London itself. Walking its streets, visiting or revisiting its churches (including the plaques marking the sites of the long lost ones), and simply calculating its distances and sightlines, provided perspectives that it would be impossible to glean from any book; this despite the fact that the City which Matthew Quinton knew fell victim successively to the Great Fire (of course), the Victorians, the Luftwaffe, venal planners, incompetent politicians, and mediocre, grossly over-rated architects.

Particular thanks must go to Matthew Baylis, Peter Bumstead, Frank Fox, Adam Georgie, Malin Joakimson, Geoff Lavery, Peter Le Fevre, Professor Steve Murdoch, Dr Gijs Rommelse, and Frits de Ruyter de Wildt. Peter Buckman, my agent, and Ben Yarde-Buller at Old Street Publishing, provided their customary encouragement and critical input. Gladstone's Library, Hawarden, is truly a national treasure, a residential library where authors can find peace, quiet, and inspiration. It was there, and on the walks around the adjacent Hawarden estate, that I developed the plot of *Death's Bright Angel*, and the library's excellent resources also provided me with several of the books I needed for my research. Finally, thanks as ever to Wendy for her love, support, encouragement, and invaluable advice and criticism.

J D Davies
Bedfordshire
15 December 2015